Deathwind
of the Border

Irv Lampman

PREMIUM PRESS AMERICA
NASHVILLE, TENNESSEE

Deathwind of the Border by Irv Lampman
© 2010 Irv Lampman
Published by PREMIUM PRESS AMERICA

ISBN 978-1-933725-18-5
UPC 797190101685

Cover and page design by Armour&Armour
www.armour-armour.com

Images courtesy of Antique Military Rifles, Malene Thyssen

Printed in the United States of America

To Mom and Dad Lampman, the world's greatest parents

To Sandy, my little lady who saves my life

To Dave Friske, who'll ride the river even when the boat's leakin'

To Helen and Jim Vest, our best friends who got us married on the mountain

To Winston Whitford, thanks for a lifetime of friendship

To Don Lampman, who spent many days and nights in the woods around the home place as we grew up and on to manhood. Don died in 1962 but has never been forgotten.

To everyone who ever spent some time camping in the wilderness and loved the sight of a great eagle riding the currents high above the land he rules or seen the awesome sight of a thunderstorm in the woods or the smell of the woods after such a storm or the bugle of an elk, this book is dedicated. The frontier is gone but the stories passed down to us from our forefathers still thrill the reader.

Foreword

I would like to say that I was like any other boy growing up in the late 1940s and early '50s who grew up on a steady diet of the Wild West — at least Hollywood's version. When TV was in its infancy, every Saturday morning after chores, I could be found in front of the black and white set watching the Lone Ranger, Roy Rogers, Gene Autry, The Cisco Kid, and any number of celluloid heroes.

I was blessed with a mother who was an avid reader and instilled a love in me for books and who made sure I studied and became a good reader. Then came Christmas 1954. Someone in the family gave me a book called *The Spirit of the Border* by Zane Grey, and lightning struck. The book was about the scout and frontier guardian Lewis Wetzel. Wetzel was a historical figure and, unlike the tall tales told about Davy Crockett and Daniel Boone, his adventures are historical fact. In fact, Daniel Boone himself said in later years, "Next to Lew Wetzel, I was but a babe in the woods." Teddy Roosevelt once said of Wetzel, "Lew Wetzel was the greatest one-man army known to man!" While Daniel Boone and Davy Crockett represented the bright side of the frontier, Wetzel represented the dark and terrible side.

When on a trip to Wheeling, I stood at the foot of McCulloch's Rock where Major Sam McCulloch leaped his horse to everlasting fame from that day forward to be known by the Indians as the "Flying Chief." I visited the old pioneer cemetery where Colonel Zane, Silas, Jonathan, and both Bessie and Betty sleep the sleep of tired pioneers.

Closing my eyes for a moment, I pictured the frontier villages as they must have looked when the settlement had just begun. I saw the verdant forest, the cabins and farms of the pioneers and the bloody old fort, smoke blackened and glowering over the valley, and the mighty Ohio, winding its way south on its never-ending journey to the sea.

Stretching imagination to its limits, I saw Colonel Zane sitting on his porch smoking his pipe, Betty and Bessie churning butter and welcoming visitors to the Colonel. Wetzel and Jonathan were leaning on their long rifles with news for the Colonel coming down river. It came to me that boys like myself, at least the boy I was in the late '40s and early '50s, before television, all of us are now at retirement age and all of us who remember reading about this strange terrible character from the books of Zane Grey, are now ready for another story about this border nemesis, this dark, mysterious terrible character whom very few pioneers had ever seen but of whom all knew.

After forty years of researching this man and his exploits, my excitement has never dimmed. If this book causes the reader to become as intrigued by Wetzel as I have been, the writer will be well repaid.

I would like to add that this book is also meant as a love story. The love of freedom that started as a spark from the pen of one Thomas Payne in a booklet titled "Common Sense" and became a raging inferno in the hearts of Americans that has never been extinguished.

Remember, America was built not with an olive branch but with a long rifle and a tomahawk.

Prelude

In 1768, Colonel Ebenezer Zane along with his brothers and some other brave souls arrived in the Ohio country. He moved his family to a place called Redstone, and in the fall of 1769 he explored the country more extensively. On a bright morning in September 1769, he came out on the bluff above the Ohio River on the headwaters of Wheeling Creek. The beautiful spot more than fulfilled his wildest imagination, surpassing any land he had ever seen. Not a sound disturbed the silence of the wilderness except now and then a songbird sent its melodious notes coursing down the valley.

Colonel Zane erected a crude cabin. Along with his brothers, Jonathan and Silas, he took possession of his rights in the west. Strong arms wielding axes soon opened a clearing, letting sunlight into the forest. So begins the story of Fort Henry and the settlement of the Ohio border country.

ONE

Late afternoon, many years ago, about five miles west of what is now Zanesville, Ohio, a group of Shawnee Indians had halted for the night. Their hair was worn in a scalp lock with eagle feathers thrust into it. Their bronze faces were adorned with bars of paint designed to make their countenances even more frightening. All wore buckskin leggings and breechclouts along with vests of buckskin, all covered with dark, horrible stains. On their belts several tufts of hair were tied, giving mute testimony to the success of this raid. This marked the group as a war party. One scalp in particular was a reason for pride in this bloody camp. Long and blonde it was, and covered with blood. The length of it left no doubt as to whose head it had adorned. It was the scalp of a white woman.

After a quick meal of venison and dried corn, the warriors sought their blankets, leaving one on guard. Twilight came and went, and the night spread its soft mantle over the camp. A great horned owl flew past, trumpeting its booming cry through the forest. A panther slipped by and, scenting the hated man-smell, fled like a shadow through the darkness.

The night hours dragged on. A soft breeze fanned the tiny flames of the fire. The one left on watch awakened his replacement and then sought his blankets. The sentinel settled himself with his back against a blackened stump left from some long-ago fire and sat listening to the night sounds. Despite himself, he began to doze.

Just as the first light of dawn filtered through the trees some slight sound reached the sentinel. The watcher sat up, alert now.

Then from far back in the depths of the forest, a long low moan like the whisper of the night wind sighed through the trees. The Indian guard vanished like a wisp of smoke into the darkness. A second tribesman awakened; rising to his feet, he noticed the absence of the guard. Then, from far back in the gloom beyond the glow cast by the fire, came that same low moan. It swelled hauntingly on the night air, rising to a spine-terrifying wail then dying away.

The change in the Indian sentinel was striking and immediate. He drew his tomahawk and backed against a tree. His eyes bugged out and sweat popped out of his face. The light from the fire danced on the blade of his tomahawk. This Indian, at home in the wilderness and a dweller of the forest, was trembling.

A whispered summons awakened a third Indian, who sprang up in confusion. Hardly had he gained his feet when the short, spiteful crack of a rifle shot sounded. The Indian collapsed against the tree without a sound. Then a huge dark shadow sprang from the brush and ferns ringing the glade with a roar so terrible that it was questionable whether it came from a human throat. It cut down one, two, three Indians as it moved among them. One powerful warrior — well-known among the tribes for his strength — attempted to grapple with the dark form. How pitiful was his strength now. He died with a knife buried deep in his heart.

Then as suddenly as the battle erupted it was over, with warriors either writhing in agony or lying silent on the moss and leaves. The huge dark shadow disappeared like a phantom into the depths of the forest. That same quivering wail swelled hauntingly on the wind, then died away.

The woman lying silent with her husband and children at the cabin along Mulberry creek was avenged.

TWO

Colonel Ebenezer Zane was the first settler in what is now West Virginia, founding the city of Wheeling in 1769. He was soon joined by the Eberlys and the Rosencranzes, who moved across the Alleghenies to occupy some of the free land that had become available after the treaty of Fort Stanwick in 1768.

Upon the bluff overlooking the Ohio River, the settlers erected Fort Fincastle to protect the fledgling settlement. As the American Revolution dawned, this imposing structure was renamed Fort Henry after the firebrand of the Revolution, Patrick Henry.

The British wanted to capture the fort, to cut off George Washington's retreat west and give them unfettered access to the river. They enlisted the services of the renegade Simon Girty and several other lesser-known renegades to enrage the various Indian tribes in the area against the white settlements. Fort Henry bore the brunt of these attacks.

The American Revolution was a hard and bloody time. There was no law but Colonel Zane's word, and his bordermen enforced it.

On one particular afternoon Colonel Zane heard that a flatboat from upriver had just pulled up at the dock. Anxious to hear any news from other Colonies, the Colonel waited impatiently for the riverman to come ashore.

"Hey, Mike," he called. "How's times on the river? Any Indian sign?"

"We seen feathers all along the ridge above the river but they didn't bother us. I'll tell you one thing, Colonel, I had a tingling in the back of my neck all the way from Fort Pitt to here. Suppose you heard about the family getting wiped out on Mulberry Creek?"

"No, I haven't heard a thing. You hear what tribe they think did it?"

"No, but I heard there was a white man with them — big fella wearin' feathers just like the Indians. The little boy lived just long enough to tell the authorities up there what he saw."

"Well, Mike, what do you think? You gonna be able to keep on bringin' supplies down the river?"

"We'll try, Colonel, but if the Indians get any worse we'll have to think twice about it. What the devil possesses these people from the east to come out here when they have no experience whatsoever in what it takes to exist out here?"

"Oh, I think it's what we all came west for, Mike. More land, freedom to make your own way and raise your family with some kind of future. Trouble is, out here, you make one mistake and the future can end mighty quick."

"That's the God's truth, Colonel. Well, I'm off for a bit of rum, and then I'm gonna sleep for a good two days."

"I'll talk to you later, Mike. I'll send Jack up to Mulberry. We need to get a stockade put up for those people and lay in supplies for them. Food, powder and lead — all they need. I'll be danged surprised if they're even close to being ready to face a siege."

"Keep me posted, Colonel. I hear anything from the other rivermen, I'll do the same."

"Good enough, Mike."

The Colonel headed up the path to the fort. As he went through the gate he saw his brothers Silas and Jonathan sharing some coffee at one of the tables in the courtyard.

"Hello, Eb," Jonathan greeted him. "Have a seat."

The brothers all favored each other, yet Eb and Silas were very different from Jonathan. The borderman was quiet, and for some reason a terrible gloom seemed to shadow his features. He spent little time in the settlement, making his home in the trackless wilds watching the river or the trails for even the slightest sign of Indians.

He preferred the solitude of the forest to the noise and confusion to be found in the settlements. Most of the time he and his friend Lew Wetzel hunted the renegades that haunted the trails and the outlying farms that circled the fort and village — men like Bones, the Girtys, and Jake Hanlon, who some said was the worst of the lot. More than one family had been wiped out. Mother dead, father killed, the children with their brains bashed out against a tree or carried off to the renegade dens in the Indian villages or back in the woods where their screams could be heard echoing through the forest.

Hanlon was a beast, a man in name only. Colonel Zane had ordered Jonathan and Wetzel to put an end to Hanlon's bloody trail no matter how long it took.

"Jack, have you heard anything about that family being wiped out on Mulberry Creek?"

"No, but I'm meeting Lew tomorrow at noon and I'm sure he'll know about it. He's been hunting for some sign of Hanlon up that way. Not much gets by him."

"Well, after you meet him report to me. Then we need to get some men and supplies up to those folks at Mulberry. I doubt if they've even got a stockade up yet."

"Well, I'll tell you something, Eb. If they haven't, they've got precious little time. Lew says there's Injun trouble all up and down the river. He's predicting bloodshed this summer like we haven't had in years."

"Well, if Lew says there's trouble brewin' we'd best believe him. I'm off to supper and I'll be waitin' to hear from you as soon as you've got something for me."

"I'll pull out for Mulberry at first light day after tomorrow," Jonathan said.

"Get together whatever supplies you think those folks will need. I'll scout for the wagons. We need to get them up there as soon as we can."

THREE

Daylight found Jonathan on the trail to meet Wetzel. This was Jonathan's favorite time in the woods. It had rained during the night, and wild denizens of the forest were out enjoying the warmth that the morning sun brought. Squirrels barked from the trees or frisked across the ground. Crows cawed from a distant hilltop, and a lordly elk, roused from his bed, snorted at the borderman and then bounded away through the forest. Jonathan breathed deeply of the fragrant, pine-scented air. This to him was better than any town could be.

Suddenly a minute sound reached the borderman's ear. His woodcraft picked up a wrong note in the symphony of forest sounds. He sank into the brush along the trail and pulled back the hammer on the long rifle. His dark eyes glistened.

About three hundred yards away across the plain, three, four, five dark figures glided over a ridgetop then sank into the grass out of sight. Jonathan recognized them as a war party of Shawnees by the way they traveled.

The woodsman proceeded on his way, pondering what a war party of five Shawnees this close to the fort meant. He decided they posed no threat — Eb always had sentries posted, and five warriors stood no chance attacking the stockade at Fort Henry.

About six miles from the fort, Jonathan walked out on a cliff and gazed across a beautiful valley of broken forest, with a meandering brook and moss-covered stones. He whistled the birdcall of an oriole, and a couple of minutes later the call of a cardinal came from across the valley. Jonathan seated himself on one of the stones and waited. A few minutes later a step sounded behind him and the tall form of another hunter dressed in buckskin seated himself across from him. The newcomer was a giant figure far over six feet with coal-black hair and eyes and a pale face like chiseled marble. Extremely broad shoulders tapered to a narrow waist.

Wetzel — for it was he — took the sandwich of meat and cheese Jonathan offered and nodded his thanks.

"How's things at the fort?" he asked.

"Tolerable," Jonathan replied. "Heard there's been trouble up along Mulberry?"

"Yeah, and there's liable to be more. Shawnees are up in arms about those new people movin' in. But that ain't the worst of it. I found tracks of a white man, big feller judging by the shoeprints. Tracks I ain't ever seen before. But this fella was right there when the killin' was done. Left his track right in the blood of the little girl."

Jonathan asked, "Well, what's to be done?"

"Find the villain and kill him!" Wetzel replied.

"I like your idea," Jonathan grinned. It was a grin without humor. "You see anything of a bunch of Shawnees headed down from Mulberry?"

"There were twelve. Now there's only five. I lost their tracks when they took to the river and I had to cut across country to meet with you."

"I run across them this morning. I laid low so's I could be here on time. Didn't see no white man with them, though."

"Well, he's around somewheres, you can be sure of that. When we find him he's gonna take up residence in a hole right where he falls."

"Eb's sending me up to Mulberry tomorrow to deliver a couple of wagon-loads of supplies and get a stockade started for them folks. It'll probably take about a week," Jonathan said.

"Well, I'm gonna see Eb tonight. After that I've got a couple things to do and then I reckon I'll catch up with you on the trail. I figure if there's anything will draw the varlets out it'll be two wagons loaded with supplies."

"I reckon you're right as rain," Jonathan said. "I'd sure be glad if we get up there without trouble. Those folks need all the help we can give them, accordin' to Eb."

"Well, I'm headin' in with you. We'll meet with Eb and then maybe I'll pull out with you at sun up."

The two bordermen set off for the fort. And somewhere at an Indian camp a bloody renegade planned his next raid of murder and mayhem, unaware that two bordermen were planning to end his bloody trail. The breeze sighing through the branches might have told him that *le vent de la mort*, the Wind of Death, was on his trail.

FOUR

That evening after supper Colonel Zane and his wife sat on the porch enjoying the evening as a cool breeze was coming up off the river. A purple haze showed the last light of day, and the lonely call of the whippoorwill echoed down from the hill. The fragrance of honeysuckle wafted on the breeze.

"I never tire of sitting here and just drinking in the beauty of this valley, Eb. It's such a shame that so much blood has been spilled over this ground," Elizabeth Zane said.

"Yes it is, Bessie. I know just how you feel. Unfortunately I'm afraid there'll be a lot more spilled before it's over but I believe peace will come. I only wish that I hadn't brought you out here. That's my only regret."

"Hush, Eb. Do you think I'd have been content to stay back east while my husband and the rest of our family was out here? No dear, my place is with you."

"I know that, Bessie, but when I hear of awful things like those killings up at Mulberry, it makes me wonder if it was the right thing to do."

"Yes, Eb, it was. The time will come when the bloodshed will all be over. These forest trails will be tilled fields. Our children will see that time. I don't know if we will."

"What's this?" Colonel Zane rose to his feet. The tall form of Wetzel came up the path and stepped up on the porch. He leaned his long rifle against the wall of the cabin and handed a couple of turkeys he'd brought to Bessie. "Here are a couple of turkeys for you, Bessie. They'll be my contribution toward a nice dinner!"

"I declare, Lewis Wetzel, you know you're welcome to dinner anytime, turkeys or no. I'll just get these plucked."

"Bessie, could you make some coffee, please?" the Colonel asked.

When his wife had gone into the house, Zane turned to the hunter.

"All right, Lew, if you have any bad news, out with it!"

"Eb, we've got a damn maniac out in the woods somewhere. I've found his tracks around at least four killin' sites. He was the bastard that murdered that little boy. Hit him with a tomahawk, then stomped out his brains. The mother and father were stomped to death too. Eb, I'm gonna find this villain and when I do, I'll put an end to his killin' right then and there.

The Colonel looked at the hunter's face. His black eyes glittered with a fire that was hard to look into. The cold face became even colder, a mask of deadly purpose.

"Did you catch any of the Injuns that was with him?"

"Caught up with them at Green Meadow. Killed six, but there was no white man with them."

"Well, Lew, follow his trail and kill him. Keep me posted on whatever you find out. Oh, here's Bessie with the coffee."

As the Colonel and his visitor sipped their coffee Betty, the Colonel's sister, joined them.

"Why, Lewis Wetzel, coming to call and not even letting me know you're here."

"I been pretty busy, Betty. I'm glad to see you though. I want to tell you to stick close and be careful for a while. There's terror afoot in this land. I'll let Eb know when it's safe."

"Why, Lewis, you don't mean someone might want to hurt me?"

"It's wus than that, Betty, wus than that. Well, I'm off, Eb. I'll keep in touch with you through Jack — I'm goin' with him up to Mulberry. I'm gonna scout ahead to clear the trail for the wagons."

After the hunter left, the Colonel and his wife remained on the porch enjoying the evening. Elizabeth broke their comfortable silence.

"What did Lew think? More Indian trouble this summer?"

"'Fraid so, Bess, I'm afraid so. Some renegade, Lew doesn't know who yet, has been stirring the Shawnees up for murder raids against the settlements. Lew says it's some kind of maniac. Stomped a little boy to death at Mulberry."

"My God! Eb, what's to be done?"

"Nothing much for us to do for now but keep close and be on our guard. I'm sure of one thing. If Jack or Lew find this monster his trail will end mighty quick."

Bessie turned to the task of cleaning and preparing the turkeys Wetzel had brought. Both Jonathan and Wetzel usually brought either a turkey or a haunch of venison or buffalo. Elizabeth Zane was grateful for Wetzel's friendship with her husband and Jonathan. She knew that the safety of the little settlement at Wheeling depended on the bordermen.

FIVE

Meanwhile at an Indian camp about twenty-five miles from Fort Henry, a hurried conference was in progress. An Indian chief in full ceremonial dress sat in a place of prominence. Many warriors sat around in a circle. The fire's glow illuminated the warriors' faces, painted in the stripes and bars of war paint arranged to make them appear as fearsome as possible.

Standing and speaking was a huge figure arrayed in a garish costume. But when he turned to address another of the warriors his face was most striking. A more villainous face could hardly be imagined. A scar from eyebrow to chin from a knife fight was set off by a blank eye, blinded by some long-ago wound. No smile ever adorned that face, for it would have found itself a stranger.

"The war has begun to drive the white man back across the mountains. Before we fought to keep our land. Now in the people's lodges, warriors by the hundreds are painting for war. The Shawnee, the Huron, the Delaware, all tribes must unite. I say kill the white man, his wives, and his children. Kill his cattle, burn his houses and his barns, leave not a vestige of him to stain the land.

"The Black Serpent has spoken."

He sat with his arms folded. The chief rose to his feet. The glow of the fire shone on a noble face. When he spoke, his deep sorrowful voice reached every corner of the council.

"Grey Eagle has heard the Serpent. He sees the young men of his village preparing for war. Grey Eagle loves his people. He loves his young warriors who have never seen war. He loves the young women who have never seen a father or husband or child dead from a white man's bullet. They have never seen the snow in winter stained red with blood. Grey Eagle is sick of war. He is sick of killing. He will lead his young warriors in war, but his heart is sick because of it."

Having said this, the chief — respected by all the Indians who had won the right to wear the eagle plumes — took his place among the seated warriors. Another stood to address the group, which leaned forward in anticipation. It was plain this was a war chief highly respected as a war leader.

"Red Fox has heard the Serpent and Grey Eagle. Red Fox too says kill the white man. My question is addressed to the Serpent. Will the white father from across the big water come to the aid of his white brothers if we attack them?"

"No. The white men now fight among themselves over this land. Your land."

"I say that we go into the land along the river and kill all we find and burn the cabins and barns. That way it will be difficult for the paleface to survive the winter."

"Is it agreed?'"

"Yes!" sounded from hundreds of throats.

"Is it agreed?"

"Yes!" again erupted from hundreds, followed by their deep, booming war cry. The clouds of war and bloodshed now threatened every settler on the border.

SIX

The trip up from Fort Henry to Mulberry was uneventful. During two nights camping on the trail nothing disturbed the travelers' rest. Wetzel and Jonathan watch from the shadows to spot any invader, but none showed himself.

On the third day they spotted the settlement along Mulberry Creek through the trees.

Wetzel stayed in the woods until they were sure there were no Indians at the settlement. The giant hunter was so recognizable to even friendly Indians that his presence could get a bloody confrontation going.

Jonathan helloed the settlement as he approached it with the wagons. Several sturdy frontiersmen hurried to meet them.

"No stockade," Jonathan thought to himself. "I'm damn surprised any of them are still alive."

"Hello, neighbor," said one of the pioneers, offering his hand. Jonathan shook it as he introduced himself.

"I'm from Fort Henry," Jonathan said. "My brother Colonel Zane sent me to help you folks get a stockade up."

"I'm Henry Baxter, founder of this settlement. Do you really think a stockade is necessary?"

"I sure do. Heard you had a settler and his family wiped out a few days back!"

"Yes, that's true, but I thought it was probably an isolated incident."

"Mister Baxter, there's four hundred Indians and God knows how many renegades prowling the woods all along the river. Every one of them would like nothing better than to kill everybody in the settlement. You have women here?"

"Yes, my wife and daughter, and the other men's wives."

"Well, have you ever heard what some of these villains will do to lay their hands on a white woman? Yes, I think it's necessary for you to get a stockade up as soon as possible. My companion will scout the woods so none of the reddies can sneak up without us knowing about it. There's eight or nine rifles in the wagons along with food, powder, and lead. Best get it under guard."

"Yes, sir, Mr. Zane. Boys, hop to it!"

The rifles and powder and lead were stored away in one of the sturdier cabins. Within two hours the pioneers were in the forest cutting trees to build a stockade.

During a break, Baxter said, "You and your friend are welcome to take supper with us, Jonathan."

"Well, I will, but I don't think Wetzel will want to come in."

"Wetzel. I've heard that name somewhere."

"You could hardly be out here on the border without hearing Lew's name."

"Lew Wetzel. Now I know. He's the Indian fighter!"

"So am I, Mister Baxter. I hope we can keep the Injuns off you until you can get that stockade up."

"I sure thank you, Mr. Zane. You and Wetzel."

"Just be sure and keep a close watch on that powder and lead. It would be worth its weight in gold to any Injun that could take it."

"What about hunting parties? We've got to hunt for provisions. If what you say is true, we need to get some meat laid by and curing."

"I wouldn't send out any men till we've had a chance to scout the whole area around the settlement. No Injun's gonna get away with hiding in the woods or killin' anybody while we're here."

SEVEN

Within three days the stockade was up, and work had begun on a blockhouse with a bastion at each corner. Jonathan had instructed that a catwalk be built all around the inside of the stockade fence. They cut holes for rifle ports so the men could fire through them with their long rifles. Day and night the sound of hammers could be heard. Jonathan and Wetzel scouted the woods surrounding the settlement, preventing any surprise by the Indians. Within a week the stockade and the blockhouse were finished. The fledgling settlement was beginning to take shape, and Jonathan and Wetzel made plans to leave. Baxter called Jonathan into his cabin.

"I've got a little surprise for you, Jonathan," he said, opening a crate in the corner. "Take a look in there."

Jonathan couldn't help but smile. In the crate were the barrel, carriage, and two wheels of a ten-pounder cannon.

"That ought to be a surprise for any of the Injuns that want to raid us, don't you think?"

"That gun can make the difference of you surviving a siege or not. Wait till they're bunched and blow them right out of their feathers."

"When are you and Wetzel pulling out?"

"In the morning, we're gonna scout the Shawnee towns to see if we can cut sign on the renegade that's got the Injuns all stirred up."

"Well, we all appreciate what you've done for us, and please thank your brother and the people at Fort Henry for their help."

"I'm glad things worked out. I'll be gone by sun up, so good luck."

"Same to you and Wetzel."

The men shook hands, and Jonathan headed into the forest to meet his companion.

Anyone who has spent time in the wilderness knows that the most pleasurable time is twilight. Stern and hard as a borderman's life was, devoid of wife and children and a home, he has the quiet substitute of twilight in the forest.

The hoot of an owl from a tree, the howl of a wolf from a distant hilltop, the restless crickets and the sweet smell of wood smoke on a soft breeze with the hint of rain all blend together into a wilderness symphony. When the moon rises over the mountain to bathe the forest with its gentle light, one could almost picture a land where no tomahawk had ever been raised in anger and the crack of a rifle shot or whistle of a bullet had never disturbed the tranquility of God's green earth as it was meant to be.

Jonathan and Wetzel sat together that evening. Little talk was needed. They both knew that come morning they would start on a bloody trail that could have but one end: the death of the monster they hunted, and possibly one of them. There was no mercy nor any compromise in their dedication to their terrible purpose. They slept, wrapped in the velvet darkness of the night. This to the bordermen was home.

EIGHT

Bret Tomilson was finished plowing for the day. He looked across his twenty-odd acres of new-turned earth and laughed at the birds that swooped in to dine on the worms that were suddenly available.

Bret knew that he would never be a rich man, but with a pretty wife, son, and another child on the way, the settler thanked God for the blessings He had bestowed on them.

Bret unhitched the horses from the plow and headed for the barn. He was looking forward to a cool dip in the creek and then a warm supper with the companionship of his family. He was sure that Milly would have a piece of apple pie for him, and he'd thought up a new story to tell his son Davey about bars, bufflers and Injuns. As he reached the barn he heard a cardinal whistle. He looked in the direction of the call; he thought it sounded strange. That was the last thought Bret would have in this world. A bullet struck him dead center in his forehead, and all thought and sight and sound were gone.

Milly heard the shot as did her son. She ran out to see her husband lying in the doorway to the barn. She screamed and began to run to him, but an arrow struck her just between the shoulder blades and a second later a tomahawk was buried in her skull. A warrior grabbed her hair and with a slash of a scalping knife ripped her blonde curls free. He swung high his bloody trophy, sounding the war cry. Davey Tomilson managed to get off one shot before he too fell victim to a rifle ball that made a bloody hole in his chest and left a gaping crater in his back. He too fell victim to the scalping knife. An hour later the buildings were burning. A huge figure with the face of a Gargoyle howled a laugh of madness as he celebrated this bloody massacre of his own kind. The glow from the burning cabins lit the night sky. By morning only smoking ruins and bloody corpses were left to mark the end of a family's dreams of a new life on the frontier. The sole survivor of the bloody rampage, Davey's dog, crawled to the feet of his master and raised his voice in a mournful howl of anguish.

Excerpt from the
Journal of Harriet Bonnet Smith

Most times only the outlying farms were in danger from the Indians. Colonel Zane's vigilance at the fort kept the people in the village fairly safe but many times outlying cabins were attacked. Most times the mother and father were killed and the children carried off. At such times, the Colonel would send Wetzel and Jonathan to kill the beasts that did these things. Unfortunately, their ability to save the captives was very difficult because the Indians, if they suspected that they were pursued, would kill the hostages.

NINE

A few days later the word reached Colonel Zane about the Tomilson killings. The sturdy pioneer was as angry as he'd ever been. Bret Tomilson had been a good friend of his, and the Colonel was determined that the men who committed this atrocity would pay with their lives. He had sent scouts out to find Jack or Wetzel. More worrisome than the death of the Tomilsons was the fact that even more would die. The hellish fiend who had done this thing would keep on killing until he was stopped.

The Colonel had stopped by the blockhouse to confer with Silas when a man came running in the door.

"It's Jack and Wetzel, Colonel. They're comin' in!"

The Colonel waited on the steps of the fort as the two bordermen came up the path and stopped in front of him.

"What's up, Colonel?" Wetzel asked.

"Bad business, Lew. Bad business."

The bordermen leaned their long rifles against the wall of the blockhouse and squatted across from the Colonel.

"You remember Bret and Milly Tomilson?" The bordermen nodded. "They got that farm out about ten miles or so."

"Well, a couple of nights ago they were murdered and burnt out. Their boy was killed too. All three scalped. This has got to stop now!" he shouted.

"We'll head out there right away. See if we can find a trail," Wetzel said.

"You got any ideas about who might have done this thing?"

"Eb, we've got a walkin' breathin' murderin' demon out there in the woods. He enjoys killin' and he's gonna be hard to ferret out."

"Well, take all the time you need. Don't worry about anything else for now. We've got to put an end to this monster as soon as we can."

"Sam Brady says he talked to a couple of Hurons he ran across. Even the Injuns are scared of this fella. Says he comes from the Old Ones or some such like," Wetzel said.

"The Old Ones. Sounds like some kind of Indian superstition."

"Maybe so, but he is a butcher if there ever was one. When we get out there to the Tomilson cabin I know the track I'm lookin' fer," Wetzel said. "He left a track at the cabin up on Mulberry. He has a big foot, long and wide as I ever seen. Judgin' by the depth he's got to weigh nigh on three hundred pounds. Can't be too many men like that on the frontier."

"Well, find the son of a bitch, Lew. Tomilson was a friend of mine."

"You can count on it, Eb." The giant hunter's low voice hissed, and his eyes shone with an unearthly fire.

"Report to me every few days," the Colonel commanded. "I don't think anyone would try to take the fort right now but we've got too many outlying settlers. They're the ones I worry about."

"See you later, Colonel. We're pulling out right now."

"Good luck, Jack, Lew. Take whatever supplies you need."

It took the bordermen about three hours to reach the Tomilson homestead. They took grim notice of the three graves on the hillside above the burned-out house.

There had been too much milling around in the farmyard for the hunters to find the track they were looking for so they ranged in ever-widening circles searching for a trail. That afternoon just at sunset they found it. There in soft soil was a huge footprint where a man had stepped over a log.

"There's the bastard's track, Jack, as sure as you're born. I know he's the one we're looking for, but I wonder who he is. I've never cut his trail before."

"How'd he get tied up with the Shawnees so quick?" Jonathan mused.

As it was late in the day the bordermen camped in the forest for the night and would pick up the trail in the morning.

TEN

About a week after Jonathan and Wetzel discovered the track at the Tomilson homestead two men stood at the edge of the Ohio River about fifteen miles north of Fort Henry. One was dressed in the uniform of a British officer, regal and military in bearing. The other was a giant, dressed in the buckskin garments of an Indian chief. But as he turned to address the Englishman the horror of his face was revealed. It was the face of what was fast becoming, according to the pioneers, the Gargoyle of the frontier. Hard and cruel was that face, its one eye staring in a pitiless look of evil. As the speaker became more agitated the scar running down his face stood out more and more.

"How is your project with the local aborigines going?" the British officer asked.

"Well as can be expected. I've got them stirred up and ready for the warpath."

"I heard something about some killings around here. You wouldn't have anything to do with that, would you?"

"That's none of your affair, Major. You want the Injuns stirred up then that's what you'll get. But it's gonna take some killin' to get them fired up."

"The killing of women I can't condone. We're not savages."

"I don't give a particular damn what you condone or don't condone. You ain't runnin' the show out here on the frontier, Major. I am. And I'm gonna kill as many of these pilgrims as I can. If I could get the Injuns to kill every settler out here I would. I want this country clear of settlers."

"But the General will not stand for it."

"To hell with your General!"

"They may hang you."

"They might try. But this country will run with blood first."

"What makes you hate your own kind like you do? I've got a job to do but you, you enjoy this blood-letting."

"That's my business. You just stay out of my way."

With that the monster vanished into the forest. The British officer shivered even though the temperature was extremely warm. He wondered what the hell he was doing on this bloody frontier dealing with a ghoul. He fervently wished he was back in London.

ELEVEN

The next day Wetzel and Jonathan approached the Shawnee villages. They had tracked the huge footprints for miles to the edge of the Ohio where the monster had apparently taken to a canoe. That night they crawled to a cliff overlooking the village. While one slept the other kept watch. They were hoping to get a look at their quarry and possibly get a shot at him. Wetzel's small bore was accurate up to three hundred yards, which put the village well within range.

Now it became a waiting game.

:::

It was with great pleasure that Colonel Zane and his wife received a most distinguished visitor when Daniel Boone stopped by on his way to Kentucky. And the two pioneers had been able to spend a few hours catching up on the news and share a bottle of the Colonel's fine wine. Boone, however, brought some disturbing news.

"Colonel, a few weeks ago I found an old fella I knew scalped and near death. I did my best for him but he died the next day. Afore he did, though, he told me that some demon came out of the woods and murdered his partner and scalped him. He said the fiend was a huge man with a horrible face. And the worst of it was, he said, the monster was laughing as he butchered his partner. Laughing! Can you beat that?"

"Unfortunately, I can, Daniel. We've had seven people killed all around here, and Lew says it's the same man. And now it sounds like he's been visitin' over your way. But we've got Lew and Jack on his trail. If they get a chance, that will be the end of him. I've no doubt about that."

"I wonder why we've never had trouble with this villain before. We've never seen his track around Boonesboro until just lately. Where did he come from and how come he's here?"

"Well, Daniel, I guess we'll just have to be on our guard and wait to see how Lew and Jack come out. They'll get him sooner or later, I'm sure of that."

"The problem is, he can do a hell of a lot of damage while we wait."

"I'm afraid that's so, Daniel. I'm afraid that's so."

"Well I'm headed back to Boonesboro, Eb. I'll have Kenton and a bunch of scouts out every day till snow flies."

"If you hear anything, get word to me!"

"The thing I'm most worried about is what this villain thinks he's got to gain. I think there's more devilment afoot."

After Boone left, the Colonel walked down to the fort to see his brother. Silas was a sturdy pioneer whom the Colonel depended on for consultation and to command the fort when the Colonel couldn't be there.

"Hello, Silas. I've got some news and I need for you to call a meeting of all the men that's old enough to carry a rifle. Tell them to try not to panic the women and children but be sure everybody comes to the fort and brings their families. The women can have a quilting bee or something."

"Are we in for a siege, Eb?"

"I don't think so, but till I hear from Jack or Lew I don't know. I don't believe the tribes are united enough to attack the fort, but with this renegade stirrin' them up, who knows."

"I'll have everybody I can find here at seven o'clock. I'll send out riders to the outlying farms, but who knows how many of them we'll find home."

"Well, do your best, Silas. The Shawnees are gathering, and I'm afraid there's gonna be hell to pay."

"I'll get started right now."

"Good. I'll get Bessie to get something going for the women."

Silas headed off on his errands, and the Colonel headed back to his cabin. He wondered when he'd hear from the bordermen.

TWELVE

About thirty miles into Ohio from Wheeling a beautiful area of rolling prairie had been settled about three years before by about four families. The soil was rich loam and they had hogs, cattle, a few chickens, and a pretty good crop of youngsters growing up to carry on their family name. Ole Jensen, the head man of the settlement, looked out across the land and thanked God for the years of prosperity that he'd enjoyed.

He had just turned to go into the barn when a peculiar whistling noise went by his ear. He didn't have to hear the roar of an overcharged rifle to tell him he was being shot at. He raced to the back of the barn, dove through the window, and sprinted for the cabin. His wife had heard the shooting and had the door open for him as he plowed through. Shooting had broken out in different parts of the settlement, and his brother and several of the other men took up the battle. A group of Shawnees broke from the trees and charged the cabin, led by a huge man with the face of a monster swinging a tomahawk. Ole fired, and one of the warriors screamed and clutched at the bloody mess that had been his face. He dropped like a stone. By this time the Gargoyle had reached the door and attacked it with his tomahawk. Ole tried to fire through the rifle slits. He must have come close because the monster let out a howl and leaped back out of sight of the window.

By this time five warriors lay dead in the yard. They obviously had not expected to meet such a withering fire from the settlers. The warriors withdrew to the shelter of the trees to plan their next move.

The settlers were busy reloading rifles, bandaging wounds, and watching the trees for a return attack. Ole had a shotgun that he used for bird hunting. But now he loaded the weapon with musket balls. At close range this was a devastating weapon. The rest of the afternoon was spent with the settlers and the Shawnees sniping at long range at each other. The pioneers were feeling indeed fortunate that no on their side had lost their life. As darkness descended, the settlers waited with terrible misgivings. Now that it was dark the advantage lay with the attackers.

Ole cussed himself for all kinds of a fool for not putting up a fort. But in all those years, there had been no trouble with the Indians. Some of the natives had come to trade for tobacco or flour but the visits had been friendly. So Ole could hardly believe this unprovoked attack. Something had to have set the Indians off.

Three times during the night they charged the cabins but were beaten off. The Gargoyle had not been seen again, and Ole believed either he had been wounded or was back in the woods hatching some new deviltry.

The next morning as the pioneers were preparing for another assault, the acrid smell of smoke reached them and to their horror they saw that the wheat fields had been set afire. The hardest thing Ole Jensen had ever been forced to do was to stand by and see a whole summer's crop go up in smoke. The pioneers were now faced with starvation or abandoning their homes and fleeing either to Fort Henry or Fort Pitt to the north. That is, if they survived the next few hours. Suddenly a clear, ringing rifle shot rang through the clearing. The Shawnee chief with the war bonnet collapsed like a rag doll. Another rifle roared with a heavy bellow, and another Shawnee warrior clutched his chest and collapsed in a heap.

The Indians, facing an unseen enemy from the rear, sprang up in confusion. Again came that short, spiteful crack of a rifle. Another warrior dropped like a stone. This was too much for the survivors, and they fled into the forest leaving their dead behind.

"Hello the cabins," came a voice from the woods.

"Come on in," Ole called.

Two buckskin-clad figures came from the woods. One approached the door to the cabin while the other stood leaning on a long black rifle.

"Pretty lively set-to you've had here!"

"Sure has been, Jack. Glad to see you. I tell you I thought we'd had it till you and Lew showed up."

"You know what got them stirred up?"

"No, and that's the hell of it. I haven't had any trouble with them. Never have had since we been here. How come you and Lew are over this way?"

"Trackin' a fella. Big fella been doin' a lot of hell-raisin' all up and down the river."

"Say, I think he was with this bunch of Shawnees. Got a face like a monster. Big scar and all."

"That's him. Well, I think you'll be all right now. Head for Fort Henry; Eb will help you with shelter and get you set up for next crop season. Tell Eb we'll see him day after next."

"Sure will, Jack. Thanks again to you fellers. Say, you think Wetzel will get a hold of that son of a bitch?"

"Count on it, Ole."

"Well, it's all up for that damn renegade then."

"Just a matter of time, Ole. Just a matter of time."

"Good. Best news I've heard all year."

THIRTEEN

Jonathan and Wetzel picked up the renegade's trail on the outskirts of the village. It went east toward the Delaware town. Jonathan headed for Fort Henry while Wetzel stuck to the trail. The bordermen knew that Colonel Zane had to be made aware that this was something that defied the normal renegades' way of operating. He was a cold-blooded killer, no doubt about that, but there was something else here. Some underlying reason behind the deliberate agitation of the tribes.

He had managed to stir up the Shawnees. If Wetzel was correct, his next step would be to stir up the Delawares. He would try to get them to believe that they had to take the war trail against the settlements — all up and down both sides of the river.

All day long Wetzel stuck doggedly to the trail. Because the potential for ambush was so high, the hunter was forced to make wide detours to take up the trail later on. Always he found it still headed for the Delaware town. Wetzel camped the next night within earshot of the village. The next morning found him on a cliff overlooking the village council area. As he looked down into the camp of his lifelong foes, a tremble not unlike that of a tiger rippled through the hunter's body. His great muscles bulged under his shirt and his eyes glittered with a peculiar fire. There was death in those eyes. The Gargoyle could well take notice that his continued existence was severely in doubt.

Every Indian in the village was within range of Wetzel's unerring weapon. The rifle was a very long-barreled, small-bore weapon. It was fully six feet long with a curly maple stock and silver-inlaid barrel bands and patch box. It was a gift from an old man who no longer needed a rifle — he had told the borderman he knew it would be put to good use. The hunter's grim smile said he had guessed right.

All afternoon the hunter watched and waited. As he waited he ran over in his mind the possible reasons the renegade would have for declaring a war on the white settlements. Not for money, that was sure. Maybe it was because of a thirst for blood.

Suddenly the hunter jumped in surprise. In the center of the village two men stood talking. One was Wetzel's enemy of many years: Wingenund, chief of the Delawares. The other man was huge by any standards. Wingenund was as tall as Wetzel, but the renegade stood over him by at least three inches. Wetzel couldn't see his face at that distance, but he had no doubt this was the murderer he had been trailing for so many miles — the man who had murdered and scalped at least seven people that Wetzel knew of.

The long, black barrel of Wetzel's rifle swept up level, then became as rigid as stone. There was a moment when man and rifle seemed turned to marble. Then a puff of white smoke belched forth, followed by a clear, ringing report. A small pellet of lead was on its way. The Gargoyle should have died. But as sometimes happens, fate intervened. Something fell from the Gargoyle's hand. He bent over to pick it up and just as he did something hot whistled over his head, embedding itself in a cabin wall. The beast leaped behind a tree. The Indians recognized the ring of that rifle. They raced to the spot where the shot had come from, but all they found was a couple of moccasin prints. The Wind of Death had vanished into the depths of the forest.

But that wasn't all that was left behind. A gargoyle-faced renegade knew he had come within a whisper of being dead. He had been in the middle of a village surrounded by warriors and still he was not protected. The Wind of Death was on his trail and could not be shaken.

Deep in the forest at the base of a cliff a Redcoat officer waited. He had expected the Gargoyle three days ago, but not a sign. He had heard that a village had been attacked. The renegades had been beaten back, leaving seven of their number lying still in the yard of the village. He'd been hearing some talk about something called the Wind of Death or some such foolishness —most likely some Indian superstition or bogey-man or some such thing. The Redcoat hated this wilderness. It was not the kind of place for an English officer. He hoped that these rebels would soon be crushed and he could return to England. If not, he fervently hoped to at least get back to New York and some semblance of civilization. What England wanted with this wild western god-forsaken Ohio country was beyond him.

Suddenly a twig snapped in the forest. He turned to see the Gargoyle coming toward him.

"Thought you'd be here sooner. I'm tired of this bloody waiting. Are you getting anything accomplished?"

"Don't get your bloomers in an uproar. The Delawares and Shawnees are talking. The Delawares will take the war trail anytime now. There's just one problem."

"What's that?"

"I want more money. I came within a whisker of getting killed. Twice! Once at that village we attacked and then at the Delaware village. Some-body took a shot at me from better than three hundred yards. Indians said it was the Wind of Death."

"The Wind of Death? Sounds like some kind of ghost or haunt or something the Indians dreamed up. I think you're letting this bloody bor-derland get to you."

"Ghost, hell! The bullet I dug out of the cabin's wall wasn't fired by no ghost. If I hadn't dropped my pipe and bent over to pick it up I'd have been dead as last year's geraniums. No, sir. I want twice as much gold as I was promised and a safe passage to wherever I want to go after this bloody Insurrection is over."

"I cannot make any commitments on my own. I will have to consult with my superiors. You must wait until I can talk with my General. In the meantime keep working on the Indians."

"Not on you life, mister. I'm taking cover and ain't coming out till I hear from you. Otherwise you can find somebody else to start your damn Indian war!"

"There is no one else. We need the Indian tribes stirred up to keep the settlers busy so they can't help in the Colonies' war for independence. If you refuse to help now at this most critical time I will see you taken back to England in irons and hanged. Do I make myself clear?"

The Gargoyle turned to stare at the British officer. Years later the captain would still remember, saying it was the most evil look he had ever seen.

"Don't you threaten me, you struttin' bandy rooster. One word from me and the Injuns will tie you to a tree and roast you like a suckling pig. Do I make myself clear?"

"All right, all right. It makes no sense to quarrel among ourselves," the Redcoat said. Suddenly he felt very cold. A chill seemed to penetrate right down into his soul.

"Well, you go talk to your superiors. How far is it to where they are?"

"About two days' journey."

"All right. I'll wait one week. After that I'm leavin' the country."

The renegade turned and disappeared into the forest. The Redcoat heaved a great sigh of relief. He was lucky to be alive. He fervently hoped he would live long enough to see his sweetheart, mother, and family back in London. The chances, he thought ruefully, weren't that good.

FOURTEEN

Far away from that spot, about five miles north of Fort Henry, Wetzel had struck the track of a British officer. The pioneers and Indians wore either work shoes or moccasins. This was the track of an army officer. He followed it until the Redcoat mounted a horse. Again his suspicions were confirmed. The Redcoat rode an unshod horse to blend in with the Indian ponies.

Wetzel pondered what this might mean. A British officer could hardly be riding near the fort. He would be spotted in a minute in his red coat. That could only mean he was a spy up to some unknown devilment. Wetzel set off for the fort. He knew Colonel Zane needed to be notified of the spy in the area as a possible saboteur. The British had sent spies before. Now that George Washington had begun to have some small success in the east, the British were becoming more and more desperate. They had used renegades like the Girtys before. However, never had a British officer been linked directly to the Gargoyle, the monster of the frontier. To Wetzel it meant the a move against Fort Henry or possibly Fort Pitt might come in the very near future.

Some of the men called renegades had become so as a matter of survival. Simon Girty, facing a hangman's noose, had abandoned his post. He was soon welcomed by the Indians. His brothers James and George had long since become villains many times more savage than the Indians. Not so Simon. Many times he had tried to intervene on behalf of white captives. However, he was opposed to the civilization of the frontier because civilization meant the end of safety for himself and his brothers. The

British therefore enlisted the white renegades to stir up the Indian tribes to make war on the settlers to keep civilization in Kentucky, Ohio, and what would become West Virginia from expanding. The British could see the handwriting on the wall and knew the pioneers must be stopped or the Colonies would expand ever westward and become impossible to control. Simon Girty had led attacks on Boonesboro and Fort Henry and had generally raised havoc for years all along the frontier. But many of the atrocities he had been accused of had really been committed by other renegades, including his own brothers. Because of Simon's aversion to the needless shedding of blood, his value to the British was limited. Not so other renegades. For promised gold or land or safety after the revolution, they were willing to do anything to wipe out the white settlements.

On the other side were the bordermen. The Zanes, the Wetzels, the McCullochs, Williamson and Metzors. These men were the guardians of the frontier. Sam Brady and Simon Kenton were also members of this brotherhood of the border. Colonel Zane in later years said that without these great men the civilization of the Ohio country would have taken many more years and many, many more lives.

FIFTEEN

That evening after supper Colonel Zane and Bessie were again relaxing on the porch of their cabin. Jonathan had come in a couple of days ago and notified the Colonel of the fight at the small settlement. Colonel Zane had got the people settled in new cabins, and they were adjusting well to their new life at Fort Henry.

It was a beautiful night. The mists were settling down over the river and the moon was just coming up. The crickets set up their incessant hum and a whippoorwill called from the forest.

"Beautiful night, Bessie."

"Yes, it is. It's like heaven," she said.

"It sure is like heaven. If we could only have peace in this valley."

The Colonel stood up as a huge dark figure came up the path and up the steps.

"Good to see you, Lew. Any news?"

"More questions than answers, Eb. Everything all right here?"

"Yes, for now. Daniel was over a couple days ago. Says they been seein' signs over by Boonesboro. Sounds like the fella you been tellin' me about."

"That ain't the worst of it, Eb. I believe we've got a British officer in here workin' with the renegades stirrin' up the Injuns to attack the settlements. That big renegade came damn close to bein' a dead renegade. I believe the devil himself must be lookin' out for that villain. I damn near got him, had him dead to in my sights but he bent over just as I shot and the bullet missed him by a hair. I also found tracks of a British officer not five miles above."

"You think we're in for a siege then?" the Colonel asked.

"I'd bet on it, Colonel. Unless we can get that Brit and the renegade. And it won't be just here. It'll be killin' and blood from Fort Pitt to Boonesboro."

"Well, Lew, what's to be done?"

"I'm gonna pick up that Redcoat officer's trail in the morning. Jack's going with me. Maybe if we're lucky the two will meet up and we can get 'em both."

"How're the people we sent over? Ole and his folks?"

"Doin' just fine, Lew. Said to thank you and Jack again. I'm hopin' we can get enough cabins up. We can always use more men that can handle rifles in the event of a siege."

"Well, judgin' by what I seen during the fight at the village, Ole and his boys will do to ride the river with. Every damn one of them can shoot!"

"Lew, you've got your orders. Kill that damn renegade and either capture or kill that British officer. We need to stop this damn thing in its tracks."

"I'm leavin' in the morning. We'll let you know as soon as anything happens. Keep sentinels out. Watch the river. I'll tell you one thing. You better keep the women in the stockade till this thing's over."

SIXTEEN

The next morning Wetzel and Jonathan hit the renegade's trail four miles north of the fort and a mile farther on what Wetzel had hoped for happened. The British officer's trail and the renegade's both struck off together toward the east. To the bordermen this meant that the villains were traveling together to meet somebody. All that day the trail led east, never varying except to avoid some especially thick brush or an open prairie. The renegade was precious shy of his skin so he avoided the open glades when he could. Late that afternoon a couple of shots were heard far off to the east, one the crack of a rifle and the other the boom of a fowling piece.

Then a few minutes later the rifle cracked again. Then silence. As it was approaching nightfall, it was too late for the bordermen to hurry through the forest after the renegade. Either they could lose the trail, or they could come upon the renegades too fast and take a chance on flushing them and missing a shot altogether. That night the hunters camped on the renegades' trail. Jack and Wetzel had a meager meal of jerky and dried corndodgers. Starting a fire would have been especially dangerous in this country where both Delawares and Shawnees were thick. The slight smell of wood smoke could set off an alarm like a clanging bell. Again while one man slept, the other kept watch.

The morning found them on the trail. It was absolutely necessary to go as carefully as possible. Not only was an ambush something to think about but also it was important not to leave a sign of their passing. No broken twigs, no footprint must be left to alert their enemies of their presence.

Shortly after noon they came out on a grassy plain. It was a beautiful place ringed by cliffs and wooden hills. About halfway across was a burnt wagon. A dead man lay by one of its wheels, his face blown away by a rifle slug and his scalp missing. A couple of feet from him lay his wife. She also was dead, murdered and scalped. In the wagon was the naked body of a girl around nineteen or so years of age. Wetzel and Jonathan wasted only a few minutes in sad reflection on the tragedy, and then left on the renegade's trail. To bury the people would have been a declaration of their presence in the Indian country. Their job was to be as stealthy as possible, kill the monster and his partner, and get back to Fort Henry.

Jonathan's jaw was set and a dark and terrible gloom had settled over his face. An unearthly light glittered in Wetzel's eyes. There was no mercy for the outlaws. The Wind of Death was on the trail, and it could only end in the villain's grave.

Near sunset the bordermen came across the trail of five Shawnees. Wetzel was all for hunting them down to keep them from hindering the hunters' work later on. It wouldn't do to come upon their quarry only to have the Shawnees show up at the worst possible moment. They followed the trail until dark and just as the light was almost gone they saw a flicker of firelight through the trees. The bordermen picked a spot and waited. They knew full well that the best time to hit the Indians' camp was near dawn. While one of the bordermen slept the other kept watch.

The moon rose to its zenith and started its age-old journey across the sky. A wolf came by on the track of a rabbit and then, sensing the men, vanished into the forest. An owl hooted from a treetop. Millions of insects droned their incessant sounds. The first ray of dawn tinged the eastern sky. The Indians slept. Suddenly two shadows leaped from cover. The Indians died almost before they could open their eyes. Wetzel scalped the dead Indians and then dipped their eagle plumes in blood and stuck them in the bark of a tree near the fire. They were now a challenge and a threat of death to every Indian everywhere. The bordermen were disturbed by what they had found. Two of the Indians were Huron, traveling with the Shawnees. This told them that the various tribes were joining forces to make a concerted move against the settlements, just as Wetzel had thought.

The two hoped with a little luck they would come upon their quarry by noon. But their hopes were dashed by a rain that moved in and wiped out any sign of the trail. They tried to pick up some sign, but the rain poured down in sheets. The powder in their rifle pans was soaked, and their buckskin garments were heavy with water.

"We'd better get dried out and then get back to Fork Henry. Eb needs to be aware of what's going on. I think we've got a full-scale Injun war on our hands," Wetzel said gloomily.

"Damn, if we could have found those villains we might have stopped this thing. Now who knows where they are," Jonathan replied.

The next morning the rain had stopped and the sun came out warm and bright. The hunters drew the charges in their rifles, reloading with fresh powder from their powder horns. After putting dry priming powder in the pans, they were ready for the trail.

Two days traveling brought them to Fort Henry. They found the fort in a state of excitement. The bordermen headed straight for Colonel Zane's cabin. They found the Colonel sitting on the porch talking to two men in the uniform of the Continental Army.

"Lew and Jack, I'm sure glad to see you. Gentlemen, let me introduce you to my brother Jonathan and Lew Wetzel."

"Wetzel, I've heard some stories about you."

The giant bordermen shook hands with the soldiers and then took a seat by the corner of the porch. Jonathan sat down at the table with the Colonel and his guests.

"Jack, the Major here says that here is a concerted effort by the British to inflame the tribes against the settlements. He's been in contact with Daniel Boone at Boonesboro. Simon Girty is over there stirring up Blackfish and the Shawnees in Kentucky. His brothers James and George are raisin' Cain up around Fort Pitt. I've asked if Washington can send some men to reinforce the Garrisons including Fort Henry, but unfortunately there's none available."

"Well, I think these men should be made aware that it's already started. Wetzel and I found a man and woman scalped not twenty-five miles from here. Their daughter was assaulted and murdered with them. We caught up with the Injuns that did it. There's three dead Shawnees and two Hurons out on the prairie. But the thing is, it's not a good sign when the Shawnees and Hurons are teaming up. That means there's gonna be a concerted effort against the whole frontier very shortly."

The Army officer nodded. "General Washington understands that. He asks that you hang on as best you can. We've found out that a network of spies have been at work recruiting white renegades from Ohio to Virginia. The Girtys are at the forefront of the renegades but this Gargoyle, as you call him, is at it too."

"How goes the war, Lieutenant?" Colonel Zane asked.

"Just between you and me, not that good. We've got supplies this year — that's better than last year. But we still haven't got near the men we need. That's why we can't spare anyone to help you folks out here on the frontier. I will send some more rifles and I've got a few light cannons I can send to the forts but right now it's all I can spare."

"Do you have any names of these infiltrators, Lieutenant?"

"Not at this time. We do know that they are Tories and that most of them are at home on the frontier."

"Wetzel, do you have any ideas?"

"I'm going back out and watch the trails to the Delaware village. I think sooner or later I'll get another try at that big ugly villain. This time I'll make a better shot."

"Jack, what are your plans?"

"Reckon I'll go with Lew. Two men can keep a watch better. If we can get him I'll bet it will go a long way to puttin' an end to this devilment that's stirring on the border."

"All right. Keep me informed. Anything else, Lieutenant?"

"Not right now. There'll be some rifles and a small cannon coming downriver on a flatboat sometime in the next two weeks."

That night Colonel Zane and Jonathan and Wetzel sat on the porch of the cabin smoking their pipes. There was little need for words. Each knew the next few weeks would decide the fate of the white settlements on the border — and possibly the fate of the fledgling country. If the covert operations of the British operatives in the New World were successful, it would set the border aflame. Boonesboro, Fort Pitt, and Fort Henry would be gone, leaving nothing but ashes blowing in the wind. The three men shook hands.

"Good luck, Jack, Lew. Keep me posted. I don't need to tell you how important this is."

The next morning was a beautiful clear day for traveling. The bordermen crossed the river and struck the trail for the Delaware town.

SEVENTEEN

The summer days dragged on and were mostly uneventful. The wheat fields became golden and were harvested, their bounty stored in the granary or ground into flour. Hay fields were cut, and the dried hay put into barns for the livestock to eat for when the snows became too deep. The women were busy drying apples and putting up preserves. Jonathan made periodic trips to the fort to confer with Colonel Zane. The bordermen had very little to report. The Gargoyle seemed to have disappeared as if the ground had swallowed him. No British officer had been spotted, or even his boot tracks.

Several cabins had been raised along the river to accommodate the new settlers from the burned settlement. A flatboat had arrived with a small cannon, as well as extra rifles with powder and lead. Most of the pioneers thought that the talk of a siege was just that, talk. There had been no further raids. But Colonel Zane knew better than to become complacent.

Simon Kenton came over from Boonesboro to confer with the Colonel. Despite scouts continuously checking the trails no sign had been found either of the Gargoyle or the British officer.

Daniel Boone had been scouting himself for over three months and yet no sign had been found. But that was soon to change.

The fall was coming and there would be clear, crisp mornings and cold, clear nights. The children would be starting school, and the Colonel was glad that the kids would be in one place and easier to keep an eye on. The women were busy making quilts and preparing for a long winter.

EIGHTEEN

As early fall came the pioneers began the chore of woodcutting. Many, many cords of dry wood had to be cut from the forest. Blowdowns and dead trees all had to be cut to the desired length, loaded on wagons, and brought into the woodsheds and stacked to wait for winter when they would be needed. When the cold moved in, the wood meant warmth. Many of the fireplaces could handle four-foot logs. One of the greatest joys of frontier life was sitting in front of a cherry fire with the sweet smell of wood smoke and the crackling of the flames.

One crisp fall morning as a wood-cutting party wound its way into the forest, they had just began the task of cutting up a huge blowdown when an Indian war whoop split the silence of the forest and feather-bedecked warriors sprang up from all sides. One of the pioneers died with an arrow through his throat. His body had not hit the ground before a warrior pulled back his head and slashed off his scalp. Shots were being fired from all sides. The pioneers took cover behind the wagons and a couple of dead oxen. Arrows and bullets thudded into the carcasses and wagons. Now the pioneers' firing became more accurate. Warriors died on all sides of the clearing. The settlers were expert in the use of the long rifle. One had a fowling piece loaded with several lead balls in each barrel. At close range it was a devastating weapon capable of shredding flesh and bone. An Indian charged the man with the shotgun, swinging high his tomahawk. The frontiersman swept the weapon up and triggered both barrels. The body of the Indian was literally picked up and thrown backward, his face and most of his upper body disappearing in a cloud of smoke. Suddenly firing came from another area. A group of frontiersmen had arrived from the fort to relieve the beleaguered party. The Indians grudgingly gave ground and finally withdrew into the forest, leaving their dead behind. Three of the settlers had been wounded and only one killed. They felt very fortunate indeed. The dead Indians were left where they fell. After the wagons were loaded with wood they headed back to the fort.

Colonel Zane waited impatiently for Jonathan to come in. He knew now that they would have to be on their guard every moment. More wood had to be cut. There was hunting to do to lay in a supply of venison. But there would be no letting down of their guard. The Colonel expected his brother sometime the next day. That night after supper a knock came on the door. When the Colonel opened it he expected Jonathan. He was a mighty relieved man to see Wetzel and Jonathan both standing there. The three men shook hands warmly. Mrs. Zane bustled around to get up some food and a pot of steaming coffee.

"Heard you had some excitement the other day."

"I'm afraid you heard right. Have you fellas had any luck?"

"No, we haven't. We have watched every trail, every village, and not a trace. Either the renegade has left the country or he's found a place to lie low."

"No trace of any British infiltrators, either."

"Well, we were mighty lucky. But Jenks was killed. Hugh Bennet and Dave Pike were hurt pretty bad. They'll be laid up awhile but they'll live."

"I'm headed out there to see if I can cut sign of the people we're lookin' fer," Wetzel said. "I think there was a white skunk in the brush pile somewheres."

"Find him, Lew. Find this beast and put an end to him once and for all. That's the only way we'll ever have peace in this valley."

The giant hunter rose to his feet. His cold face looked even colder. His eyes burned with an unquenchable fire like the fires of hell itself. He held out his hand and shook hands with the Colonel. He nodded to Jonathan and then closed the door behind him. In his later years, the Colonel would remember that night. And shiver.

NINETEEN

In a Redcoat camp far away from the western settlements a meeting of the minds was just getting underway. Several British officers were present, as was the bane of the border Simon Girty. Wingenund was there, as was Pipe and Half King. Also present was that monster of the border, the Gargoyle. This congregation of villains had gathered for one specific purpose: to kill as many of the white setters as possible, burn the settlements, and wipe their memory out of the Indian land. To Simon Girty it was a matter of survival. If the Ohio Valley was settled for good it could no longer provide a safe haven for him and his Indian brothers. Wingenund was there because he was the leader of the Delaware. His people had been lied to by the white man until he could no longer tolerate it. Pipe was the Indian enemy of all white men, and never had there been a crueler countenance on the face of any Indian. And last was Half King the Huron. These were the representatives of the Indian nations. The fire gave a hellish cast to the circle of faces. Girty had just gotten up to speak.

"People of the forest. I say to you that we must stop the incursion of the palefaces into our hunting grounds. They kill the game; they fish out our streams. They build their homes right in the middle of your lands. The Wind of Death still moans through the forest, and warriors die. No longer shall we let this continue. I say unite. Kill the whites. What we don't kill, drive back over the mountains. Simon Girty has spoken!"

Pipe now arose to address the gathering of Indians.

"Pipe says kill all the whites. I will pledge a hundred warriors. Pipe has spoken!"

Half King the Huron now rose to his feet. "Half King pledges three hundred warriors. Kill the white invaders. Half King has spoken!"

The Gargoyle rose to his feet. The firelight's red glow made the man's evil face even more distorted. "Brothers, I bring you good news. I have talked to the Great White Father from across the big water, chief of the Redcoats. They have promised that if we will make war upon the towns of the white man he will send many Redcoats and big guns that are as loud as the thunder as it plays among the clouds and fires bullets that can knock down the largest stockade that the white man can build. I am your friend and I tell you that unless you join forces with the red-coated soldiers, the whites will rise up and kill all of the Indians. As we speak there are plans by General Washington to wipe out all of your villages and steal your land. I have spoken!"

A red-coated officer now stood and moved to the center of the circle. "Brothers, I come to you to confirm what this man has said to you. The Redcoats are now fighting the Bluecoats to see who will be here to rule the men of the forest. If you help us you will again rule your land. No longer will the Indian fight alone against the white invaders. What say you?"

The war whoop sounded from a thousand Indian throats. Warriors leaped to their feet, brandishing their knives and tomahawks. Simon Girty nodded in satisfaction, and an evil smile played over the face of the Gargoyle.

And far away the Wind of Death prowled the forest glades and prairies. Savage as a tiger and absolutely fearless, Wetzel knew that sooner or later he would strike the trail of the man he was looking for. He made a vow that before another year passed the monster of the frontier would lie quiet on the moss and leaves. The hunter knew that anybody moving through the Ohio traveled well-worn trails. The forest in many areas was just too thick to bring wagons through. Most of the Indian trails were little more than worn tracks made by deer or bison. Wetzel had spent most of his days hunting Indians, ambushing the trails and bridle paths. There were well-traveled roads also, and Wetzel knew that the British would come on horseback. This would give him the best chance of getting a shot either at the renegade or a British officer. The hunter believed he knew which trail a large force of spies or infiltrators would use to cross the river under cover of darkness, then head into Ohio.

The hunter took a post in a small hidden cave overlooking the trail. During the day he could watch for any movement on either side of the river. At night he could work his way down to overlook the trail within forty feet of where people would pass.

He settled himself for a long wait. So patient was this terrible man-hunter that he would wait until he turned to stone if it meant a chance to kill the quarry he had come to destroy.

Summer dragged on, and gave way to autumn. Colonel Zane had the new settlers set up with cabins, rifles, a small stockade, a supply of powder and lead; they were prepared for a protracted siege.

Daniel Boone had been by for another visit, and Simon Kenton was prowling the woods around Boonesboro scouting for any sign of the British spies or the renegades. Sam Brady had been up to Fort Pitt, but again nothing was seen.

TWENTY

The frosty mornings came. It was time for butchering, bringing the harvest in, from apples and hickory nuts to pumpkin and squash. The frontiersmen were busy hunting deer, bear, woods bison, squirrels, rabbits and turkey to provide for the long winter to come. All knew that when the snow fell at least they could breathe a little easier because the Indians rarely attacked in winter.

One frosty morning Colonel Zane had just come in from feeding the cattle and sat down to a breakfast of ham and eggs and some baked bread with Bessie's preserves. He couldn't help thinking how lucky he was to have a pretty wife and a young son as well as the good luck he'd had settling the Fort Henry area. There was talk of a road project that would keep him busy for years. And so far, there'd been no Indian attacks to deal with at Fort Henry, although he'd heard of sporadic attacks in some of the outlying areas. Wetzel had been in to report that so far he hadn't seen any renegades or Redcoats crossing the Ohio. But Colonel Zane and his bordermen knew that just because there hadn't been a sighting didn't mean that the threat of attack was nonexistent.

:::

On one quiet evening after a hard day in the fields Colonel Zane was entertaining guests. Captain Boggs had come over from the fort, Jonathan and Silas were there, and the Colonel's sister Betty had persuaded Wetzel to come. It was a beautiful autumn evening with a huge harvest moon in a cloudless sky. A wolf howl split the silence. Wetzel rose to his feet, listening.

"Look here, Lew, wasn't that a real wolf howling out there?"

"Reckon so, Eb. But it might not be a bad idea for you to move the party indoors. You never know when a red wolf will show up."

Betty grasped Wetzel's arm and looked up at him. "No need worryin', Betty. I'll take care of you," Wetzel said with his rare smile.

The Colonel headed his guests into the cabin where a cheery fire in the fireplace lighted the room with its warm glow. Wetzel and Jonathan said their goodbyes and glided out into the darkness.

"I'd judge Mr. Wolf had best be making tracks," Captain Boggs remarked.

"I reckon Wetzel will come back, or Jack will, and let us know what's up. I'm sure it wasn't a genuine wolf or Lew wouldn't have told us to move inside."

As Wetzel and Jonathan approached the hill where the wolf call had come from an owl hooted. By a slight variation in the call the bordermen knew it was not the feathered hunter of the woods it pretended to be. At once came the wolf call again. Wetzel motioned for Jonathan to stalk the owl while he glided off to find the red wolf up on the hillside.

Wetzel moved slowly and deliberately toward the wolf call. No twig cracked under his feet. Not a rustle of a leaf or any sound came to give a warning to his quarry. His moccasins allowed him to feel the ground and avoid anything that might give him away. His eyes glittered with a light that boded ill for his enemy. Just ahead of him something moved in a clump of brush off to his right. Suddenly the call of a wolf came floating on the wind and was answered by the owl on the other side of the hill.

The hunter hunkered down behind a boulder to wait. On the other side of the hill Jonathan was approaching the place where the owl was hooting. Suddenly from the hill came a soft, low moan. It swelled mournfully, rose to a blood-chilling wail, and died away only to start again.

A dark form rose from a place of concealment to run past Jonathan. The borderman pounced upon him like a panther. His tomahawk rose and fell. A short choking cry emerged, but that was all. Only the moon was there to bear witness to the woodland violence. The short, spiteful crack of a rifle split the night only to die away after echoing down the valley. The wailing, strangling death cry of an Indian came on the heels of the rifle shot. Jonathan smiled grimly. At least the forest was cleared of two would-be killers. Just then the dark form of Wetzel stood beside him.

"Well, there's two more that won't be around to bedevil this fort this winter," Jonathan said.

"You notice what kinda guns those varmints was carrying?" Wetzel asked.

"No, why?"

"Brown Bess muskets. Top of the line. Pretty fancy for Injuns."

"Now where you reckon they got 'em? I haven't seen any sign of supply wagons come into Ohio. None around the fort, either," Jonathan mused.

"I'm afraid we've been snookered looking for wagons, Jack. I think they've brought 'em downriver and then took them overland to the tribes. But what worries me is what else did those Redcoated villains bring with them?"

"What do you mean?" Jonathan asked, but he was afraid he already knew the answer.

"Cannon," Wetzel said grimly.

"Well, if they've got cannon we better find 'em and take 'em out before next spring. I don't figure they'll be ready for a full-scale assault before then," Jonathan said.

"We've got to find that ugly-faced snake and kill him. He's the key to this whole mess," Wetzel said.

"Well, where do we start?" Jonathan asked.

"Well, I guess there's only one way," Wetzel said. "We'll have to check every path leading to the villages. Shawnee, Delaware, Huron. If they're here we'll find 'em. It's not that easy to hide a cannon."

"It's not that easy to hide a Redcoat either. They're mighty proud of their uniforms."

"Well, we'd best get back and let Eb know what we found," Jonathan said.

"He'll have to double the watch now."

"I don't look for an attack so late in the year, but who knows."

Colonel Zane received the bad news from Wetzel and Jonathan with the same courage with which he had kept his settlement alive when so many settlements had been burned to the ground and their residents scalped and murdered. He knew his bordermen would prevent any surprise attack. And he was sure that before spring was over, the renegade and his British companions would be dead. In the meantime he had the men stationed on the stockade and in the blockhouse. The women were busy making bullets, pouring molten lead into bullet molds, letting it cool and then opening the mold to let the bullet drop out. Each bullet had to be examined to make sure it was perfectly formed so it would fly true. As the cold winds of winter blew down off the mountains and the snow piled up, the pioneers settled in for a long cold winter, feeling comparatively safe.

Not so Jack and Wetzel. They knew that the Indians normally preferred to stay in the villages and leave the making of war for the spring, summer, and fall. But with the British involved, who knew what devilment could be cooked up?

The snow made it almost impossible to travel the trails so the bordermen had to content themselves with watching the river, manning the blockhouse, and fighting off the wolves that tried to get the livestock now that game was scarce. For Wetzel especially it was a trying time, but he was not a settler, and neither was Jonathan Zane. To these men winter was a time to spend pacing not unlike a caged tiger. Both the bordermen knew that it was a matter of utmost importance to find the camp of the British and the Gargoyle before they could get set for war. That would set the border aflame from one end to the other.

Jonathan spent a lot of time at the Colonel's home when he was in the settlement but he spent most of his time listening to the conversation rather than joining in. Both he and Wetzel were stone-faced, taciturn men living a life that was cold and dark and bloody. Colonel Zane never tired of trying to encourage his brother to court some of the girls in the village but as Jonathan said once, "My life is the borders, my sweetheart the

North Star." Wetzel seemed to care very much for the Zane family and spent many hours at the Colonel's cabin but his home also was the trackless wilds, the only place he felt truly comfortable.

TWENTY-ONE

One cold blustery day in February, Colonel Zane and John Harper were engaged in one of their favorite pastimes, a game of checkers. Suddenly a knock sounded upon the door. On the porch the Colonel found four officers of the Revolution. Ushering them into the dining room, the Colonel took their coats and motioned for them to sit down. After pouring each a glass of fine brandy to warm his visitors the Colonel asked, "And to what do I owe the honor of this visit, gentlemen?"

"Colonel, we know now that there's an army of three hundred British regulars ready to move into the border country come spring. They'll have over four hundred Indians ready to come with them against the settlements. The big thing is they've got ten cannons with them, twenty-pounders. The stockades won't stand against that."

"Well, gentlemen, what would you have us do?"

"Colonel, if I was you I'd abandon Fort Henry for the time being. Take your families back to Virginia."

"Give up all we've worked for all these years! No, sir! Not on your life. We've worked too hard, shed too much blood on this ground to have a bunch of Redcoats and renegades take it from us."

"Well, Colonel, I know how you feel but those cannons make the difference. Fifteen minutes after they open up there won't be anything but matchsticks left."

"Can Washington send some help?"

"I'm afraid not, Colonel. We've got all we can do to hold Cornwallis from running rampant all over the Colonies."

"Well, then the only thing is to have Jack and Wetzel find where that renegade is with those cannons. If we're lucky maybe we can send them east to use on the Redcoats. All I know is, we will not tuck our tails between our legs and go sneaking back east."

"Nothing cowardly about it, Colonel. If I was you I'd be thinking of my womenfolk and kids."

"I'll let you know, Captain. Right now I'm gonna talk with Jack and Lew and get the feelin' of the other men. I'm pretty sure what they'll say. They've got women and kids, too. But we all came here for new lives. We didn't plan to get dragged into the Revolution, but the British are bringing it right to our door."

"Well, it's your funeral, Colonel. If you locate those guns let us know. Then maybe we can send some help. Right now we've got all we can do to survive!"

Just between you and me, Colonel, Washington's in bad shape. If he don't have some victories pretty soon he's gonna lose half his army. He's low on food, clothing, ammunition, and most important, shelter! One of the men who came back from there said it's gonna be a hell of a time for those boys if they don't get help, and soon!"

"Well, you can take a couple of wagonloads of corn and flour. I'll get as many as have them to give some hams. It won't get them through the winter, but at least it will help some."

"Colonel, anything you can do to help will be greatly appreciated. If we could get all the settlements to kick in, it would help immensely."

"Well, try Boonesboro. Talk to Daniel Boone over there. I'm sure he'll help if he can," Colonel Zane said.

"I'll do that, Colonel. I wish more people would do what you're doing. I'll convey your feelings to General Washington. And I hope your bordermen can find these infiltrators. I'm afraid if they don't, we'll see total war up and down the border."

"Well, if anyone can find them it'll be Jack and Lew. I've counted on them for twelve years, and I'm sure I can depend on them to come through this time too."

"Well, we'd best be getting on our way back, Colonel. We'll stop at the Fort for supplies. Goodbye and good luck."

"Here, give this to Silas," the Colonel said, handing them a note of authorization. "He'll help as best he can."

After his visitors left, Colonel Zane walked down to the fort. He found it well manned, with the pioneers taking turns on the catwalk and manning each bastion. The one bulldog cannon was aimed down the trail leading up from the river. The Colonel felt comfortable with the fort's state of readiness.

He found Wetzel and Jonathan in Wetzel's cabin going over some maps of the Ohio country.

"How's it going, gentlemen?"

"Well, we're checking every square mile of the country along the river," Jonathan said. "There's about three caves big enough to hide some wagons. Then over around Half King's village there is about four or five that could be big enough. I reckon we'll start with those as soon as spring comes."

"I just had a visit from the army from back east," the Colonel said. "They told me that they now know that the cannons from back east are headed this way. He recommended we close the fort and head back to Virginia. I told him that all the Indians and renegades in Ohio wasn't enough to drive us out of this country."

"We'll be movin' out soon as the winter breaks," Wetzel said. "They can't stay hid forever."

TWENTY-TWO

The winter dragged on. February came with its cold windy days and clear cold nights. The pioneers could do little but care for the livestock and wait for spring. Wetzel and Jonathan spent many hours in Colonel Zane's cabin playing cards or checkers with the Colonel and telling stories to the children. Betty and the Colonel's wife were working on a quilt with a flag of the thirteen colonies sewn into it. Wetzel told tales of Indians and animals and a ghost story or two. Betty tried her best to get Lew to dance when the Colonel picked up his fiddle. He finally did cut the rug with her once. They made a striking couple with Betty's colorful dress twirling and Wetzel's long hair flying. When combed out and let down, it reached within a foot of the ground. In his mind, he couldn't cut it because it would tell the Indians that he feared them — every warrior in the Ohio territory wanted that scalp. It would make any brave a chief if he could say, "See, I have stopped Deathwind's bloody trail."

The Colonel watched as the borderman danced. Zane knew the hunter as well as any man on the border. When he was in need of information about what went on in the forest around the fort, Wetzel went out to find out what was needed. When a girl was kidnapped, mother and father killed, Wetzel and Jonathan took the trail alone to bring her back and spill the blood of the villains, red or white, who had perpetrated this atrocity. On the frontier there were no juries or prisons. Colonel Zane had to make the decisions of life and death for men who broke the law. His bordermen were the police force that brought the frontier's murderers and outlaws to justice.

When Jack and Wetzel were in the village the pioneers felt a lot safer. Wetzel sometimes took part in foot races in which he was hands-down the fastest runner on the border. On some occasions Wetzel would join in the shooting contests. Colonel Zane looked forward to these shooting matches with delight. One of the contests that the riflemen on the border engaged in was called snuffing the candle. It consisted of placing a candle at various distances in the dark and snuffing it with a rifle bullet. Jonathan could do it consistently at a hundred yards. One evening Colonel Zane asked Lewis to try it. The candle was placed at a hundred fifty yards. Wetzel checked the wind. There was no breeze. The long black rifle rose to a level and stopped. A red flame burst forth, followed by a sharp crack. The candle was dark. Wetzel had made a shot that many pioneers said couldn't be made.

Such were the bordermen. Such were the men that, when spring came, would find the lair of the Redcoats and renegades and put an end to their conquest of the forts along the Ohio.

Wetzel and Jonathan both knew that if the cannons were brought to bear against the wooden stockades of Fort Henry or Boonesboro there would be little chance of any of the pioneers surviving.

:::

The month of March passed with only a whimper. The geese were flying in their wedges across the sky. The melting snow made the streams and the river crowd their banks. Betty saw a robin in a tree outside her window. The first of April came and Lew and Jonathan knew it was time to hit the trail.

The night before they left, the bordermen and the Colonel walked down to the river. It was a beautiful spring evening. The frogs were croaking, insects buzzing and a whippoorwill called from down the valley. A beautiful half moon sailed high into the heavens.

"Sure is a wonderful night," the Colonel said.

"This is the kind of night that makes you know what you're fighting for," Wetzel remarked.

"Don't worry, Eb," said his brother. "We'll find the villains. And when we do the ground will turn red with their blood."

Colonel Zane nodded. He knew that as sure as the sun rose and set, someday soon the renegades would sleep on the moss and leaves. In their eyes would be the realization that the Wind of Death had settled with them for their evil deeds.

TWENTY-THREE

In a bluff about ten miles north of Fort Henry and across the Ohio was a huge natural cavern hollowed out over millions of years by the mighty motion of an ancient river as it wound its way south. Jonathan and Wetzel headed straight for it; they'd decided it was the largest and most likely place to hide a cache of weapons. They knew that the whole area was probably crawling with Indians. It was a council rock where the Shawnees held their ceremonial celebrations and a meeting place for peace talks between the tribes.

The bordermen arrived at the river in late afternoon. They knew that the best time to check out the cave was after dark. They had a meal of sandwiches from their knapsacks and streamwater to wash it down. They risked no fire to give them away with smoke or a glow after dark. They made no sound to alert an Indian warrior that Deathwind had entered the sacred grounds.

That night as they waited for moonrise the sweet smell of wood smoke reached their nostrils. Somewhere close was a campfire.

The moon rose into a cloudless sky. As it looked down over the forest it saw soft shadows that glided silently from the cover of the thicket toward the cavern. An old wolf on his nocturnal prowl had detected the smell of something delicious coming from the area of the cave, but then it caught the scent of two more of the hated man things. The wolf didn't like the odds and glided past on his way to seek easier prey.

A wise old buck whitetail had come to the edge of the water to dip his velvet muzzle in the coolness of the river where he saw a tiger-like shadow rise from a clump of bushes and then sink into the ground. The old buck put its head down to glide silently away. He hadn't got as old as he had by being careless.

On the edge of the cave two dark forms rose to their full height and stepped inside. Two forms wrapped in blankets were sleeping near a cherry fire. They looked to be not much more than boys. Wetzel and Jack Zane stood over them. Killing them would only serve to warn the Indians that there were intruders in their hunting grounds.

"Reckon we'll let 'em go," Wetzel said. "Nothing but a couple of kids up here tryin' to win their eagle plumes."

"You letting an Injun off the hook?" Jonathan asked incredulously.

"Reckon so. We'll probably end up having to fight 'em a few years from now anyways. No sense lettin' Half King and all the rest of those butchers know we're here."

The bordermen backed quietly out of the cave. They had seen no sign of wagons, cannons, or British regulars. They crawled into their blankets that night knowing that time was a luxury they didn't have. Even now the Indians were growing in strength and urged on by Girty and the Gargoyle. They would be ready soon to set the border aflame.

Meanwhile, across the border in Canada a wagon train was headed south laden with cannons, kegs of powder, and bars of lead all guarded by a long column of British soldiers. On one of the wagons sat a huge figure with the face of a monster and a soul to match.

In each soldier's mind was the desire to take the cannons south to destroy the settlements and help defeat the Colonies. These obstinate Colonists had embarrassed Cornwallis for two years and were a long ways from defeat.

The wagons rolled along. The Redcoats marched along behind with a few of the Shawnees out front. The Gargoyle rode the lead wagon. It was extremely stupid to be out there in the open but a renegade such as he was never known for his intelligence. Simon Girty on the other hand was always in the forest and haunting the thickets always on the edges of cover.

The renegade was feeling a twinge of conscience but he knew that conscience was the one thing he could little afford. Simon Girty was precious shy of his skin and he didn't look forward to having his neck stretched. Girty also knew that the frontiersmen from hell to breakfast were out for his scalp. Daniel Boone had lost one of his sons in Kentucky. The Girty brothers had attacked and murdered family after family in Kentucky and West Virginia and because their name was Girty, Simon got the blame along with them.

Simon Kenton had sworn to kill Girty, as had Sam Brady and Jonathan Zane, but the man that Girty feared above all others was Wetzel, the Deathwind. Wetzel would not just kill him — he would make him cuss his own mother for giving him birth, Girty was sure of that.

The renegade's eyes sought out the cliffs above the wagons and the rocks at the river's edge as the wagons rolled slowly inexorably south. Simon Girty knew that if the bordermen knew where they were at this moment he would be dead within twenty-four hours. No doubt about that. No matter that he traveled with three hundred Redcoats and close to fifty Shawnees. Nothing would save him. Sometimes Simon Girty wished that he had never left Canada.

Suddenly one of the wagon wheels broke and the wagon tilted, throwing the driver off and frightening the horses. Girty was extremely delighted that it wasn't a wagon with either powder or cannons but only a general supply wagon. Otherwise it could have caused a delay for a day or more for repairs.

The British captain rode over to berate Girty about the broken wagon. "I thought you said these wagons were trail-worthy?"

"They are, Captain. I didn't say they wouldn't break a wheel or wagon tongue. That's just the way it goes on the road."

"Well, you bloody well better remember that any delay jeopardizes our mission."

"I know that better than you, captain. It's my hair that's on the line even more than yours. I'm the one that's got those damn bordermen hunting me."

"You sound like you're afraid of two men. What can they do against all the men we've got here? Getting a little spooky, aren't you?"

"Listen, Captain, you haven't been out here on the frontier for more than a year and you haven't been trailed by these damn bordermen like I have. Wingenund isn't afraid of the devil himself, but even he has a healthy respect for Wetzel. The Indians all call him Deathwind. They say the death wind blows through the forest when Wetzel's on their trail. Maybe you'll say I'm crazy but I've heard that damn wind, and it chilled me clear to the bone. Damn right I'm spooked."

"Well, if it'll make you feel better, I'll send out ten or fifteen regulars. If those bordermen are snooping around we'll bloody well settle their hash damn quick."

"Captain, if you'll forgive me for sayin' it, you're crazy. Have you ever been hunted by somebody you can't see? Somebody that can kill you from two hundred fifty yards. You can't ambush them and you can't trail 'em. Just how in the hell you think you're gonna settle their hash?"

"Well, anyway, it appears as if they've got the wagons fixed so I suggest we get back underway, Mister Girty."

"Very well, Captain."

As the Redcoat officer turned to head for the front of the column Girty called to him. "Oh, Captain."

"Yes?"

"Keep your head down!"

"I'll do that, Girty."

The British soldier was far out of his element. Every bird, every animal, every leaf spoke to the bordermen, and not a sound did they make as they stole onward through the forest.

TWENTY-FOUR

The column continued south. If this wagon train got through to its destination it would be the end for many a fledgling village. The brush would soon cover up the scenes of tragedy. The grass would grow green and the blackness of ashes would disappear and the bones of men, women, and children would bleach white in the sun.

At another time in anther place, the Redcoats would try to justify what they did by saying it was war. No matter that they planned to unleash hordes of howling devils upon settlers who had no idea what was headed their way. By the grace of God the pioneers knew what was coming. But being prepared was no guarantee. The frontier would be aflame and the streams would run red if Girty and the Redcoats had their way.

:::

Along a chain of low hills about twenty miles west of the Ohio, the dark figure of a man carrying a long rifle crept along the edge of a clump of trees. He never stepped out into the open, always moving rapidly from tree to tree. As he crossed an open space the sun brightened his face. It was Jonathan Zane. He and Wetzel had split up that morning to check several trails that might be wide enough for a wagon to pass through. They had hoped to find a trace of the enemy wagontrain, but so far no such luck. Jonathan completed the circle of the hills and approached a standing stone where he was to meet Wetzel. He had just reached it when the tall form of Wetzel stood beside him.

"Any sign of what we're looking fer?" Wetzel asked.

"Nary a sign. If they've brought wagons through here, they had to fly."

"Well, we'll camp here for the night and head over to Shawnee rock in the morning," Wetzel said.

"I hate to say it, but we're running out of time. If those cannon get here before we can head them off, the border is in big trouble," Jonathan said.

"Jack, if you needed to bring in wagons and you didn't want to let anybody know it, where would you bring them from?"

"Hard tellin'! We know they didn't cross the river. Maybe I'd bring 'em down the trail from the north along the river."

"What's north of here?" Wetzel asked in his deep voice.

"Canada, by God!" Jonathan exclaimed.

"Right! I reckon you've hit the mark!" Wetzel's eyes were burning like torches.

"Girty's bringin' 'em down from Canada. The British supply the guns and Girty brings 'em down while that big ugly villain works up the tribes!"

"I believe we've nailed 'em," Jonathan said. "Now where do we look for 'em?"

"Comin' right down the trail from Canada, straight along the Ohio. That's where we'll look for 'em starting in the morning," Wetzel growled.

"There's a bridge over Pine River they'll have to cross," Jonathan said. "And if they are comin' that way, then that's where we'll hit 'em."

Wetzel nodded. His jaws clamped like a steel trap.

TWENTY-FIVE

Morning found Wetzel and Jonathan on the trail. It was a bright spring morning with mists off the hills and valleys making it slow going for the bordermen. Fog hung over the low areas and might conceal an enemy. Once they surprised a huge old whitetail buck that bounded away through the forest. This worried the bordermen, for a running deer could alert a native scout. Crows cawed from a treetop and squirrels barked from tree limbs at these intruders in their forest home. The bordermen's top priority was to avoid the Indian scouts, get to the gorge without alerting the Indians, and stop the wagons.

Suddenly Wetzel halted, raising his hand. Something on the trail ahead had struck a discord with the hunter. They spent long minutes watching the trail to spot what had alerted Wetzel. He had almost begun to think he was mistaken when a wild commotion burst from a thicket down the trail and a huge turkey gobbler took flight. The gobbler had seen something. A minute later one, two, three dark forms glided across an open space in the thicket and disappeared in the forest beyond.

The bordermen knew that though they had seen three Shawnees, the Indians many times would leave a sentinel behind bringing up the rear. They waited long minutes and sure enough the bordermen saw another dark form gliding along behind the other Indians. Wetzel's eyes glittered not unlike a tiger about to spring. Even though they had another more important job to do, the hunters' thirst for Indian blood was strong.

Wetzel and Jonathan waited a few more minutes then proceeded cautiously on their way. Seeing the Shawnees this far north told the bordermen that what Colonel Zane had feared was true. Girty and his ugly companion had managed to get the tribes to join forces against the settlements. If they managed to get the cannons, Fort Henry, Boonesboro, Fort Pitt were all doomed. It was imperative that they stop the wagons at the gorge. And if they could get a shot at Girty or the Gargoyle they would take it as a welcome bonus. It would go a long way toward clearing the border of a monstrous thorn in the settlers' side.

Meanwhile at a cabin about twenty or twenty-five miles from Fort Henry, a farmer and his wife and children set about the day's chores. The oldest son had just taken a basket of corn to feed the hogs while his father was pitching hay to the cattle. The new spring grass was not yet long enough to let the cows graze upon it. The delicious smell of fresh baked bread reached the boy's nostrils and his stomach rumbled in anticipation of a slice or two smothered in fresh churned butter. Made a fella feel awful lucky to be alive. His sister had just come out to the clothesline to hang up the family's clothes when their old dog started barking insanely. The boy dropped what he was doing and sprinted for the house. His pa always said that old hound could smell an Indian a mile away, and the boy knew the only thing that would set the dog barking like that was Injuns. The boy ran into the house, followed closely by his father and sister. The door was slammed shut and barred. The heavy shutters on the windows were closed, leaving only rifle ports. Now began a waiting game. The morning dragged on; noon came and went. Not a sign of an Indian could be seen. On the edge of the clearing a flock of birds burst from cover with a whirring of wings. Still no Indian could be seen. But once in a while the dog rose to his feet with a growl.

The chickens scratched in the dirt of the yard and the cow bellowed from the barn. Soon it would be time for the evening milking.

"If they're gonna start something I wish they'd get to it," the boy said.

"Don't wish for that, boy. It'll come soon enough if they're out there."

The sun had made its trip across the sky and was headed toward the horizon in the west. Suddenly the father's rifle snarled from the window toward the barn. An Indian's strangling death cry sounded. An arrow thunked into the barred door of the cabin. That was all.

"Maybe there were just two of them," the boy said hopefully.

"Not likely, but we'll wait and see. When it gets dark, if there's more of the sneaks out there, they'll probably try somethin' then."

Suddenly another rifle shot split the silence and echoed away down the valley.

"Ho the cabin. Sam Brady here!"

"Brady. Thank God, we thought we were goners!"

"Well, there's one sure thing. If you don't get to Fort Henry, you will be. I got the last of your visitors. He's lyin' over by the barn. But I've seen tracks of Shawnee and Delawares all over these woods. Get your wagon loaded, and we'll get started for the fort at midnight."

"How can we give up all we've worked for here? This is our home!" the woman said.

"Ain't much of a home if you end up buried in it or burned at the stake. Maybe after this is all over you can come back."

"Well, hard as it is, I guess that's the best thing to do."

"I'll stay on guard for the night in the woods. I can cover you better from there. Be ready at midnight!" Brady said.

"We'll be ready, Brady. There's four of us, and I suppose we'll try to bring the cow and the horses. We'll turn the pigs loose and let the chickens fend for themselves."

"Good! See you at midnight." Brady headed into the forest and was soon lost to view. The pioneer family turned to the task at hand with heavy hearts.

At the darkest hour, true to his word, Sam Brady was at the door. He helped wrap the wagon wheels with hides to muffle the sounds of them over rocky ground. The axles were well greased so no squeak would give them away. They tied the dog's jaws shut so no bark would betray them. Silence was their best ally now.

Slowly, ever so slowly, they eased down the road toward Fort Henry. They made fifteen miles the first night — it was very slow going with the cow and the wagon. They cold-camped on the trail. Brady absolutely forbade any fire. The smell of wood smoke could reach the nostrils of a warrior and spell disaster. Even pipe smoke was something too risky to gamble with. The next day about noon they topped the hill above Fort Henry and a little later were inside the stockade. They felt very grateful to Brady and lucky, lucky indeed.

Excerpt from the
Journal of Harriet Bonnet Smith

Many families with burnt-out cabins and their crops destroyed arrived at Fort Henry with little more than the clothes on their backs. At such times Colonel Zane would do his best to provide shelter and then it would fall to the women to help provide clothing for the women and girls. Mostly if every one gave something, this could be readily accomplished.

TWENTY-SIX

Thirty miles above the pine river gorge on the trail from Canada, Wetzel and Jonathan had found what they were looking for. On the trail below their place of concealment was the renegade's column. First came five Shawnee scouts spread out to look for any threat on the trail ahead. Behind them came a hundred and fifty British regulars with their spit-and-polish Redcoat uniforms and gleaming rifles. They were ready for battle. Next came eleven wagons with covers over what they contained. Then a hundred fifty more Redcoats and five Delawares bringing up the rear. Off to the right in the shadows of the rocks and scrub grass rode the renegade Simon Girty and the Gargoyle. Wetzel and Jonathan wished with all their hearts that they could drop the renegades from their saddles right then but it was not to be. No warning must be given to the column until it was too late to save the dastard's plans.

Jack and Wetzel withdrew and headed back into the forest. About a mile in they stopped.

"Any ideas?" Wetzel asked.

Jonathan shook his head. "We don't have enough powder in our powder horns to blow that bridge."

"Right down there is all the powder we need," Wetzel said.

"Trouble is, they might take a dim view of our borrowing some of it," Jonathan said.

"Well, come tonight we're gonna find a way to separate one of those wagons from the rest. Maybe if one of those teams got scared they'd wreck one of those wagons. In the confusion we'll help ourselves to a keg of that powder. They'll leave the horses hitched. That's the mistake we been lookin' fer."

That night the Redcoat camp was something to behold. The fire they built was huge and bright enough to be seen for miles. Like Wetzel had it figured, they left the horses hitched to the wagons for a quick getaway down the trail. They sat around the fire smoking their pipes, and the smell of tobacco could be detected for miles. The bordermen marveled at the Redcoats' stupidity. They couldn't help but smile at what must be going through Simon Girty's mind. Girty and his brothers James and George had lived by stealth and wood lore — knowing how to be hard to find in the woods. To him it must seem the Redcoats were trying to be detected. After the Redcoat camp had settled down for the night the bordermen crept up to within bowshot of the wagons. Jonathan had fashioned a bow out of a tree branch, good enough for their purposes. Releasing a blunt-headed arrow, Jonathan smacked a horse in the rump. The result was immediate and dramatic.

The horse leaped in the traces as a second arrow hit him again. The team bolted down the trail scattering rifles, a cannon, and powder kegs. Wetzel was waiting by the trail, and he grabbed two small kegs and leaped away. Up the trail the bordermen could hear the Redcoat captain shouting orders to his men. Then came Girty's hoarse yell cursing the horses and everything four-legged in the general proximity. Confusion reigned supreme. The team had broken loose from the wagon and fled full speed down the trail, hauling hoofs for other parts. The bordermen were confident that the Redcoats and renegades would figure that something like a panther or wolf scent had frightened the horses. They wouldn't be looking for the bordermen. With a full moon to light the trail, the hunters traveled most of the night. They knew that to stop the wagons they would need all the time they could get.

Meanwhile, the Redcoats had finally managed to get the horses calmed down and returned to the camp. They had finally managed to establish some semblance of order.

Simon Girty was poking around where the horses had been tied. The captain walked over and asked, "What are you looking for, Girty? The boogeyman?

"Captain, if it's what I suspect frightened the horses you might end up wishing it was the bloody boogeyman."

"Still looking for those bloody bordermen, are you, Girty?"

"Might be, Captain. It just might be. If they know about these cannons you damn well better believe they'll be after us like thunder after lightning. You can bet on that."

"Well, as there isn't a thing we can do about it tonight and as we've a long day tomorrow I suggest we get some rest. We have the Indians to keep watch, and I can't believe anyone would dare attack a camp this size!"

"Captain, I'm afraid you have a damn dear lesson coming to you. If you're lucky you'll live through it." Girty sounded so almighty sure of himself the Redcoat couldn't help being a little less confident than he had been.

The renegade had lived in these wild lands for a long time and had risen to a level of respect among the Indian tribes rarely achieved by a white man. He must know what he was talking about or he wouldn't have lived this long. But the Redcoat's big downfall was his inability to adjust to a different warfare. In England the British soldier was used to lining up in mass against a foe that lined up across a disputed battleground. After firing their muskets they would fix bayonets and then charge to combat with their foes. It seemed they never learned to adjust to border warfare against an unseen foe who could kill from an unheard-of distance. A foe who would shoot from cover and even the Indians in years of unrelenting warfare had been unable to kill or capture. The Captain, though he would never admit it to his superiors, fervently wished that this damn revolution was over, win or lose. Let the damn rebels have this bloody wilderness.

TWENTY-SEVEN

The next morning Wetzel and Jonathan reached the bridge over Pine River. They spent most of the day scouting to make sure no Indians had yet reached the area. No sign of their red foes could be seen. In order for Wetzel's plan to work they must wait till nightfall to plant the two kegs of powder. No fuses could be used, for the burning length could be discovered. Both kegs would be tied together against the support of the bridge. Then at just the right moment when the wagons were on the span crossing the river, a well-aimed bullet from Wetzel's rifle would hit the keg and set off the charge.

After making their plans, they went back up river to find the Redcoat column; it was right on schedule. The Redcoats and renegades would arrive around 10:00 a.m. the next morning. Everything must be in place by then.

That night before moonrise the bordermen were ready. At twilight the kegs were tied. The support poles of the bridge would be taken out with the detonation of the kegs, dumping the wagons with their cargoes of powder, cannons, and muskets along with as many of the Redcoats and renegades as possible into the river. The only thing left to do now was wait. Wetzel said the Indian scouts would not get into the river to check the pylons. If they crossed the river and continued scouting ahead then the plan would work without a hitch.

Sure enough, the next morning three Shawnee were observed crossing the bridge and carefully surveying the road ahead. They continued on their way, not thinking to look under the bridge. A few minutes later marching feet and creaking wheels and snorting horses could be heard, and the column pulled into view. The Redcoats crossed the bridge and regrouped on the other side. Just as the wagons were strung out on the bridge Wetzel's rifle cracked with its short, stinging sound and a second later a tremendous explosion roared skyward, sending pylons, rails, boards, wagons, horses, and Redcoats into the river. Jonathan had taken up a position behind the wagons and now sent an arrow of fire into the rear wagon teetering on the bridge. Another tremendous explosion rent the air.

Above the bridge and wagons rose a huge black cloud of smoke billowing skyward. Wetzel and Jonathan shook hands in satisfaction. The cannons would not be used against the settlements this summer.

Simon Girty cussed horses, Redcoats, and bordermen in particular. All the work of bringing the wagons and cannons was gone for nothing. Along with it went Girty's chances of security. The Redcoat captain was busy getting what was left of his column reformed. A few of his men had managed to drag themselves out of the river. But over eighty men had been lost along with all the wagons and powder. The Gargoyle had disappeared back into the forest.

Girty walked up to where the Redcoat captain was talking to his men.

"Well, what do you think about these two bordermen now, Captain?"

"Damn you, Girty. Damn you and those bloody bordermen and this bloody wilderness. If I have my way I'll see them hanged. And as far as I'm concerned you look too damn satisfied to suit me. Maybe I'll see if I can fit you for a noose, too."

"You try that, Captain, and you'll have every damn Indian on the border against you in a second. Your scalp will look damn good on some chief's lodge pole."

"All right, all right. Forget it. What's to be done now?"

"Well, we've still got over a hundred ninety men. I'll get us to where we can meet up with the camp at Redoaks. We'll get them ready and attack the settlement without cannons."

"You think we can overcome them, Girty?"

"Well, I don't know, Captain. You got any better ideas?"

"One sure thing: it's gonna be a lot harder without the cannon. Our ugly friend is gonna have a lot harder time getting the Injuns moving, specially after they find out those damn bordermen are on our trail."

"To hell with the bloody bordermen. We'll roast them in the same fire as the rest of these colonials."

"Ain't as easy as it sounds, Captain. We might be lookin' up the bore of old Deathwind's rifle right now."

"You don't think they'd hang around after this day's work?"

"Can't tell, Captain. Wetzel's been after my scalp for years. Unless I'm damn lucky he'll get it, too. But I ain't gonna make it easy for him."

"Well, let's get goin' for the Redcoats' camp then. I've got orders to set this damn frontier ablaze this summer, and that's what I bloody well intend to do Girty! Let's go!"

"Aye, aye, Captain," Girty nodded.

As the Redcoat column began the long march the captain shivered and his eyes sought the cliffs around the trail and the brush and trees and anything that might conceal a foe. Despite himself he couldn't help feeling the sights of a long rifle on the back of his neck.

Wetzel and Jonathan searched long and hard for the Gargoyle's trail. The renegade was cunning and devious in the woods. He traveled only over rocky, hard ground. Once in a while he broke a twig or overturned a leaf or branch, but these mistakes were few and far between. But gradually it became apparent that the Gargoyle was swinging east toward the Shawnee towns. The bordermen knew that in order to head off the attacks on the settlements that summer the Gargoyle must be destroyed along with Simon Girty and their henchmen among the tribes. There was Fort Pitt, Fort Henry, Boonesboro, and Short Creek to name a few. Pipe and Half King along with Wingenund and Tarhe Huron, were all joining forces to purge the Ohio country. The Redcoats no doubt would make another attempt to bring in cannons. It was just a question of how.

TWENTY-EIGHT

Colonel Zane welcomed the news from Jonathan of the destruction of the munitions train at Pine River with relief. The Redcoats might get a siege together, but they would not have the cannons and gunpowder to do it with.

Jonathan reported that Wetzel was hot on the trail of the Gargoyle and that Simon Girty and the Gargoyle were in cahoots with the British along with the Indians. Jonathan had set up a system of scouts to watch the river. Both he and the Colonel believed that the Indians and the British might try to slip across the river from Ohio to surprise the garrison at Fort Henry.

Wetzel was trying to find where the Gargoyle and Simon Girty had holed up. Simon Girty was with the Delawares, but the Gargoyle had disappeared like the Earth had swallowed him. No tracks, no sightings. Wetzel had spent days watching the different camps, but no sign had he seen.

The hunter had hoped that he would have a chance to end the Gargoyle's killing once and for all, but no opportunity had presented itself.

One afternoon about two weeks after the dumping of the supply wagons into the river, Wetzel noticed a great commotion in the Delaware towns.

War whoops rent the air: the screeching signaled the arrival of someone very important. Then into the village at the head of three hundred Huron warriors rode Thunder Cloud, war chief of the Hurons. Well did Wetzel recognize that war bonnet. The hunter had spent many a day in ambush waiting for that strong face to ride into view. Wetzel would have loved to put a bullet right in the middle of that forehead.

Between Thunder Cloud and Wingenund, there were over five hundred fifty warriors preparing to set the border aflame. God help the settlements. Some of them, like Fort Henry or Boonesboro, might survive, but many of the smaller white villages would not stand in the face of such an overwhelming force.

Men and older women and children would most likely be killed outright or burned at the stake to please Pipe or Half King. The older girls would be carried off to satisfy the perverted wishes of the renegades. Wetzel knew he had to get back to Fort Henry with the information for Colonel Zane. With one last glance at Thunder Cloud from his glittering eyes, the hunter left on the trail to Fort Henry.

Two days traveling put Wetzel on Colonel Zane's doorstep. The Colonel paled when he got the report on the doings at the Delaware camp. Over the years the Colonel had began to think of the settlers, their wives, and children as his family. A man can face death with impunity. With his rifle and tomahawk he can fight to the death. But when his loved ones are facing a bloody death at the hands of Indians and renegades then it is an altogether different thing. The Colonel knew that should the total force from the Delaware camp come against his settlement, the chance of survival would be slim. But he also knew that Jonathan was there to lead his men and Wetzel was in the woods to warn them at the slightest sign of the enemy. The Colonel knew that the terrible borderman would kill either Wingenund or Thunder Cloud if they set foot on this side of the Ohio. Wingenund or Thunder Cloud would die with a small bloody hole from Deathwind's rifle. The hunter could put a bullet in the eye of a squirrel at more than a hundred yards. In the woods he was like a lion stalking his prey. The sighing of the winds in the trees might well tell the Indians and renegades that Deathwind prowled the forest and, should they cross the river, it would cost them dearly. Jonathan was here and there and everywhere scouting the fringes of the woods while the pioneers did their plowing and seeding. At night he met with Wetzel to discuss the strategy the hunter had come up with.

Jonathan Zane was by far the most untamable of all the Zane brothers. Colonel Zane, Silas, Isaac, and Andrew all fought Indians when need be, but to Jonathan the whistle of a bullet and the screech of a dying Indian was music to his ears. He was a fitting companion for Wetzel.

Like Wetzel, Jonathan was not at home in the settlements. He loved the silence of the deep wilderness. He loved the quiet in the forest, the smell of the trees after a rain, and the verdant green of the unbroken wilderness. To Jonathan it was more home than a village could ever be. He did enjoy his visits with his brother and listening to the conversations of his sister and Mrs. Zane and telling stories to Noah, the Colonel's son, but soon the restlessness would come upon him. It was a relief when he was in the forest again. He was, after all, a borderman.

TWENTY-NINE

Colonel Zane believed it was of utmost importance that Boonesboro and Short Creek be warned. Daniel Boone was a good frontiersman and would, if he had the time, be able to mount a good defense against the Redcoats and the renegades. Boone was fortunate that Simon Kenton called Boonesboro home. Sam Brady frequented Boone's cabin and was there to visit on many occasions. And a member of the Wetzel family, Jacob, spent a lot of time in Boone's settlement.

Several weeks went by and nothing was seen or heard of Girty and the Gargoyle or the Redcoats. Wetzel spent his time scouting the woods to try to pick up some sign of the renegades. Evidently they were lying low waiting for the Redcoats to move.

One morning as Wetzel crossed a valley the quick notes of a catbird struck a discord in the wilderness symphony. He didn't need the rasp of a blue jay to tell him that somewhere not far ahead was another man. Wetzel shrank into the bushes beside the trail. He'd scarcely concealed himself when the sound of Indian voices reached his ears. A tremble like a tiger about to spring upon his prey rippled through the hunter's powerful frame. What a change had come over the hunter's face. The jaw had become set. The dark eyes had begun to burn with a fire unearthly in their dark depths. Thus he changed from borderman to Deathwind. He was now focused on the purpose that had been his life's work, the killing of Indians! The Wind of Death blew over the hills and vales. The terrible borderman desired only to spill more Indian blood.

The voices became louder, and then an Indian warrior glided into view. Five more followed. The long black barrel of Wetzel's rifle swept to a level and stopped. A red flame and a puff of white smoke belched forth, followed by the short, spiteful crack of a rifle shot. The first Indian dropped without a sound. Wetzel sprang up and took to his heels, long black hair streaming behind. The Indians discharged their muskets and, whooping like demons right out of the abyss, took off in full pursuit. Wetzel's figure, large target though it was, was almost impossible to hit so rapidly did he dodge in and out among the trees. But then he began slowing down. Supposing either the hunter had been hit or was out of breath the Indians charged on in full pursuit. Like other fighters of the period Wetzel had perfected the ability to reload his rifle while running at full speed. This skill he employed now. Turning suddenly, he shot the first Indian dead. Again he bounded off at top speed. Twice he reloaded and two more Indians lay dead. The last warrior, seeing he was the only one left, broke off the pursuit and disappeared back the way he had come. Wetzel waited awhile then returned up the trail to scalp the dead Indians. This let the Indians know that Deathwind was on the trail. Other Indian fighters such as Boone or Jonathan Zane didn't take scalps. Wetzel was known for it.

One of the most famous of the Indian chiefs of that time was Wingenund, chief of the Delawares. A braver, nobler Indian chief never lived on the border. One of the most respected of the Lenanape, the Wolf Clan, he was well known as a terrible warrior in battle but was one of the strongest advocates for peace on the frontier. One of his sons had led an attack on Boonesboro and Fort Henry. Wingenund was there when Colonel William Crawford was burned at the stake in revenge for Colonel Cresap's raid on Logan's Village. In the annals of Indian history, no more moving speech was there than that given by Logan.

"I ask the white man when did he come to Logan Village thirsty and I gave him nothing to drink. When did he come hungry and I didn't give him food? When was he wounded and I didn't bind up his wounds? Such was my love for the white man that during the last bloody war I didn't take the war trail, and remained in my tipi. The warriors of my village said, 'Logan is a friend of the white man.' A few years ago a troop of white soldiers under Colonel Cresap attacked and burned Logan's Village killing my wife, my children, father, mother, sister and brother. There runs not one drop of blood belonging to Logan in any living person. Logan has made war. I have taken my revenge. Now Logan is sick of war. Our young men die. The Redcoats want us to go to war against the white settlements. Deathwind's bloody trail continues. It is enough. Logan will not lead his people in war. But not because of fear. Logan never felt fear. Who is there is mourn for Logan? There is not one. Logan has spoken."

The Gargoyle did all he could to win Wingenund and Logan to the Redcoat cause. Aided by Simon Girty he made plans to march on Fort Henry. While Wingenund held Girty in high regard, he had nothing but disdain for the Gargoyle. The man's cowardice under fire, his habit of disappearing when Deathwind was in the area, all spoke of a coward.

There was an enmity between Wetzel and Wingenund but neither accused the other of being a coward. There was hatred, yes. A blood enmity, but no disrespect.

On one long afternoon the council met as a preparation for going to Boonesboro. Girty had laid the groundwork for a full-scale attack on Boone's settlement.

Two hundred British and over two hundred warriors were prepared for battle. Girty had hoped to intimidate Boone into giving up by bluffing about the British cannons. He had no way of knowing that Jonathan Zane had already warned Boone that the cannons were at the bottom of the pine river.

Boone had called in all the villagers from the outlying farms and was prepared to fight to the last man to defend his settlement.

Girty was addressing the circle of chiefs and warriors.

"Warriors of the Delaware and Shawnee, first we hit the village of Boonesboro, then Short Creek. After these villages have been burned we go to Fort Henry at Wheeling Creek. Girty knows that the people of the forest are brave warriors. They will fight to take back their lands to protect their families. They know that unless these white intruders are driven from the forest they will spread like locusts over the prairies and woodlands until even the graves of our ancestors will have to give way. People of the forest—Delaware, Huron, Shawnee—come now with Girty. Kill the whites, burn the forts, purge the forest. Will you follow me?"

One long war whoop rent the air. Five hundred warriors lent their voices to the thunder of the force ready to march on Boonesboro.

On the way to Boone's settlement were two or three small villages that had little or no ability to defend themselves. One, Shelby's Fort, was not really a fort at all but only a few cabins with a trading post and a general store. The founder of the settlement, because relations had been good with the Indians, had never felt a stockade was necessary. However, he had not taken into consideration the renegades, the Redcoats, and the Gargoyle. No one could possibly have anticipated the Redcoats working with the Indians to kill every man, woman, and child on the border.

Excerpt from Journal of Harriet Bonnet Smith

To give an idea of the dread of the Girtys that ran rampant all over the frontier was when mothers felt danger was imminent only had to tell the children, "Stay in the clearing or stay in the cabin or Simon Girty will get you!" That was all that needed to be said. The children were terrified of the name of Girty.

THIRTY

The attack came one early morning without warning. The settlers at Shelby's Station had just finished the morning chores and were having breakfast when the first war whoops came from the woods. Shelby heard the first shots and ran out the door to see what was happening. He died right there on the steps of his cabin. Some of the men tried to put up a resistance, but the massive attack by the Indians rolled over the pioneers like an unstoppable wave. A great fire was ignited in the center of the group of cabins, and men, women, and children were thrown screaming into the fire. The renegades took two or three of the older girls. One girl grabbed a knife from an Indian and, after seeing her mother and father murdered, plunged the knife into her own heart.

The Indians ran rampant through the village scalping the dead and dying. Some of the scalps were ripped off of still-living people. The Redcoats held back, appalled by this bloody orgy of butchery. One face alone showed no horror at the awful carnage. The Gargoyle smiled in satisfaction at what to him was a great victory.

Four hours after the attack the cabins had been reduced to ashes. Over twenty bodies were stripped and lay bleeding in the sun, and a smoldering funeral pyre sent tendrils of smoke skyward. The smoke filled the air with the stench of burned flesh. The column of Redcoats and Indians and renegades left on their way to Boonesboro.

Some people said these were times that tried men's souls. And they were. And on the frontier the devil's own angel prowled the forest. And he was called the Gargoyle, his soul more disfigured than his face, an awful caricature of a human being. Even James and George Girty, well known for their depravity, paled in comparison with this monstrosity. Killing pleased him; torture was his brand of enjoyment. Not one shred of decency dwelt within him.

Searching the forest for him was the Wind of Death. Some day Deathwind would find him and exact a terrible vengeance.

It was because of the Gargoyle that the border ran with blood and death voiced his kill scream into the sky.

THIRTY-ONE

In Colonel Zane's cabin the mood was somber. Wetzel had just come in to report on the massacre at Shelby's Station. The Colonel, strong man that he was, was shaken down to his soul. Over three dozen men, women, and children tortured and killed. Girls carried into captivity to a terrible fate.

"Lew, do you think there's any chance one or both of those girls might be alive?"

"No telling, Colonel. Those people are on the way to Boonesboro. It may be they've got the kids with them. I don't know. Maybe they haven't had time to pay the girls any attention yet!"

"Do you think there's any chance to get the girls away from that monster?"

"I don't know, Colonel. Jack and I will give it a try if you say so."

"By all means, Lew, give it a try if you think it will work. I don't know how we could live with ourselves if we didn't at least try."

"We'll leave within the hour, Colonel. I need to stock up on some fresh powder and get Bessie to pack some meat and cheese. There won't be much time to cook anything if we're gonna catch up with those villains before they hurt those girls."

"When in the devil do you think we'll have to worry about those howling devils making it to Fort Henry?" the Colonel asked.

"I reckon about a month, Colonel. They've got a fight on their hands at Boonesboro. I hope those people at Boonesboro will get some rein-forcement from Fort Pitt."

"I'd send some help myself, Lew, but we need every man we've got!"

"And then some, Colonel. And then some!"

"Well, good luck, Lew. Report to me as soon as you can. Let me know if you've been able to help those poor girls. Without rescue they'd be better off dead!"

"We'll be in touch, Colonel."

"Good luck, Lew. I'll be waiting to hear."

After Wetzel left, the Colonel sat on his porch smoking his pipe. Suddenly a boy came running from the fort.

"Mr. Zane sent me over from the fort. Said for you to come down right away. Important."

Colonel Zane grabbed his rifle and powder horn and a bullet pouch and hurried for the fort. As he reached the blockhouse he saw a large crowd of the towns people had gathered.

"He's right in there, Colonel."

"Who's in there?"

"Why, General Washington. He just arrived. Your brother Silas is with him."

"Well, I'll be danged!" The Colonel could hardly believe his ears.

As he walked in the door the great man stood up and offered his hand. "Hello, Eb. It's been a long time."

"Too long, George, or should I say 'General'?"

"George will do between friends, Eb. How's Bessie?"

"Just fine. And Martha?"

"Just fine, Eb. Only thing is, this war is taking a lot out of all of us."

"I imagine it has, George. But for what it's worth the war here on the border has been just as bloody. Right now we're being bedeviled by a damn fiend right out of the bowels of hell."

"Yes I know, Eb. And that brings me to the purpose of my visit. Besides seeing an old friend."

"What can I do to help, George?"

"Eb, the Redcoats have made up their minds to take over the Americas all the way from the New York harbor to the Ohio. In order to do that they're gonna have to take the forts out here on the border. I'm sending a group of frontiersmen under Nathaniel Greene to reinforce Pitt. I can send you thirty men and a bulldog cannon, but the key here is to find this renegade they call the Gargoyle and if it's possible hang him to the highest tree. If you can't do that at least kill him."

"You can rest assured of that, George. My bordermen are on his trail right now."

"I know your brother, Jack. Fine man but who is this fellow Wetzel?"

"Lew Wetzel is the greatest Indian fighter we've got out here. Jack is only a shadow of him. I grew up with Lew back in Virginia. He was like all of us, all full of vinegar and full of life. But he was faster and stronger than all of us. He lost his family to the Indians and he's been an Indian hunter ever since. He'll get that damn renegade; I'll bet my shirt on that."

"Well, I'm glad to hear that, Eb. I'll breathe a lot easier knowing that. Now is there anything else I can do to help you meet this threat?"

"No, George, I guess we're as ready as we'll ever be. What about Boonesboro?"

"I've sent some men to help Colonel Boone. Couldn't send a lot, but I hope they'll be enough."

"I don't know if you've got the word yet, but we've had a massacre out here a few days ago. Shelby's Station was wiped out to the last person and burned to the ground. That renegade kidnapped a couple of girls. Jack and Wetzel are taking the trail right away. Maybe we'll get lucky and that beast will be dead before they reach Boonesboro."

"I hope so, Eb. That would go a long way toward our long-term goals. Well, I must start back."

"Will you stay for dinner, George? Bessie will be devastated if you don't."

"Tell her when this is over I'll be back to see you and I'll bring Martha for a nice visit. But right now I must get back. But I've got one last question."

"What's that, George?"

"Who is this Gargoyle anyway? None of our people can find any trace of where he came from. We know about all there is to know about Simon Girty and his brothers, but we haven't even got a name on this fellow."

"We don't know any more about him than you do, George. Only that he's a fiend right out of hell. He seems to enjoy killin' like nobody else we've got out here. Before last summer he'd never been heard of on the border."

"Well, when you get him let me know, Eb. I need to be informed!"

"Will do. Well, goodbye, old friend. Keep your head down."

"You too, Eb. Say hello to everyone."

"I'll do that, George. Good luck."

As he watched his old friend ride off, Zane thought about the good times they'd had in Virginia before the move west. Colonel Zane, General Washington, Daniel Morgan, Nathaniel Greene and Ben Franklin had all had frequent visits at the Colonel's fireside. Ben Franklin in particular had spent many hours whiling away evenings over a game of chess with the Colonel. Daniel Morgan and the Colonel along with Daniel Boone and a Mr. Lincoln (the great grandfather of the future president) spent many hunts after deer, bear and wild turkey in the Virginia mountains.

After Washington was on his way Eb stopped to talk to his brother Silas. He found him at the blacksmith shop talking with the smithy about a plow that was bent out of shape from hitting a rock in the field by the river.

"How's things, Silas?"

"Oh, all right except this damn plow is keeping me from getting my spring work done."

"We've got some jawin' to do over some news I got. How about stopping by the house this evening?"

"Sure, Eb. I'll be by around twilight. Anybody else you need?"

"No, I guess it's something the two of us need to talk over. Jack and Wetzel have left already."

"Okay, Eb. I'll see you this evening."

"Good enough."

Colonel Zane headed home, whistling thoughtfully.

THIRTY-TWO

Wetzel and Jonathan headed cross-country to intercept the column headed for Boonesboro. That was the first place to look for the Gargoyle and the white girl captives. If the renegade and the captives weren't there then they would backtrack the column and find where the beast had left the column with his captives.

The Redcoats weren't hard to find. The bordermen arrived in the late afternoon of the second day and found the column about forty miles from Boonesboro. Jack and Wetzel took up a position on a hill overlooking the trail. They were not disappointed. The Gargoyle and his captives marched along in the center of the column. A rope went around each girl's waist, and the renegade held the other end.

The bordermen both silently renewed their vows to make the frontier demon pay a terrible price for his evil ways, but right then their priority had to be to get the girls away from him. That night after dark the hunters crept up to within a very few yards of the tent where the girls were being held. An Indian guard was stationed at the door to the tent, which was closed and laced tight. This should work in the bordermen's favor.

At the rear of the tent another warrior stood guard. At midnight Wetzel silenced the rear guard with a knife slash that almost took his head off. Jonathan slit open the rear of the tent and silently awakened the girls. Luck was with them, and they got away safely. Daylight found the bordermen and their charges far away from the Redcoat camp. Another day should find them back at Fort Henry.

The Gargoyle was literally beside himself. Losing his captives enraged him to the point he literally foamed at the mouth. A more disgusting spectacle could hardly be found. There was no doubt in the mind of the captain of the Redcoats that he was dealing with a man who was unbalanced. Simon Girty agreed wholeheartedly with the Captain's assessment of the man, but as they were committed to the attack on Boonesboro and they needed the Gargoyle and his Indian allies, both Girty and the Redcoats agreed not to place any trust in the man but to use him as need be.

Simon Girty knew that only the bordermen from Fort Henry could have pulled off the rescue of the two girls. He knew that with Wetzel and Zane stalking the Redcoats and the rest of them, his own life was not worth spit.

As the column moved on toward Boonesboro, two more isolated cabins fell victim to the raiders. Two more families were left scalped and bleeding. As the Gargoyle had promised the border was awash in blood.

At Boonesboro, Daniel Boone, his brother, and Simon Kenton were checking the fort's supplies to make sure water barrels were full, every extra rifle had been cleaned and loaded, powder kegs were stored safely. The women were busy tearing bandages and making sure there would be standing by to cool the rifles. In those days the rifles had to be cleaned to remove fouling, wiped dry, and reloaded. Boone knew that this would be a fight for the very survival of the settlement.

On the second morning after the men from Washington's army arrived the familiar whoop came from the forest surrounding the fort and hundreds of Indians appeared in a circle around the perimeter of the fort. Simon Girty could be seen on his black horse talking to an Indian chief with a long feathered war bonnet: Thunder Cloud, chief of the Hurons. Further down the Gargoyle danced in glee and motioned with his tomahawk. The Redcoats formed on a knoll about two hundred yards from the stockade gate.

"Ho the fort" came a call from Simon Girty.

"What do you want, Girty?" Daniel Boone yelled.

"Boone, I'd like to avoid bloodshed. If you will surrender, I'll see that you're given safe passage back across the river."

"Sorry, Girty. We know about Shelby's Station, you damn murderer! You'll never take a man, woman, or child alive out of this fort. We've got a few surprises for you. If you want a fight bring it on!"

The Indians and renegades disappeared into cover wherever it could be found. Puffs of white smoke seemed to blossom from everywhere and war whoops came from Indian throats. Bullets pattered like hail on the stockade fence, and the pioneers returned fire in a thunderous roar. The smoke instantly engulfed the fort, leaving only war whoops from the Indians, hoarse yells from the men in the fort, the roar of rifles. A blast from a cannon from the fort and the acrid smell of black powder smoke all combined to make a terrible scene of battle. The British formed up and with bayonets fixed headed for the fort. Their red coats made a wonderful target for the frontiersmen. A sheet of flame burst from the portholes of the fort, and the first line of Redcoats wilted like weeds in a hot sun. The remaining soldiers withdrew out of range behind cover.

"Hurrah," somebody yelled. "Those lobsterbacks won't try that again."

It was bloody battle that continued all afternoon. The defenders inside the fort had lost three dead and eleven wounded, five of them seriously enough that they couldn't return to the fight. The Redcoats had lost thirty of their men in the first charge at the fort and ten since then. The long rifles in the hands of pioneers who depended on them to put meat on the table made for a deadly fire.

Simon Kenton was here and there and everywhere. The deadly fire from his rifle had sent a bullet into a warrior heart every shot. The Indians had learned to respect the fire from that rifle. They charged three more times that afternoon and three times they withdrew, leaving a large number of their companions dead upon the field. As darkness descended over the battlefield and the fort, the defenders were grateful for a few minutes' respite from the din of battle. The moon came up, bathing the battle scene in its gentle light. Daniel Boone and Simon Kenton held a hurried consultation.

"We need to be on our toes, Daniel," Kenton was saying. "The Injuns have been mighty quiet for the last three hours or so. We can expect some devilment, you can count on that."

"What do you think, Simon?"

"I think they'll try to hatch some scheme to set fire to the fort. That's the most likely."

"Well, I think we'd best get out there on the catwalk and try to head off whatever ungodly thing they come up with."

As Kenton and Boone gazed out on the valley it was hard to believe that this beautiful clearing had ever been the scene of chaos and bloodshed as it was now.

But there on both sides the valley were exposed dark terrible stains in dried pools. Blood soaked the catwalk of the fort and the soil of the yard before the fort. It was hard to believe that out there somewhere back in the forest was a fiend right out of hell. The Redcoats were to be damned for bringing this devil to the doorstep of the fort. They knew that within the walls of the stockade were women and children whose only crime was to want to make out a living in a hostile wilderness. People, who after this revolution was fought, would be needed to carry the settlements onward whether they be under British rule or under the flag of a new nation.

The life of the people on the frontier was hard even without the Indians and renegades and now the Redcoats who had come to bedevil them.

Diseases such as pneumonia, smallpox, and yellow fever were a distinct possibility, along with the wild animals and snakebites that were a constant threat. But the pioneer of the 1770s and '80s were of hardy stock. They raised their own vegetables, grew apples, and gathered berries to make jam and preserves. The men hunted the deer and bear that were thick in the forest. Wild turkey, squirrels, and woods bison were there for the taking. These people would not be driven from their homes while breath of life remained. Girty would do well to remember that.

THIRTY-THREE

Suddenly on the hill west of the fort a huge fire was seen and then it came down the hill, rapidly approaching the stockade. Daniel and Simon knew it for a fire on a wagon. The terrified horses pulling it were screaming in fear of the flames behind them. Kenton's rifle sounded and one of the horses dropped in its traces, effectively stopping the wagon short of the stockade. Boone fired and the other horse died kicking on top of its companion. Boone hated this killing of the horses but it was either that or the death of every man, woman, and child in the fort.

Nothing else happened during the rest of the night. The light from the burning wagon lit the yard in front of the fort so to make the Indians' creeping up closer to the stockade impossible.

Dawn came early over the hills around Boonesboro, and the glow of the early morning sun shown brightly in the lines of Redcoats and Indians. Smoke from the cookfires headed skyward. The fires showed that the Redcoats and Indians had no fear of anyone coming to help the defenders.

Inside the stockade the pioneers rested and thanked their God that they had been allowed to survive the night.

Daniel Boone went from bastion to bastion to see how his people were doing. He counted five dead and nine wounded, three seriously. Not bad next to what the Indians and Redcoats had lost.

"Ho the fort" came the hoarse voice of Simon Girty.

"What's on your mind, Girty?"

"Have you reconsidered my offer now that you've had time to think about it, Boone?"

"I've considered it and we don't believe one word you say, Girty."

"You know you're all gonna lose your lives?"

"Maybe so, but you're not gonna have our women to rape and our men to burn at the stake. You wanted this fight, Girty, now by God you can have all the fight you want!"

"All right, but don't say I didn't warn you."

Girty raised his hand then dropped it. Again a horde of howling devils started for the fort. Again a sheet of flame and a roar from the defenders' rifles greeted them. Dead warriors again littered the yard in front of the fort. Some of the Indians reached the stockade fence and attacked it with their tomahawks. Suddenly gallons and gallons of boiling water was poured over the fence and down upon the attackers. The women from the fort had entered the battle. Hoarse yells and screams came from the horde of Indians as they retreated in confusion.

As the Redcoats were massing from one side of the hill to the other the Redcoat officer raised his hand to commence the battle. He never knew it fell. A puff of white smoke belched from the top of a cliff at least three hundred and fifty yards distant. A clear stinging report reached their ears. The British officer fell like a log from his horse, a small round hole dotting the center of his forehead. The Redcoats stopped, aghast at the death of their leader. Simon Girty knew the ringing of that rifle. He dove for cover and shouted "Deathwind!" The Indians in one howling horde raced for the top of the cliff, but they found nothing. The Wind of Death was gone.

Twice more the Indians attacked the fence and twice more they were beaten back. The Indians were beginning to get discouraged; over one hundred of their number littered the ground in front of the fort. The British captain lay dead, and they were no closer to reaching their goal. Simon Girty was for breaking off the attack, and the Gargoyle had disappeared. Finally at sundown the attacking force vanished into the forest as quickly as they had appeared. After dark Kenton and one of the other scouts went and returned a couple hours later to report the attackers were gone. The siege of Boonesboro had been broken.

Girty and his brothers all knew that Wetzel had sworn to take their scalps. Simon Girty had made up his mind long ago to head for Canada when the revolution was over. All three brothers knew that while Wetzel and Jonathan Zane lived, their lives weren't worth a pinch of powder.

THIRTY-FOUR

The next morning found the villagers of Boonesboro starting to pick up the pieces of their lives. They were deeply touched with sadness. Twelve of their men had died and over fifteen were wounded. But the pioneers were of sturdy stock. There were funerals to hold and cabins to raise to replace the ones that had been lost in the siege.

Boone knew that the rifle shot that killed the British officer came from Wetzel's rifle. Every one on the frontier knew the sound of the rifle that Wetzel carried. No other man on the frontier could have made that shot. Boone knew that Wetzel had left on the Gargoyle's trail. The monster had not been seen since the British officer had been killed. Wetzel would not waste any time in picking up the beast's trail. Boone was satisfied that the hunter would never rest until that evil monster of the frontier was dead.

The next day, about forty miles back toward Fort Henry, Wetzel was hard on the renegade's trail. The Gargoyle was making little effort to hide his tracks but was hurrying east with all possible speed.

"Going east to meet somebody," Wetzel muttered to himself.

The question was, who? Simon Girty was still with the Redcoats as far as Wetzel knew. The Indians were headed back to their villages to re-group and get ready for the next foray against the whites.

"Makes no difference where the villains going. If I can catch him his trail will end right there," Wetzel said to himself.

The hunter spent that night curled up under the side of a fallen tree. He awoke sometime around midnight to see a flicker of lightning in the southwest. Before dawn a heavy thunderstorm swept the area effectively wiping out any trace of the beast he was trailing. Wetzel cussed the luck that again had robbed him of his chance to rid the border of the beast that haunted the pioneers and their families. The hunter spent better than half a day trying to pick up the renegade's trail but no sign could he find. Finally he gave it up as a lost cause and struck out for Fort Henry.

Colonel Zane had heard with satisfaction of Wetzel's killing of the Redcoat captain at Boonesboro. A messenger had arrived just that afternoon with the news from Daniel Boone that Boonesboro had survived. The Colonel had sent for Jonathan to inform him of what had transpired at Boone's settlement, and just as he walked out on the porch he was pleased to see the tall figures of Wetzel and Jonathan approaching. The Colonel shook hands with his bordermen and offered each a cup of coffee.

"Lewis, I just want you to know that was a good job killing that British captain. People are already talking about that shot. They say it was over three hundred and fifty yards."

"I'd rather I'd got a shot at that ugly villain or Simon Girty. And then of course there was Wingenund too, but I didn't get a shot at any of them."

"Any luck trailin' that monster? I can't wait for you to tell me that either you or Jack have killed that animal."

"I trailed him from Boonesboro, Colonel, but that thunderstorm we had wiped out his trail. Seems as if his luck's still holdin'."

"How did the folks at Boonesboro come out, Lew?"

"Well, I didn't wait to see the end of the siege but near as I can figure they did pretty well, considerin'. Girty gave 'em a chance to come out but old Daniel told him to go to hell. He did the right thing. If they'd a come out and surrendered I wouldn't have given a pinch of powder on their chances of seeing another day. Them howlin' devils would have killed every one."

"Well, Lew, I need you and Jack to stick around the fort tomorrow. We've got a barn and a cabin raisin' and I want you fellas to keep an eye out. I don't think the Indians will try anything, but with this skunk out there prowlin' the woods, who knows?"

"We'll be here, Colonel. If trouble does come it would come from some isolated Injun tryin' to win his eagle feathers. The Reddys aren't gonna mount a siege this soon after Boonesboro."

One of the most enjoyable times for the pioneers was a barn and cabin raisin'. There would be foot races, horse races, wrestling matches, shooting matches, and the women would bake pies and cakes and there would be heaping plates of turkey and venison and when available some beer! Because of the difficulties of the times, good times came less and less on the frontier, so everyone was looking forward to the celebration. A young couple was planning to be married in about a month, and the Colonel wanted a cabin and a barn for them to start life with. The Colonel was happy to see new families in his settlement.

The only way a settlement could grow and thrive was new families starting up and then children who would grow into sturdy people to continue on. The country would need people to push on westward across the Father of Waters as the Indian called the Mississippi. Pioneers who by horseback, on foot into the Rockies, by oxen or horse-drawn wagon pushed westward, ever westward to the Pacific. This was ever the dream of the American pioneer.

The Colonel had a vision that one day Wheeling would grow into a thriving city — what Daniel Boone had begun in Kentucky Colonel Zane had begun at Wheeling.

As the celebration began some of the boys were having a foot race. The women were there with their new bonnets and dresses. The tall figures of Wetzel and Jonathan Zane stood watching over the proceedings, leaning on their long rifles.

One of the boys was Kent McCorry. He was a tall boy of about fourteen who was already showing signs of growing into an exceptional rifle shot and woodsman. Next to Wetzel and Jonathan he was about the fastest runner in the fort. The boys lined up for the race, and the Colonel gave the signal to go. The boys took off at the furious pace, but it was no contest. The McCorry boy outdistanced his companions with no other boy even coming close.

The cabin raising went off without a hitch and a great time had been had by all. Late that afternoon the pioneers had a great feast and, as Wetzel had predicted, no Indians showed themselves. The Colonel and his wife were there to welcome the pioneers from the next settlement downriver. The Colonel had been able to convince them to get a stockade up and to agree to come to Fort Henry at the first sign of trouble.

::::

Far away from Fort Henry at a Redcoat camp an angry discussion was taking place. One participant was a British general of distinguished bearing and noble appearance. Another was Simon Girty, and the third was the Gargoyle of the frontier. The General was angry; that was plain.

"What the bloody hell happened at Boonesboro? I've got forty dead and seventy wounded, and one of my most trusted officers dead with a bullet through his head."

"They were well prepared, General," Girty replied. "They must have had reinforcement from somewhere. Boone doesn't have that many fighting men."

"Who killed my officer?"

"I can tell you that, General," Girty said. "It was that Indian hunter from Fort Henry. Wetzel's his name."

"You mean to tell me that one man came into the middle of five hundred and killed a British officer? That's bloody well impossible."

"He killed your officer at better than three hundred and fifty yards, General."

"Unbelievable! Who the bloody hell is this man Wetzel anyway?"

"The Indians call him Deathwind. He makes a noise in the forest that would chill your blood. I've heard it and I know. The Indians, the superstitious fools, think he's some kind of spirit or ghost or something. He's a cold-blooded killer of Indians! He's a friend of Eb Zane, the commandant of Fort Henry. Him and Jack Zane were probably responsible for dropping your powder and cannons into the Pines River."

"Listen to me, Girty. My superiors are very unhappy with the way this border war is going. My career is on the line, and I'm not letting some bloody Indian killer in some bloody little frontier outpost destroy it, do you understand me, Girty?"

"Well, General, I . . ."

"Do you understand?"

"Yes, General!"

"You find this Indian killer and you kill him no matter what it costs, do you hear me!"

"I'll do my best, General."

"I said, do you hear me, Girty?"

"Yes, General."

"Very well. Dismissed," the General said with a wave of his hand.

Girty walked out and breathed a sigh of relief. South America was nice this time of year. So was Canada. No matter where he was, it was a hell of a lot safer than here right now. He marveled at the General's stupidity. He talked as if killing Wetzel was no problem at all. Every Indian in the Ohio country had been trying to do that for years, and the General thought he could do that with no problem. What a jackass.

Meanwhile, the word from the Colonies wasn't good. It was great for the British but bad for the colonials and the pioneers.

The Redcoats were running over Washington's forces, and the Continental Congress had fled to a new location to continue working on a constitution. How Washington was going to pay his army was anybody's guess, and desertions were running rampant. As has been said before, survival of Washington's army and the success of revolution hung by a thread.

Colonel Zane received the discouraging news from a flatboat coming downriver from Fort Pitt. Wetzel and Jonathan had been gone for a week hunting for some trace of the Gargoyle. There had been word of another cabin burned out and a family murdered and scalped. The Colonel knew that sending out an armed force to hunt the monster would not bring results. The trackless wilds were not for pioneers or even militia. It must be left to the bordermen to rid the frontier of this beast, but to Colonel Zane it was a frustrating thing. To hear of families that he knew murdered, people who had spent time at his home killed, was more than the soft-hearted Colonel was willing to tolerate. But along with the frustration was the surety that his bordermen would kill the monster, of that he was certain. As sure as the sun rose and set, the bones of the renegade would be bleaching in the sun before long. The problem was, God knew how many more people, good people, people whom the frontier could little afford to lose, would die in the meantime.

Colonel Zane was a good man, a God-fearing man and as such he cared about the families that had followed him into the wilderness to carve out homes from the hostile country. Many of them had already paid with their lives and many more would fill unmarked graves before peace came to the Ohio country. But peace would come, of that the Colonel would content himself.

THIRTY-FIVE

One sunny afternoon the Colonel had just returned from a visit to a settler's cabin downriver. He was sitting on the porch waiting for supper when he saw Sam Brady coming up the path from the road. Brady stopped before the porch.

"Howdy, Colonel."

"Howdy, yourself. Come up here and sit yourself. Bessie, bring us a cool drink, maybe some cider."

"Sure will, Eb."

"Good to see you, Sam," Bessie called from the kitchen.

"What brings you over this way, Sam?"

"Daniel wanted me to stop by and let you know how things are at Boonesboro."

"The folks over there getting over the siege all right, Sam?"

"Just fine, Colonel. I wondered, have you had any luck figuring out who this Gargoyle fella is or where he came from?"

"None at all, Sam. Most of the renegades out here we can trace where they came from. The Girtys, for instance. We know they deserted from Fort Pitt. Some of the others are traders who came over from the old country. They aren't necessarily renegades, but they live with the Indians. But this Gargoyle fella seems to have appeared out of nowhere."

"Well, I can't seem to learn anything either, Colonel. Even some of the friendly Injuns at Fort Pitt don't know anything. All they'll say is he's bad medicine. And they don't want anything to do with him. That's all they'll say. You know, Colonel, I talked to a French trader who was in the village when Bill Crawford was burned at the stake. He said that the Gargoyle was there, and he was laughing with glee when they made Crawford walk around on hot coals, and he was leaping and dancing like a demon when they tore the scalp off the poor tortured soul before he was even dead. For what it's worth, I think this man is worse then the Girtys. I think there are people on this Earth who are possessed by something right out of Hell. That's the only answer."

"Well, that's maybe so, but it still don't tell us who he is."

"No, that's true. But it can tell us what kind of animal we're fighting. I hope Jack and Wetzel will kill this beast. Because if they don't there's gonna be a lot more killing out on the border."

"Tell me what you're thinking, Sam. Do you think we'll have a siege here at Fort Henry?"

"Well, not right away. The Redcoats are gonna have to get an officer in here to tell them how to make war against Fort Henry first. It's gonna be up to the Gargoyle and Simon Girty to keep them together. Otherwise the tribes will all go their way and none of them are strong enough by themselves. They need to be united in order to pose any threat to you here at Fort Henry."

"Well, whatever comes we'll be ready, Sam."

"I'd like to ask you something, Colonel. How in the hell can two men hope to kill this renegade when he's right in the middle of all those Indians?"

"I wish I knew the answer to that, Sam. I've lived with Wetzel for all these years, and I still don't know. But I'll tell you one thing: they will kill him, of that I am sure."

"Sure hope you're right, Colonel. We'll I'm off now. Daniel asked me to deliver his message. He sends his best. Wishes you good luck."

"Watch your hair, Sam."

"I intend to, Colonel. You best watch yours and your family's. I wouldn't be surprised to have one of those skulkin' varmints sneakin' around here to try for a shot at somebody."

"I don't doubt that. I'm hopin' Jack or Wetzel will get back before long. There ain't an Indian alive who can conceal himself for long with the bordermen here."

"Well, good luck, Colonel. Bessie, thanks for the cider."

"You're welcome, Sam. Stop by anytime."

THIRTY-SIX

West Virginia is called the mountain state. Everywhere are pines, oaks, maples, birch, elms and hickories. Wetzel and Jonathan knew that if the Gargoyle had gone to the Colonies to meet with the British Generals he would most likely pass through here on his way back to Ohio. The bordermen positioned themselves on the cliffs above the one road coming from Virginia to Ohio. They believed that sooner or later the renegades would pass this way.

The hunters settled down to wait. The mountains were beautiful that time of year. There was a spring coming from the rocks where they camped that provided them with cold clear water. Everywhere was a verdant green. Deer were common and one afternoon a huge old black bear raided a honey tree right below their hiding place. To most people such a wait would become boring but to the bordermen it was home.

They watched the trails for two weeks. Nothing. They finally had to admit that their plan was not working. But they felt that it had not been in vain. They knew that if the Gargoyle hadn't come this way at least they also knew that no British had come this way either. The bordermen knew that the Redcoats would bring in a replacement for the officer that had been killed at Boonesboro. Therefore Fort Henry had time to prepare for a siege. Wetzel thought maybe the next attack would be against Fort Pitt. However there was no way of knowing for sure.

The bordermen finally gave up on a bad cause and struck out for Fort Henry. They figured it would be about time to report to Colonel Zane and find out if there was any news about the Gargoyle. Jack and Wetzel were both hoping that there were no more burned cabins and dead settlers left in his wake. The girls Jack and Wetzel had saved settled in at Fort Henry with a settler's family. Jack and Wetzel hoped there wouldn't be any more murdered families and kidnapped girls to try to rescue. Too many times rescues went wrong and captives were murdered before they were saved.

As the bordermen crossed a ridge about ten miles above Fort Henry there was the trail they had been looking for - the huge track of the Gargoyle and also the boot tracks of four men in British combat footwear. The hunters took the trail at once. The tracks were at least three days old, heading in the direction of a crossing place above the fort. The bordermen cussed their luck while they had been camped above the road the renegades and the British had slipped by them and was probably safe in Ohio by this time. Jack and Wetzel turned to Fort Henry. Colonel Zane needed to be notified that the British had new officers to join with the Indians and plan with the Redcoat army to attack Fort Henry, Fort Pitt, and again have another attack at Boonesboro. There's no doubt about it this was a very dangerous time on the border for every man, woman, and child. Simon Girty, the Gargoyle and the Redcoats like fiends out of hell would be dedicated to burn the settlements all up and down the Ohio and to see the last vestige wiped out.

The bordermen arrived at Fort Henry at around 3 in the afternoon. They noticed a large group of people at the fort and headed that way. They found Colonel Zane talking to a much agitated man on horseback at the hitch rack.

"Afternoon Colonel." Wetzel greeted the Colonel.

"Jack, Lew. I'm sure glad to see you. This is Tom Haberman. He's been sent from Washington. He's got a message for us."

"Colonel I need to talk with you in private." Haberman said.

"These are the bordermen I told you about. I want them in on it."

"Very well, Colonel. Where do you want to talk?"

"At my cabin in an hour."

"Very well, Colonel. Which cabin is yours?"

"The one on the hill."

"Very well, Colonel I'll be there."

The Colonel led the way up the hill to his cabin. His wife saw them coming and brought out some steaming cups of coffee.

"Any luck, Lew?"

"We found the trail not 15 miles north of here. Girty helped them slip by."

"So the Redcoats must be joined up and all of them safe in the Delaware towns by this time."

"That's what I'm figuring Colonel. Girty is gonna help them get the Injuns stirred up again. What's this fella from the Colonies got to say?"

"I have no idea but he'll be here in a few minutes and then we'll know."

"Just then a knock came on the door. The Colonel opened the door to find the man from the Colonies on the porch. "Come in Mr. Haberman. We're looking to hear what you have to say."

"You have a wonderful little village here Colonel."

"Thank you, sir. Now what is it you have to tell us?"

"Gentlemen, it has come to the attention of the Continental Congress you have a bad problem out here. About a month ago a Redcoat spy was captured and before he was executed he was persuaded to tell us some very interesting facts. He told us that a man from a British prison, a homicidal maniac was pardoned by the English Crown and sent here to do a job. This man has killed before in British possessions all over the Empire. He was scheduled to hang until it was discovered that through his father he has ties to the Indian tribes in this area. The British government wants to destroy the western settlements in this country and they will do anything to accomplish their goals. This man is here now working with Simon Girty and his brothers to arouse the Indians to a fever pitch. We are expecting a massive attack on either Wheeling or the Kanawa settlements within thirty days maybe less. General Washington has asked me to give this man's name to you. His name is Colin Damonic. He was charged in a shipboard trial right in the West Indies. They say he killed three men in that fight with his bare hands. His pardon is contingent on getting the tribes to wipe out these settlements you folks have established out here. He is a man that enjoys killing and he must either be killed or he will accomplish his goals make no mistake about that. I heard that the British lost a wagon train out here with cannon and gun powder."

"You can thank Lew and Jack for that Mr. Haberman. There's also a British Captain that will never see England again."

"Well, at least you're putting the fear of God into the Redcoats. That's something but it's gonna take more than killing one man to stop the bloodshed out her. First we must put an end to Colin Damonic. Then Simon Girty must be stopped from spreading his poison among the tribes."

"That's easier said than done. Girty has all the Indian tribes in his pocket. He has shown some compassion for white captives yet he was there when Colonel Crawford was burned at the stake and didn't do anything to stop it but maybe he couldn't go against Pipe and Half King."

"How's the war going back east?"

"Gentlemen, I don't have to tell you its been a terrible struggle. Desertions, not any way to win decisive battles, inadequate training and supplies. But the war goes on. I believe despite all the problems that in the end we will prevail."

"How is General Washington doing?"

"He is holding up, Colonel. He asked me to send his best wishes and to tell you he has faith in your abilities. He also believes that the key to your survival is killing Damonic and the Girtys. Now one last thing, Colonel. We have learned that he British have ordered their commanders to take no prisoners. They have no place to keep prisoners and no way of feeding such a large number. Neither do they believe they can keep the Indians from murdering the captives. So you can expect no mercy. Make sure that no man, woman or child falls to their hands. Do I make myself clear Colonel?"

"Perfectly, Mr. Haberman. You can rest assured on that point sir!"

"Well, good Colonel. I'll convey your feelings to General Washington. Now is there anything we can do to help?"

"Only more cannon and powder and more soldiers if you have them."

"Unfortunately the army is stretched too thin to be able to offer any soldiers. I can send a couple of captured British cannons. I can also offer a keg or two of powder. That's about it. How do you think Fort Henry stacks up in the event of a siege?"

"As well as we can hope for under the circumstances Mr. Haberman. Lew and Jack I want you to keep trying for a shot at Damonic or Girty."

"We'll do that Colonel. We'll pull out first thing in the morning."

"Got any idea where to look?"

"I reckon we'll find the villain with the British campin' somewhere near the Delaware towns. Girty will probably be there too. It's a sure thing that he's got to get things together if he plans to come against Fort Henry. The Injuns need some pumping up after Boonesboro so that's where he'll be."

"Well, Lew, Jack, find him and kill him. Kill both of them. It's as simple as that. It's the only way to end this bloodshed."

Jack and Wetzel shook hands with the Colonel and Haberman and headed off toward the Fort.

"Well, I guess that's about all there is to say Colonel. I'll be going. I hope your bordermen are successful and kill that monster and Girty."

"They will Mr. Haberman. You can count on it."

"I will be Colonel. And so will General Washington."

After Haberman left, Colonel Zane sat on his porch smoking his pipe. His wife came out and sat down beside him. The two of them often sat in the evening just enjoying the twilight. A whippoorwill sounds his haunting cry from the hillside. As the darkness descended the frogs started their croaking from the river. An owl's booming cry came from the Island. It was hard to believe that this beautiful valley had seen so much strife and bloodshed and most likely would again. The Colonel's sister came out of the cabin and sat silently beside them. There is something in the twilight that gives a sense of peace that comes at no other time of day. The Colonel's wife slipped her hand in the Colonel's and he knew that whatever happened they'd face it together.

THIRTY-SEVEN

The next morning found Wetzel and Jonathan already on the trail. It was two days hard traveling to the Delaware town, and the bordermen knew that there was no time to waste. Both men were determined that the Gargoyle would not live to spread his poison among the tribes. They knew that the British Secret Service was ready to use the Indians and renegades to wipe out the settlements. They had to be stopped.

That afternoon they struck the trail of five Indians and a man in boots. They could tell by the way he walked that he was an easterner not used to the frontier life. Wetzel made the decision to trail them to find out who the identity of the man traveling with the Indians. They trailed the group of travelers until dark. That night the bordermen camped back in the woods away from the trail. Wetzel fully expected an Indian or two skulking back along the trail to ambush anyone that might be tracking them.

Morning found the bordermen up early and eager to be on the move. They had a quick breakfast of corn dodgers Mrs. Zane had packed for them and fresh water from a brook. They freshened the powder in the pans of their rifles and were ready to hit the trail.

As they proceeded it was a beautiful morning. Squirrels ran along the ground or barked from the trees, crows cawed from the treetops, and a blue jay scolded them from a tree limb.

"I believe we best be on our toes, Jack; you slip around the left side of the trail and I'll go right. We'll meet at noon by that big dead cottonwood sticking up ahead there. Look mighty close. I've got a tingle in the back of my neck, and it ain't ever let me down yet."

Wetzel stepped off the trail and disappeared in the forest. Jonathan moved forty feet off the trail, then a hundred yards. The borderman's method of trailing was different than that of any other pioneer.

The Indian hunter would follow the trail to ascertain its direction then step off the trail and move under cover for many miles and then pick the trail up later on. That made it almost impossible for the bordermen to be ambushed.

Jonathan moved slowly through the forest, taking advantage of every cover, from trees and moss to covered stones to ferns and brush. He kept the path down which the trail led almost always in sight. Once, a little before noon, he heard two rifle shots. One was a whip-like crack that could only have come from Wetzel's rifle and then a hollow boom that came from an Indian musket. A few minutes later Wetzel fired again.

Jonathan completed his circle of the trail and headed for the dead tree Wetzel had indicated. He saw the tall form of Wetzel standing close against the trunk of a cottonwood.

"I heard some shootin'," Jonathan said.

"Just like I thought they would, the varmints tried an ambush. Found a couple of them hunkered down in some ferns. Shot one, then took off after the other. He was a good runner but not good enough," Wetzel said grimly.

"Well, there's only four of them left. Three Indians and the white man, whoever he is."

"I figure they'll go on about fifteen miles today and camp at that grove of birch on White's Creek. We'll cut across and be waiting for 'em. I'm getting more curious all the time. I figure he's got to be somebody pretty important to send an escort of Injuns. I'd be willin' to bet that he's got something to do with the Gargoyle. I wouldn't be surprised if his trail leads all the way back to the English lords, maybe King George himself."

"Well, his trail is gonna end mighty sudden, and he's gonna rest on the moss and leaves. But before he dies he's gonna tell us what we want to know about this operation," Jonathan said. It was imperative that they learn exactly whom they were up against and what was the timetable under which the Indians and renegades were operating.

That evening the three Indians and their white traveling companion camped in a small grove of birch on the side of a bubbling creek. They ate a supper of dried corn and dried meat and retired early. The moon rose and took its journey across the sky. As the midnight hour passed the Indian sentinel awoke and stretched. Then from far back in the forest a sigh like the night wind came through the trees. The Indian guard drew his tomahawk and reached for his rifle. He called his companions, and they jumped to their feet. Suddenly a huge shadow sprang from the brush bordering the glade. Two of the Indians tried to grapple with the shadow. How pitifully weak were they in the hands of Deathwind. One died with his skull cloven in by the blow of a tomahawk. The other came in with his knife held low. The shadow caught his arm and broke it. The warrior was lifted high in the air and had his spine snapped over one of the boulders that ringed the glade. A second later a knife was buried in his chest.

In the meantime the third Indian fled from the glade. The Redcoat officer cowered against the side of a fallen tree. Jonathan Zane was holding a knife against his throat.

The British officer looked into the glittering eyes of the giant hunter and the cold face of Jonathan Zane. He knew then that he would most likely never again see the beautiful estate in England where he grew up. He fervently wished that he had never left the arms of the sweetheart who waited for him on the Thames.

"Now, mister, you're going to tell us what your mission is and who you were supposed to see. Then it will be our pleasure to kill you as quick as possible. Otherwise I'm going to spend a whole day killing you slow. Fact is, I'd rather you didn't talk — kinda be more enjoyable that way."

The British officer looked into the glittering eyes burning into his. The hunter's low voice hissed and stung like a serpent. He thought how much the glow from the fire made the giant borderman look like a demon right out of hell.

"Who are you?" the Britisher asked.

"I'm Jonathan Zane. This is Lew Wetzel."

"You're, you're the one the Indians call Deathwind."

"You got it, you low life son of a bitch." Wetzel lifted the British officer off the ground and shook him as one would a wet puppy. "Now what are you doing on the border and who were you supposed to see?"

"I'm a uniformed officer in the King's service. I am a courier sent to see a Mr. Simon Girty with a dispatch from General Cornwallis."

"Where's the dispatch?"

"It's in my saddle bag. But I ask to surrender to the ranking officer from your continental army."

"That would be Colonel Zane at Fort Henry. But tell me why we shouldn't just kill you now and save the trouble of taking you all the way back to the fort?"

"Because I am a prisoner of war. A soldier. I'm not a renegade and it would be inhuman to kill a private that is only a courier. I have no part in whatever it is that my superiors are planning."

"He's right, Lew. We are at war and he was wearing a uniform when we captured him," Jonathan said. "If we kill him, it will make us as bad as the people we are fighting."

"Well, maybe so. But make no mistake, Britisher, I'd still rather kill you. I'm friends with the people at Boonesboro and Fort Henry so if you give us any trouble any trouble at all, I'll slash you from shoulder to hip and take your scalp for a souvenir, you got that?"

The Britisher knew that he was only a whisper from death, the closest he'd ever been. He thanked God for his mercy and even began to hope he would see merry old England again.

"I will give you no trouble, sir. This war is none of my making. As of now I have not fired a shot at any of my fellow men, and I thank God now I will not have to. I am completely at your disposal, sir."

"Good. We understand each other then. What's your name?"

"My name is Harvard Posey, gentlemen."

"Posey." Jonathan couldn't help but smile.

"Yes, Posey. And I assure you it's an honorable name, gentlemen."

"All right, Harvard. You get yourself some sleep. We'll be startin' for the fort first light."

Posey shuddered as he watched Wetzel scalp the two dead Indians. How barbaric this country was. It went against everything the British gentlemen believed in. Once an enemy was dead you did not mutilate the remains. But he was forced to admit this was not a European battlefield. This was the western border of America.

The fire was extinguished, and they spent the night far back from the glade in the forest so no Indian would try to slip in to fire on them from the darkness. Posey's sleep was fitful at best, haunted by Indians being killed and a giant shadow chasing him through the forest swinging a bloody tomahawk.

THIRTY-EIGHT

He awakened to a beautiful sunny morning. Birds singing, squirrels barking from the trees and everywhere the fresh green forest. He gave thanks to God that he had allowed him to live through the night to see the sun. Last night he had not had much hope. His captors gave him some balls of corn and fresh water along with something called jerky. Then they set off toward what Posey hoped would be civilization. Zane and Wetzel moved at a rapid pace and were forced to wait for the Redcoat several times that day. That night and the next day were the same as the first, and they reached the fort at sundown. The bordermen decided to wait until after dark to cross the river. The Britisher would not be too popular at the fort. It was very important to place their prisoner under Colonel Zane's protection.

That evening they slipped across the river and quickly slipped through the sentries and up the path to Colonel Zane's cabin. They found the Colonel at his customary place for that time of evening, sitting in his rocker smoking his pipe enjoying the evening. Wetzel whistled a note that brought the Colonel to his feet.

"Hello, Jack, Lew. What have you got there?"

"Courier from Cornwallis to Girty and is surrendering himself to you. Name of Harvard Posey."

"Well, well. Come right in. Posey, is it? I'm anxious to see what dispatch you have. Jack, Lew, Bessie will still have some stew hot. Help yourself and we'll have some for Mr. Posey here, too. Now let's have a look at those dispatches."

While the travelers had a supper of stew and cornbread and coffee the Colonel pored over the dispatches.

Finally he said, "Jack, Lew, I think now we have the reason for what's been going on out here. King George wants to wipe out every man, woman, and child out here on the border. He wants to build an army in Ohio to catch Washington in a pincer movement so Washington will have nowhere to retreat. He's planning on sending a massive number of troops over the summer for an attack in the fall."

"Well, at least we know what we're up against. Well, Eb, what's to be done?"

"Well, the first thing is we have to get these dispatches through to Washington. I think this will paint a whole new picture for what's going on out here on the border and what our Redcoats are planning. They're not talking about war. They're planning wholesale slaughter."

"You got any idea who you want to send to carry these dispatches?"

"Not right now. It's gonna be a very dangerous job. If the courier is caught he'll be shot as a spy. No doubt about that."

"I'll volunteer, Eb," Jonathan said. " I know the General and I know the area where the fighting's been going on."

"I'm willing to go, too," Wetzel said.

"No, Lew. I'm gonna need you here. We're in for some ambushes and we need to catch any Indians trying to get near the fort to learn about what our defenses are like. Jack, you need to pull out as soon as possible. Get yourself some rest and get ready to go."

"I'll be ready at daylight. Lew, we need to talk before I leave. You want to walk up to the fort with me?"

"Sure, Eb. I'll see you in the morning. Were you planning to keep Posey here?"

"Lock him in the long room over the fort. I'll figure what to do with him later. It's a cinch we can't turn him loose. The people around here would string him in a minute. Things are getting mighty ugly."

"Well, we can lock him up but we can't keep him there forever. We'd best turn him over to the army as soon as we can."

"We'll do that. Lew, in the meantime we'll have to look out for him. As of now he's a prisoner of war."

The bordermen escorted Posey down the path to the fort, where they locked him in the long room. Wetzel and Jonathan shook hands and Jack went off to prepare for his long journey to meet with Washington. Both of the bordermen knew that it was a long dangerous journey Jonathan was embarking on, a journey that he might not return from.

Excerpt from the Journal of Harriet Bonnet Smith

Many times during the war years from 1775–1782, Jonathan Zane was used to carrying messages between Fort Henry and General Washington's Colonial army headquarters. A regular dispatch rider had little chance of getting through. Only a borderman with the ability to move silently and unseen was able to get through.

THIRTY-NINE

Jonathan left at dawn. He could not travel by horseback because Indian scouts would be watching the roads. He traveled cross-country through the forest. He skirted open prairies, always remaining in the cover of the trees. He spent the first night in the woods in a hollow under a log. During the night a few soft-footed animals went by sniffing at the hollow under the log, detected the man smell and scurried off. Near daylight a fat old black bear smelled at the hollow and stuck his nose into Jonathan's hiding place. The borderman slashed him across the nose, and the bear roared and took off for other parts. Jonathan was glad that he hadn't had to use his rifle. A shot would alert every Indian within miles of his presence. But the fat old bruin went on his way figuring that discretion was the best part of valor.

Jonathan traveled all the next day and night. He did run across a British patrol on the fourth day, but the borderman slipped around them. That evening he found a Continental army camp and asked to be taken to General Washington. As Jonathan traveled north through the various camps he was struck by the ragtag appearance of the army. Uniforms were ragged; rifles were stacked in a haphazard fashion. Still, there was determination in the faces that looked at him from the tents and around the cook fires. They stopped before a tent and the guide called "General Washington, sir."

"Come in, Lieutenant," came a deep voice. Jonathan entered with the guide.

"General, this gentleman says he has important news from Wheeling."

"Jonathan, by God, it's good to see you. How are things at Fort Henry?"

"Fine when I left, General. We captured a courier about a week ago and he had these dispatches with him."

The General took the bag and read over the dispatches. "Well, by God, now we know what they're up to out there on the border. If they are able to wipe out the settlements on the border then they will be able to get a pincer movement to strangle our armies. We've got to stop them at all costs."

"Got any ideas, General?"

"Not at this minute, Jonathan. I want to talk this over with my officers. Get yourself some rest and we'll meet in the morning. I want to see what they think."

"All right, General. I'll see you in the morning."

"Get some rest, Jonathan. You've did a good day's work getting me these dispatches."

Jonathan rolled up in his blankets and slept well. He was awakened after sunrise with a call at the tent door.

"Mr. Zane, the General wishes you to have breakfast with him."

"Tell him I'll be with him shortly."

"All right, sir."

As Jonathan stepped out into the morning sun he noticed a couple of wagons being loaded with cannons. Horses were being saddled and General Washington's tent was being stacked and Washington and his officers were seated at a table having breakfast.

"Good morning, Jonathan. Have some breakfast. We've come to a decision about what to do to stop the Redcoats out west."

"Well, what have you come up with, General?"

"Jonathan, we're going to lay a trap for the Redcoats at Fort Henry. We'll give you a dozen cannon and a hundred men. We'll try to move them in after dark so no one will suspect they're there. Then we'll set tight. I'm placing your brother Eb in charge. I'd like to go with you to Fort Henry, but I've got a war to win here in the Colonies. In the meantime, I'm counting on you getting my men through to the fort."

"It ain't gonna be easy, General. The Tories have men all over the place. I'm going to need experienced woodsmen that can move quiet at night."

"You'll have them, Jonathan. I'm sending Nathaniel Greene with you. He's a woodsman with all the experience you're looking for!"

"How soon will the men be ready to move?"

"Should be ready the day after tomorrow."

"Good, General. Tell the men that they need to give up smoking till we reach Fort Henry. Pipe smoke can give you away fast in the woods. Every man that has moccasins best wear 'em. We'll travel at night and hole up during the day. Make sure every man has water and corn dodgers. Maybe some jerky. There can be no cook fires. How soon will Greene be here?"

"Should be here this afternoon."

"Good. General Washington, I'll get your surprise party for the Redcoats going if I can. This is exactly what we've been hoping for on the frontier. I want to meet with Greene as soon as he gets here."

"I'll send him over when he arrives. Jonathan, I'm counting on you to pull this off."

"General, you can count on me to do the very best I can. How have things been going with the Revolution here in the Colonies?"

"About as bad as they can get. We're short of about everything but we keep going hoping it'll get better. My men are mostly now hanging on because they want their country to be free and they want a better life for their children. We've had some victories but more losses. It's been a hard struggle ever since Lexington."

"General, we've found out where the main Redcoat camp is. They're camping with the Delawares in Ohio. They have been holed up licking their wounds since Boonesboro. The one we call the Gargoyle and Simon Girty are with them."

"Oh yes, Mr. Girty. It will be my pleasure to hang him and his brothers from the highest tree in America if he ever falls into my hands."

"Well, if Wetzel gets a shot at him he'll die mighty quick along with his brothers James and George. They've been tormenting the settlers all along the border for years."

"Well, tell Wetzel he's got my blessing!"

Meanwhile in the European city of Paris, another hero of the Revolution was doing his best to bring France into the colonial war of independence. Benjamin Franklin had done about all he could to get the French to send arms, men, and funds to shore up Washington's forces and to provide much-needed naval forces. As the war continued toward a conclusion, the war on the western border would become even bloodier, and every day a matter of survival.

FORTY

That afternoon a man rode up and stopped before Jonathan's tent. He was a big man dressed in the garb of a woodsman.

"Mr. Zane, I guess."

"That's right, and you'd be Nathaniel Greene."

"The same. I'm here to help you give the Redcoats a drubbing. I've got thirty men with me, all experienced woodsmen, and every one of them would like nothing better than to kill a dozen Redcoats apiece."

"Well, there's plenty to go around out there on the border, Greene. But first we've got to get the men through to Fort Henry without anybody bein' the wiser."

"Sounds like a challenge. But we can do it. My men can move quiet as a ghost across Plymouth Rock."

"Will you be ready by tomorrow afternoon?"

"You bet. My boys could be ready this afternoon, but Washington says his men won't be ready until tomorrow."

"Good, we'll leave at sundown tomorrow. We'll travel by night. It ain't gonna be easy to move all that equipment quiet to Fort Henry. That's gonna be the challenge. Greene, have you got anybody you can trust to take a message through to my brother at Fort Henry?"

"I've got a scout who could sneak up and smack a panther on the behind."

"All right," Jonathan said. "Have him stop over this afternoon. I'll have a message for my brother for him to take through. I want Eb to know we are coming."

"I'll do that. We'll see you tomorrow sundown."

"Thanks, Greene. I'm looking forward to working with you."

The next morning was cold and gray and showing a threat of rain. Jonathan cursed their luck. It would delay them seriously if it rained hard. However, a light rain would serve to hide their trail. The day passed quickly and as sunset concealed the column of woodsmen, they were ready to pull out. As they left camp a drizzly rain set in, the kind that had them wet to the skin, but it masked the sounds of travel. The rain quit about an hour after midnight but it still kept it dark enough to help in concealing the woodsmen as they traveled steadily toward their goal.

Morning found them under cover in a large overhang with a covering of ferns and underbrush. During the day they rested, pulling the charges in their rifles, cleaning out the bores, and recharging. The weapons were an all-day job. After a few hours' sleep they were ready for their second night of travel.

Travel went well until an hour before dawn. Suddenly a sound of marching feet and rattling sabers reached them. The column sank into the underbrush. A few minutes later a column of British regulars marched by, led by an impressive officer on a white horse. Not a sound from the group of woodsmen was there to warn the Redcoats that death waited in the forest just yards away. The frontiersmen waited with cocked rifles until the regulars had marched on by. They waited for many long minutes almost without breathing until the Redcoats were out of earshot. There wasn't one of the hunters who wouldn't have given an arm or a leg to engage the British in a head-on fight but that would have ruined their mission, which was to ambush the Redcoats in Ohio. So they proceeded on their way to hold up for another day.

Twice that morning while undercover they saw British troop movements. One group of Redcoats lit a large fire and cooked their noon meal over it. They would have been very uncomfortable if they knew that not more than 100 yards away a group of frontiersmen waited with cocked rifles and drawn tomahawks with every intention of killing every Redcoat in North America. However Jonathan and Nathaniel Greene managed to control the group of woodsmen and keep them from wiping out the Redcoat patrol. The Redcoats finally moved on, and the hunters spent the rest of the day getting a few hours of much-needed rest. Twilight found them again on the trail as silently, surely they moved westward. Once they startled a huge old buck deer that bounded off with a great deal of noise and confusion. The column's horses whinnied in terror but the men driving the wagons soon had them under control, and many minutes were spent making sure that no enemy had heard the noise. Evidently nothing had been noticed by the Redcoats or — what worried Jonathan Zane and Nathaniel Green more — roving bands of Indians, for they were approaching Shawnee country. But no Indian showed himself, and daylight found them again in camp out of sight of Redcoats or prying Indian eyes. So far the trip had gone according to plan. Two more days should put them at Fort Henry. That night as they marched a fire was spotted ahead through the trees. The column halted while Jonathan and Greene crept up to find out who it was. It turned out to be a group of five Huron warriors. Many hours were spent waiting for the Indians to go to sleep. At midnight Jonathan and Green hit the camp and killed all the Hurons. Not one escaped to give warning. The column then proceeded on its way. Jonathan hoped that by the time the Hurons were missed the column of woodsmen would be behind the walls of Fort Henry. That afternoon the note of a cardinal came from down the valley, and Jonathan whistled a note in return. A few minutes later Wetzel stepped from a thicket, and a minute later was shaking hands with Jonathan.

"See you made it all right. Any trouble on the trip?" Wetzel asked.

"Not worth mentioning. How's things at the fort?"

"Just fine. Eb sent me to look you up. The messenger got there day before yesterday."

"Lew, this here's Nathaniel Greene. Greene, this is Lew Wetzel."

"Good to meet you, Wetzel. Seems as if I've heard a lot about you."

"Can't believe all you hear. Did you all get here intact?"

"Not a scratch."

"The Injuns been kicking up any fuss?"

"Not a thing happened since you left, Jack."

"Well, at least now if Girty and that Gargoyle show up we ought to be able to give him a real warm reception."

"You have a chance to get a shot at any of those buzzards?"

"Nary a sign of any of them within twenty miles of the fort. Eb wanted me to stick close to make sure none of the varmints snuck in after dark and took a shot at somebody."

"Well, we'll wait till after dark and then we'll slip the column into the fort," Greene said. Jonathan nodded.

"Lew, how's our guest doin'?"

"You mean Posey? Why he's settled in like he was born at Fort Henry. I don't guess Eb has figured out what to do with him yet."

"Who's Posey?" Greene asked.

"He's a British courier that Lew and I got a hold of," Jonathan said. "The only one happier than Lew and I to have caught him was Posey to be caught. Seems like soldierin' isn't his cup of tea."

"What you figure you're gonna do with him?"

"I'll leave that up to Eb. He's not gonna do any harm where he is."

"Well, it'll be dark in a couple of hours. Best pack up and get ready to go."

"I'll scout ahead and make sure the coast is clear. You bring 'em on in, Jack."

Jonathan nodded. "We'll cross the river right after dark before moonrise. I don't believe there's any Injuns skulkin' around but there's no way of knowing for sure. Greene, let's get 'em ready."

Right after dark the column was at the river's edge. There were a dozen canoes waiting at the crossing. The column made it across without incident and an hour later were all inside the fort. Colonel Zane was there. He shook hands with Jonathan. The borderman looked haggard from his trip. Many times the Colonel had seen his brother come in gaunt and tired but this had been a long trip.

"Good to see you, Jack. Everything go all right with George?"

"He's doing as well as can be expected, Eb. It's gonna be a long fight."

"Well, everyone knew that the Revolution would be a long bloody fight. I'm just glad he could send us some help to take on Girty and the Gargoyle. Chances are we'll have a yard full of howlin' devils some time this summer. With those extra men and those cannons we ought to be able to blow Girty right out from under his hat."

"Well, if we can and we can get the Gargoyle it'll go a long way toward ending the trouble out here."

"So what's your plan, Lew?"

"I think I'm gonna hunt for some scalps. If I happen to see Girty or that big ugly fella on the way, why I reckon I'll put an end to one of our problems out here."

"Jack, are you going with Lew?"

"I was plannin' on it."

"All right, then, I'll get Greene to watch the river to make sure we don't get any surprises. Lew and Jack, if you see any sign from any of the Redcoats or Injuns let us know."

"Sure will, Eb. We're leaving first thing in the morning."

"I'll see you when you get back then. I want to talk to the men see how they're settling in."

The next morning Colonel Zane walked down to the fort. The powder kegs were stored in the fort's powder room. The men were busy getting the extra cannon set up behind the hidden gun ports. The cannons were set up to sweep the whole of the yard in front of the fort. Now all that was left was to wait. Greene and his men set up watches all along the river so that no Redcoat column could cross the river without being seen. The Colonel was satisfied as he could be about the readiness of the fort. All that could be done now was to keep the word about the extra men from getting out.

The Colonel wondered if the time would ever come when the settlers would be able to live without worrying about the next attack. When Jack would settle down and find himself a wife and when even Wetzel would give up his bloody war with the Indians and bury the hatchet. "Not likely," the Colonel thought to himself, "not likely."

FORTY-ONE

June came with the hay fields needing to be cut and stored in the barns for the winter. Grain was harvested all under the watchful eye of the Colonel. Fires in the fields that time of year would be disastrous. The flatboats continued to come downriver from Fort Pitt with news of the Revolution. Washington was continuing the fight with some small victories. The Continental Congress was working on a constitution. On the last day of June Daniel Boone stopped in from Boonesboro. Colonel Zane took him into his confidence and showed him the improvements in Fort Henry's defenses. Boone was elated at the surprise that had been set up for Girty.

"It almost makes you wish Girty would get here sooner than later. You should be able to devastate his ranks right here at Fort Henry."

"I hope you're right, Daniel. The main thing is, we have to maintain secrecy for the plan to work. I want to get Girty and his Indians and Redcoats under those cannons. Girty is an egotist. He wants the honor among the warriors of wiping out Fort Henry. It'll go a long way toward solidifying his position as a hero and heap big chief among the tribes."

"How can a white man, any white man, make war like the Indians do on his own people, Colonel? It's beyond me."

"Simon Girty got himself into an impossible situation. He deserted under fire and if he's captured he'll be hung. He either has to make his way among the Indians or die. I'll say one thing for him. He has tried to see that white captives are treated humanely. His brothers Jim and George were the worst monsters on the border until this Gargoyle showed up. But Simon isn't as bad."

"Well, I lost a lot of good friends because of Simon Girty and his kind, Colonel. We've been under a virtual state of siege at Boonesboro on and off for years. I've told Kenton and our scouts to kill Girty the first change they get. Jacob Wetzel almost got him last year but he got away."

"Lew and Jack will settle his hash sooner or later. Of that you can be sure."

"Tell me something, Eb. How can two men hope to get Girty when every Indian in Ohio is protecting him?"

"Daniel, all I can tell you is that Lew Wetzel isn't like other men. Even his brothers will tell you that. Back in Virginia where we grew up he was stronger and faster than any of the other lads. When his family was murdered it almost killed Lew. He was very ill for some time. After that he's hunted Indians. Have you ever seen his face? There's no natural color. The medical people say it was caused by shock. He's a fast runner. He's unsurpassed with the long rifle. He's a faster runner than any other hunter on the border. Jonathan can outrun any of the men on the border, and Wetzel can run away from him. That's why he's so feared by the renegades and Indians. Jonathan learned everything he knows from Wetzel. The two of them together make a deadly combination."

"Well, if the two of them can kill Girty, every man, woman, and child on the frontier will owe them their lives."

"Well, anyway, we've got hay to get in and grain to harvest. I want to get it in before the Indians think of burning it. We've got to figure that Girty will come up with that idea sooner or later."

"Well, I'd probably better get back," Boone said. "We've still got grain in the fields, too, and if Girty can burn your fields he can burn ours. Say, Eb, how's about you and Bessie coming to Boonesboro once this trouble is over? I know Rebecca would love to see you. Jeremiah is growing like a weed and so is Israel. We've got some Kentucky bourbon that I think will be the best you've ever tasted."

"Well, we'd love to, Daniel. You know I hope the day will come when we can visit back and forth and not worry about these Indians and the Girtys and the Redcoats. If Washington can whip Cornwallis I think most of our troubles will sort themselves out sooner or later."

FORTY-TWO

The next afternoon, after saying goodbye to Bessie and Betty, Boone struck out for Boonesboro. Colonel Zane was busy for the next week getting the crops in. All in all, the summer had been going fairly well. That all changed on Saturday.

Colonel Zane had just stopped by the fort to see Nathaniel Greene and Silas. The biggest enemy the soldiers had had to face up to now was boredom. Day after day dragged on uneventfully. Then on a warm Saturday, Colonel Zane was summoned to the fort. Upon arriving at the gate he found Sam Brady kneeling over a body stretched out in a wagon. A more pitiful sight had never reached Colonel Zane's eyes. The man had been hit with at least two arrows and a bullet in his side. He had been scalped, and yet he clung to life. Colonel Zane's wife had come right away to try to ease the sufferer's pain but she held out little hope that the man might live.

"He's Burt Cole from downriver," Sam Brady said. "Him and his wife had a farm down there. They had two boys about fourteen and fifteen or so. I'm goin' down the river right away, but I don't hold out much hope for the family. I don't know how in the hell he happened to get away unless they figured he was dead."

"Well, let me know what you find out. Silas, double the watches on the river. We know there's the devil afoot; whether it's renegades or Indians we won't know until Brady gets back. It might be an isolated incident or it might be we'll have the woods full of warriors and soldiers by tomorrow. We have to assume the worse."

Sam Brady was mad. Mad clear through. Bart Cole was a friend of his.

He had spent many a pleasant evening at the Cole farm sharing an enjoyable meal and a glass of homemade elderberry wine. He enjoyed telling the boys about Injuns and bears and such. It was one thing to kill a man in war — a man knew when he was in a war. But to murder women and kids and mutilate the bodies, that was another story. As he stood in the yard of the Cole cabin he cussed every Indian and renegade on the border.

The boys had been tied to trees, shot full of arrows, and then burned alive. As an afterthought both boys had been scalped. The wife had been stripped naked, probably violated God knew how many times, and then had her brains beaten out with a tomahawk. Brady hoped Wetzel would kill every Indian and renegade in Ohio. Brady did what he could to give the family a decent burial and then hurried back to Fort Henry. The Colonel would need to know about this. The Indians were in the woods, and unless there was a stop put to it there would be many more cabins burned and more families murdered.

When Brady got back to Fort Henry he learned that Cole had died that evening. Well, maybe it was a mercy with his family gone. Cole would never have to be told of the horror of what had been done to his wife and family. Maybe if what the parson said was true, the Cole family had been reunited in a better place where Indians and renegades were no longer murdering innocent people, the sun was shining, and it was a wonderful place to be.

The Colonel was mad as hell, just like Brady. There was no tracks of the renegades, only Indians, but that didn't mean the renegades hadn't been in on the planning of the raids on the border.

The Colonel hoped that Jack and Wetzel had put a bullet through either Girty's head or the Gargoyle's. The Colonel was a good man. He was sick of hearing of families murdered and the wonderful country he had hoped to settle awash in blood.

The frontiersmen Greene had brought with him were watching the river. No sign of the Redcoats or a concentrated force of Indians had been seen. No sign of Jack or Wetzel had been seen. The bordermen would show up when they'd had some luck, the Colonel had no doubt about that.

The days dragged by. The grain was in the granaries and the hay was in the barns. The woodcutters were in the woods starting to lay in the winter's wood. The wood had to be cut in the summer so as to be dry for burning in the cold winter days that were coming. None of the wood-cutting parties were attacked. Colonel Zane made sure that heavily armed men escorted the woodcutters, but no threat presented itself.

A courier arrived from Washington requesting information on how things on the frontier were progressing. The war news still remained bleak at best. Washington was having difficulty in recruiting men for his army. The Colonel wished he had good news for the General but not a sign of the Gargoyle, Girty or the Redcoats and Indians could be found. A flat-boat coming downriver from Fort Pitt brought word of an Indian attack. A family somewhere around Fort Pitt had been attacked. They had managed to get away with their lives but only by leaving all property behind. The house, barn, and outbuildings had been burned to the ground. There was a rumor of the Gargoyle being seen at a settlement below Fort Henry on the Ohio. But he had done nothing, only walked past on the river road. Unfortunately rumors ran rampant, and there was no way to know which rumor was true.

Jack and Wetzel came in late one afternoon and showed up at Colonel Zane's cabin. They had had a long hard tramp but had located the Redcoats, Simon Girty, the Gargoyle, and some major Indian chiefs at Cincinnati in the Shawnee towns. Something was definitely going down, but no one was going in or out. They had gotten in as close as they could after dark but could not make out what their enemies were saying. Girty's harsh voice could be heard railing against the white settlements, and Wingenund gave a speech cautioning against rushing to war.

The bordermen said maybe it would be possible for the force from Fort Henry to hit the village by surprise and possibly destroy the whole group's ability to mount an attack. True, there were only a little over one hundred men available, and forty of them had to be left to protect the fort, but it was possible if the bordermen could get the group of frontiersmen in position they might wipe out the village. Nathaniel Greene was all for an attack on the village. The frontiersmen couldn't stand inactivity for long. Greene was a fighter and that's what he lived for. However, he could not move without orders. Jonathan said that General Washington had placed Colonel Zane in charge.

Colonel Zane issued orders for preparing to attack. It would take at least a month to get ready to march. While preparations were being made Colonel Zane ordered Jack and Wetzel to keep the village under surveillance and to notify the fort if the Redcoats and Indians moved out. It was imperative that they know what was going on, and if the Indians and the Redcoats were moving at all.

The bordermen left the next morning. It was three days back to the village. About one day out, the bordermen ran across a huge print on the bank of the stream. No doubt was there as to whom the print belonged. The Gargoyle. Wetzel's eyes were glowing like burning coals and his jaw set as he studied the ground for the direction taken by the renegade.

"He's headed for the Shawnee town. What do you suppose the villain is up to?" Jack wondered aloud.

"He's probably got track of some settler or somebody he can wipe out. Maybe grab a girl from. Who knows what the unnameable villain might be up to?" Wetzel growled.

"Well, I sure wish we could take his trail, but we've got to get to the Shawnee town to see if the Redcoats are still there. Much as we'd like to kill him, we'll have to let the son of a bitch go for now."

"Well, sooner or later, Lew, we're gonna catch up with him. He can't keep sneaking away forever."

"Jack, we've got to put an end to this bunch of demons. We can't be in two places at the same time, but once we get the attack on the Shawnee village over with I'm gonna take that animal's trail and stick to it till it ends in his grave."

"I'm with you, Lew. I hate to think of a monster like him laying his hands on Betty. Animal is the word for him. Well, let's get on the way to the Shawnees. Eb needs to know what's happening out there. But as soon as it's over we'll go scalp huntin'."

The giant hunter caught Jonathan's hand in a grip of iron. And far away to the west a bloody-handed renegade went ahead with his vicious plans, unaware of the pact that sealed his fate.

Jonathan and Wetzel arrived at the Shawnee village on the third day. It didn't take them long to ascertain that the Redcoats were still there. However, their ranks had been increased by at least fifty men and one large field piece. Wetzel cursed when he saw the large cannon.

"We've got to spike that cannon before the attack, Jack. If the lobsterbacks can bring it to bear on the column it could make the difference between winning this thing and losing."

"Won't do to spike it now, Lew. It will have to be right before the attack."

"You see any sign of Girty?" Wetzel asked.

"Nary a sign of the varmint," Jonathan answered.

"Well, it's a cinch the Injuns and the Redcoats won't move until he's there. I reckon he's up to some devilment somewhere."

Suddenly, Wetzel gripped Jonathan's arm. "Jack, by all that's holy, look at that."

Jonathan looked where his companion was pointing. A tall man in the uniform of a colonial militiaman stood talking to a Redcoat captain.

"He's got to be a spy. Otherwise those Injuns would have him skinned and staked out for smoking like a country ham."

Wetzel thrust forward the long rifle.

"Wait a minute, Lew. We don't know for sure he's a spy."

"What other possible reason could a man in a militia uniform be doing in that village?"

"You're right, Lew, you're right. Kill the son of a bitch."

The long black rifle rose to a level and stopped. White smoke belched forth followed by that sharp spiteful crack. The man in the militia uniform fell like a stone. A second later the bordermen were speeding away through the forest.

Simon Girty had been standing right next to the militiaman when he was shot. He had been behind a tree when the rifle shot had put a small blue hole in the man's temple, which prevented the bordermen from seeing him, and saved his life.

But Canada was beginning to look better and better to the renegade. Twice in one month he had been within a whisker of death. He had felt the cold breath of Deathwind, and he didn't like it at all.

The ranking officer of the Redcoats came running from the officer's tent. The Indians were whooping the battle cry, and the other Redcoats were all cowering behind trees.

"What the hell happened?"

"Somebody killed Baxter!"

"Somebody, hell," Girty roared. "It was that damned Wetzel from the fort."

"Well, didn't anybody get a shot at him?"

"No, I don't even know where the bullet came from. That damn rifle of his can reach out for two hundred fifty yards or more. Listen to the Indians. Hear them? Deathwind, they're yelling. They know who it was. Well, he killed our pipeline into the settlements. I worked a long time to line this up, and now it's all gone for naught."

"Somehow we've got to put an end to this damn borderman, as you call him."

"Well, good luck. Every damn Indian on the border wants to do that."

"Well, we've got General Howe and General Gage and every warrior on the border out for this Wetzel's scalp. I'm getting bloody tired of his ruining every plan I come up with."

"Well, I'm beginning to think Canada is getting more attractive all the time."

"Planning to run out on us too, Girty?"

"No, I'll stick it out, but I'm not sure if any of us will outlast this border war."

FORTY-THREE

During the early years of the Revolution the Redcoats employed many of the people in the New World who remained loyal to England, called Tories. Simon Girty and his brothers were Tories, as was the most famous traitor of all, Benedict Arnold.

For every well-known traitor, there were many who had never been heard of but were just as vicious. General Gage and General Howe and even Cornwallis himself actually recruited men as traitors to enlist in the Continental Army and work from within to destroy Washington. On the frontier many men were working with Girty to bring about the destruction of the frontier settlements.

After Wetzel shot the traitor at the village, he and Jonathan moved in a huge circle to look for any sign of Girty or the Gargoyle. The border-men knew that with the additional Redcoats who had arrived at the village, sooner or later the Indians and Redcoats would move against Fort Henry. Colonel Zane needed to know about Baxter's treachery because of the information he might have given the Redcoats about the fort's defenses, the trap that had been laid for them, and also the possible attack against the Shawnee village. The problem that faced the militia at Fort Henry was that if they moved out to attack the Shawnees, they could well be wiped out in an ambush from the village. If the Redcoats and Indians were aware of the pending attack then an opportunity to wipe out the Shawnees and Redcoats would be lost. All in all, it was a might iffy situation.

That same day about thirty miles away a cabin and barn were burning. A husband and wife and three children lay dead in the farmyard. Even thc family's dog had been killed and mutilated. All five bodies had been scalped, and the young girl had been stripped naked and violated before being murdered and scalped. A huge footprint in the dust of the yard was like a signature of the beast that had committed this abomination — the Gargoyle. In this world there are men so vicious that no crime is too despicable, no crime so evil as to be too much for the conscience to bear. This monster had no second thoughts.

That night in camp the bordermen were planning their strategy for the next day. Colonel Zane should be told of the new number of Redcoats in camp. Jonathan decided he would carry the word to Fort Henry. Very shortly a troop of militia would be pulling out, headed for the battle with the Redcoats and renegades. They needed to know the number of their adversaries.

"You figure to stay here till the militia gets here?" Jack asked.

"Unless the red varmints and the British move out against Fort Henry or Fort Pitt. It's a certainty they're not gonna sit down in the valley forever," Wetzel said.

"Well, Eb said the men would be ready to move by the end of the month. The only thing that worries me is they'll be leaving the fort way undermanned."

"That's the whole problem we're up against, Jack. And it ain't only this bunch of villains we've got to worry about. What's to keep the red varmints from sneaking down from Canada with another force to hit the fort with while we're out attacking this bunch?"

"Well, it ain't a perfect plan by any means. And another thing, Jack. Where's that big ugly cuss been keeping himself? You can bet he's up to some devilment; you can bet on that."

The hunters turned in that night, but sleep was not peaceful. Both knew that the very survival of the border settlements might be in their hands. These next few weeks could affect the frontier for generations to come.

FORTY-FOUR

At Washington's headquarters the word had reached the General about the traitor in the Shawnee camp. The word was out that the man had been shot and killed for his traitorous acts. However, the question was, how much damage had the turncoat managed to do to their plans to ambush Girty and his Redcoats and Indian allies.

On top of that, word had reached Washington that General Howe had been sent to try an encirclement of his army and end the Revolution in one swoop. The General had sent out scouts into the Colonies to keep him informed of the Redcoat's movements. Washington knew that his army was in dire need of a victory. Too many of his men were saying that the cause was lost. A lot of men had not been paid. Ammunition was running low, and if something did not happen to turn this war around the Redcoats would block off their retreat into the woods and valleys. That would be the death knell for the Revolution.

Washington had managed to survive by doing exactly what the British didn't expect him to do. The British expected a siege at Ticonderoga, but Washington abandoned the fortress on the night of July 5, 1777. Brigadier General Simon Fraser, commander of Lieutenant General Burgoyne's advanced corps, was alerted at dawn and lost no time in entering the main works from the west. Shortly after, Major General Friedrich von Riedesel, commander of Burgoyne's German forces, moved in. Fraser crossed the bridge boom to Mount Independence and began a vigorous pursuit of the Americans, who had retreated by land. He had with him eight hundred fifty men, a little over half the advanced corps. The regulars included twenty companies of light infantry and grenadiers at half strength and two battalions' company of the twenty-four-foot. Among the irregulars were rangers, Captain Alexander Fraser's marksman, a handful of Canadian militia, and some loyalists from the corps of John Peters and Ebenezer Vessup. Fraser had only a few Indians, as most of them were in the process of plundering Ticonderoga. The corps did not bring its artillery with it.

Riedesel followed with a company of elite Jagers and eighty grenadiers from Colonel Heinrich von Breymann's advance corps, with the rest of the corps bringing up the rear. Washington knew they were tired and disorganized. Brigadier General Arthur St. Clair, commander of Ticonderoga, led twenty-five hundred Americans, the bulk of his command, to Skenesboro via Castleton. At the hamlet of Hubbardston, Vermont, he left Colonel Seth Warner with a small force to collect the rear guard and stragglers and then to join at Castleton six miles north. Warner's command of a thousand to twelve hundred men consisted of three regiments of continentals, Warner's own "Green Mountain Boys," Nathan Hale's (not the spy) 2nd New Hampshire, and Colonel Ebenezer Francis's 11th Massachusetts. Warner disobeyed orders and camped for the night at the Castleton's crossroad just outside Hubbardston. This led to the bloody encounter of the battle of Hubbardston.

Between luck and ingenuity Washington's army had managed to survive. The general knew he had good officers and brave men. Because of the terrain he knew he could win this war. He also knew that if the border settlements fell at this critical time the Revolution was doomed. He knew that Simon Girty had recruited several loyalists with nothing else in mind but to destroy the colonial army. Having lost at Bunker Hill and Breeds Hill, Washington was in no mood to lose any more engagements. He had fortified Dorchester Heights, which dominated Boston, and had placed heavy artillery there as well. General Howe at first had decided to attack but then, remembering the loss of life at Bunker Hill, had thought better of it. To him Boston wasn't worth the cost in lives, so he decided to take his army and the loyalists away from the city.

No better man could have been picked to lead the colonial army.

George Washington was not only an experienced soldier who had proved himself under fire, serving with courage in the French and Indian War, but was a man blessed with luck as few generals before or since. At one battle, he had two horses shot from under him and his coat and hat perforated with bullets but none touched him.

FORTY-FIVE

One afternoon Washington was in his tent when the word reached him about the preparations for the attack being planned against the Shawnee village and the death of the spy. The General sent a message by courier notifying Colonel Zane that he was in complete agreement with Eb. Washington had ordered Nathaniel Greene to place himself and his men completely under Colonel Zane's command. Thus the stage was set for the attack to go forward.

What had not reached Washington or Fort Henry was word of an attack on a little village of several religious families on the Konawa River. The Gargoyle and his picked gang of Indians and renegades had killed every man, woman, and child. The men had been burned at the stake. The women had been raped and tortured. One little boy had been mutilated. Even veteran frontiersmen used to the violence of border warfare turned away in horror at the evil of the attack. Word had gotten around that the Gargoyle laughed and bragged to his cohorts about the atrocities at the village.

He would not have laughed so long or bragged so loudly had he known that he had been marked for death by Deathwind. Wetzel had sworn to trail him until his bones were bleaching in the sun after being picked clean by buzzards. Wetzel, once he took the trail, never wavered or gave quarter. He would stick to the trail like a wolf to a bleeding buck. The question was, how many settlers and their families would have to die before the monster's trail ended.

The borderman's life was for the most part devoid of happiness and the normal joys of family kith and kin. Oh, there was the joy of the wilderness, of night in the woods with its peaceful tranquility, the sight of an eagle flying high above the earth or a huge buck drinking at a water hole. But mostly the borderman devoted his life to seeing the settlement grow and prosper, attracting new families, new homes in the wilderness.

That was what made both Wetzel and Jonathan dedicated to the destruction of Simon Girty and his brothers and the Gargoyle. They dreamed of a time when a man could walk out on his porch and not worry about being shot from ambush. When his wife and children could live their lives without losing their scalp to a renegade's knife or being carried off to a renegade's lair.

The greatest joy for Colonel Zane was to walk out on his porch and hear the sound of hammers and saws as cabins were going up. He loved the talk of the settlers as they went about their daily routine, the sight of flatboats on the river. These were all signs that his vision was being fulfilled. When the Colonel had found his valley and first walked out upon the bluff, it was just he and his dog. Since then forty families had come to Wheeling. It had been a long, difficult struggle, and the graves on the hillside had increased in number. But in all the years the Colonel's dedication to his friends and family had never wavered. The threat of an Indian attack was always present, and since the Gargoyle had moved into the Ohio country at the instigation of the British it had become even worse. That's why the Colonel had ordered his bordermen to find and kill this fiend from hell.

FORTY-SIX

At Fort Henry there was a great increase of activity. Cannons were being cleaned and both bore and touch hole covered to keep them dry and ready for firing. The cannons were loaded on wagons with their kegs of powder. Buckskin garments were being sewed and laced; long rifles and tomahawks were being prepared for battle. Simon Kenton and Jacob Wetzel had arrived from Boonesboro to accompany the expedition. In each man's heart was the resolve that the Redcoats and renegades in the Shawnee village had to be destroyed. This threat to the settlements had to be stopped before it could spread over the border county like locusts. Jonathan Zane had come in from Ohio stating that the village had been reinforced with more soldiers made up of British regulars. Colonel Zane had made up his mind that to wait longer would only let the enemy increase his strength. Wingenund with the Delawares had not yet left their encampment, but no one knew how long they could count on the Delaware chief's remaining out of the war.

A dispatch had been sent to Washington notifying the General that the expedition against the Indian village was ready. A detachment of thirty men under Colonel Zane's brother-in-law Sam McCulloch had arrived from Fort Pitt to bolster the force that would remain at Fort Henry. Everything was ready. The decision was made to pull out the following evening. Jonathan Zane would lead the expedition and act as guide as he was most familiar with the trail to the village through Ohio. They would meet up with Wetzel about twenty miles from the village. They would encircle the village, placing cannon on the heights above the camp. All hundred frontiersmen would be ready to move into the village the minute the artillery stopped firing. The attack would then be hand to hand, tomahawk to tomahawk. Every man knew it would be a bloody encounter with no quarter given.

With tearful good-byes from the womenfolks and handshakes and well wishes from those left behind to guard the fort, the militia was on its way.

The column moved north until it reached the westward trail. By dark they were at the river. The crossing was made without mishap and, after taking a couple of hours to dry out the clothing and wagons and check the powder and cannons, they were ready to proceed. So carefully had the wagons been packed and the wheels greased that no sound was there to warn any Indian scout that might be prowling the forest. When an owl took off, booming its haunting cry through the forest, many minutes were spent listening for any sound that might tell an adversary that an enemy was in the woods. When a horse snorted, his master gripped its muzzle to quiet him. No harness jingled, not a sound was there to warn the Indians that over a hundred men were traveling ever so silently, ever so slowly, toward the Shawnee village. Jonathan Zane was a borderman. He knew how to pick the ground over which to proceed so that no sound escaped them. No rock rolled, no stick cracked underfoot.

Just before daylight Jonathan led them into a huge cave that in eons past had been hollowed out by some long-extinct river. Breakfast was cooked over a small hot fire that allowed no smoke to warn any Indian scout. A small spring of water trickled from the rocks at the back of the cave so the men filled their waterskins. Then some lay down for some much-needed sleep, while the other men kept watch. Each man fell asleep with the knowledge that this might be one of his last days on earth. But each man knew that if his life was lost in the battle to come, it would be to clear the Redcoats and the Indians and renegades from the frontier.

A huge old eagle called in a tree high above the cave entrance and, seeing something it didn't like, he glided off on the air currents. A squirrel scolded from a tree limb barking his displeasure at the intruders in his domain. The frontiersmen all slept as if dead, so strong had been the stress of moving through woods knowing that one sound could destroy the element of surprise so critical to the success of their mission.

Twilight found them again on the trail. Jonathan led them through the forest with almost ghostly silence. Once a snort deep in the forest delayed them for two hours until Jonathan and Jacob Wetzel could find out what it was. At last it was ascertained that it was an old elk that had been frightened from its bed by the column of men traveling silently through the forest. Before daylight a soft, gentle rain set in and, though it made it cold and wet, Jonathan breathed a sigh of relief. Wet leaves made almost no sound as the men passed, and the rain would wash out any trail the column might leave.

In the morning they holed up in a thicket. The sun came out and dried their wet clothing, and the men fell into an exhausted sleep. Two long, hard nights on the trail had sapped their strength, so it took most of the day to get ready for that night's travel. As they sun sank slowly toward the western horizon a catbird's quick notes sounded from a thicket. A minute later the tall form of Wetzel stepped into view. He shook hands with Jonathan and his brother Jacob and nodded to the other men.

"How are things at the village, Lew?"

"They are all there, Jack. The only one that I ain't seen is that Gargoyle fella. I ain't been able to leave to look for him because I had to be at the village to keep an eye on them. But the Redcoats are there, Girty's there, and two or three of the mason chaps."

"Have the Redcoats set up any heavy artillery or light ordinance to cover the valley?"

"None. I don't think they know that there's a force ready to come against them within a hundred miles."

"It sounds to me like our best bet is to direct our heavy fire right into the center of the Redcoats. We can send a few rounds into the Indian village. Eb has ordered that there be no deliberate killing of women and children. We are not to take any women and kids prisoner. After we leave they'll fend for themselves. To do otherwise would make us no better than the men we're fighting." Jonathan had his brother's orders to run the attack, and the other men agreed, though there were some among them who would have liked to kill every Indian in the village. Years of bloody border warfare had made them incapable of feeling anything but hatred for the Indians' men, women, and children. But disobeying Colonel Zane's orders was not acceptable. The men spent the remainder of the day checking the padding on the wheels of the heavy cannon and the wagons. The hooves of the horses were padded and everything on the harness that might make a sound was checked and rechecked so that no warning would be there for some Indian scout to pick up on.

It was agreed that Wetzel, Jonathan, and Jacob Wetzel would go in and silence the sentinels. The Redcoats would be easy to quiet, but the Indian guards wouldn't be crept up on so easily. Years of forest warfare against other Indians and the bordermen had made the Indian acutely aware of his surroundings. However, the bordermen would do the job. Not an Indian sentinel would there be to give warning.

At twilight the column began its final drive to the heights above the Redcoats' camp. Wetzel, Jonathan, and Jacob Wetzel left early, gliding through the forest on their deadly mission. Not a leaf rustled or twig cracked underfoot. No weapons made a sound. Their buckskin garments and moccasins were soft and pliable so they could slip through the brush silently. Sleepy birds twittered at the approaching dawn. Once an old cottontail bounded away through the woods.

A Redcoat sentinel was located. Jacob Wetzel silenced him with a quick but deadly knife slash across the throat. Wetzel crept up on an Indian guard at the head of the valley. No rustle of leaf or crack of twig was there to give warning. The Indian might have heard some slight sound but there was no time to give warning before a knife blade was driven deep into his heart. He died without a sound. A second later his bloody scalp was ripped off, and Wetzel glided off to ferret out the next Indian guard.

In the meantime Jonathan had killed one Indian on the other side of the camp and Jacob had killed one more British sentry. So far, so good.

Jonathan headed off to guide the heavy guns to the top of the hill above the camp. By dawn everything was in place. The Redcoat camp was just awakening when the first cannon roared and a second later a huge explosion erupted in the middle of the camp. Screams, curses, and flying bodies erupted in all directions. Another roar from the heavy cannon and another tremendous explosion in the middle of the camp sent shredded bodies flying in all directions. The Redcoat officers screamed orders at their men, and the soldiers tried their best to form ranks. Sheets of rifle fire rained into their ranks. Men were killed rushing from their tents. Another huge blast from the cannon on the hill, and more British were torn asunder. The shrapnel from the exploding cannon balls took a dreadful toll.

In the meantime another battle was raging in the Indian village. Warriors were cut down as they leaped out into the early morning sunlight. Rifle fire from the frontiersmen took a dreadful toll among their ranks. The frontiersmen then attacked with tomahawks and knives. Wetzel was here and there and everywhere. His bloody tomahawk and knife slashed among the warriors. He split the skull of an Indian warrior. Mingled with the sound of the conflict rose the hunter's mad booming roar. Even seasoned warriors wavered, then ran. Wetzel leaped on two Indians, one a huge warrior wielding an axe that the Indians used for woodcutting. The warrior raised it but there was no time for it to fall before Wetzel closed with him. The Indian, known throughout his tribe for his strength, was pitifully weak in the hands of the giant bordermen. The axe was thrown in one direction, his knife in the other. A second later the lights went out as his skull was cloven by the hunter's bloody tomahawk. With a roar Wetzel ripped off the scalp of the Indian and leaped to grapple with two other warriors.

Simon Kenton would later say that never had he witnessed anything like Wetzel's attack on the Indians in the Shawnee village. The giant borderman leaped into the midst of three or four Indians. With a sweeping motion he cut down two or three of the warriors while the other fled like sheep. Meanwhile a terrible battle was raging in the Redcoats' camp. Twice, three times more the cannon roared, shredding carnage with every blast. Some of the British regulars had managed to get a bayonet charge going only to be cut down by the frontiersmen's long rifles. With every blast from the rifles and cannons great clouds of white smoke belched forth to half-obscure the scene. The smell of blood and death and carnage hung over the valley and mixed with the acrid smell of black powder smoke, stinging the eyes.

Jonathan Zane had been taking his own toll on the Indians while searching for a glimpse of the one man he wanted to find more that any other, Simon Girty. But no sign of the renegade could be found. Either he had been pulled out before the battle began or lay dead somewhere among the Indians and Redcoats.

By noon the battle was nearly over. Whatever warriors had not been killed in the battle had fled into the forest. Only twenty or so of the Redcoat camp had survived the battle. Three or four of the officers survived, two were wounded. Ten of the attackers had been killed, and over eight wounded, three seriously. The surprise had been complete. Simon Girty was nowhere to be found. The wily renegade had slipped away at the beginning of the battle. He had managed to survive many years of border warfare by avoiding any conflict that it was possible to avoid.

Through the carnage in the Indian village stalked the terrible figure of Wetzel. The giant borderman was searching for some trace of the Gargoyle, but none was to be found. The hunter was soaked in the blood of the battle; his buckskin garments were stained with the blood of countless warriors.

Jonathan and Kenton were busying themselves with questioning the Redcoat commander. So complete was the devastation in the ranks of his command that the man was in shock. He was shaking and staring into space. Jonathan knew it would be some time before any information could be gotten from him. It was decided that the frontiersmen would pull out that afternoon and camp overnight in the woods. No use staying in the village and giving stray warriors a shot at them. The Redcoats' plans to wipe out the border settlements had been defeated, at least for a while. There had been heavy cannon captured, cases of Brown Bess muskets, and kegs of powder. The Indian stores of meat, wild rice, and dried corn had been destroyed so what warriors were left would have to spend their time lying in stores of wood, meat, and furs to help their families and the old and infirm survive the winter.

FORTY-SEVEN

The column set out around three in the afternoon. As they tramped into the forest, the smoke from the camp spiraled toward the sky in huge columns that left a glow in the sky. The twenty or so British prisoners stumbled along, shuffling as if they were dead men hoping only for a place where their bones could find a resting place. The Redcoat captain stumbled along like a drunken man. The shock had not yet worn off. When Wetzel moved to Jonathan's place in the column, the Redcoat captain happened to get a look at the giant borderman with the blood-stained garments and nearly died from fear.

The trip back to Fort Henry went off without a hitch. Colonel Zane was happy that things had gone as well as they had. He sent off a dispatch to Washington to notify the General that the British in the Shawnee camp had been destroyed and requesting orders as to what needed to be done with the British prisoners. The column was set up in the cabins at the fort. Jacob Wetzel and Simon Kenton started back to Boonesboro the next morning. All were sure Daniel Boone would be well-satisfied to hear of the success of the raid on the enemy village.

Wetzel and Jonathan stopped over in the evening to confer with Colonel Zane. The bordermen were anxious to get back in the woods to try to pick up the trail of Girty and the Gargoyle. Girty would most likely strike off cross-country for the Delaware villages. There under Wingenund's protection the renegade would feel safe. Where to look for the Gargoyle was anybody's guess. The monster had found a hole to crawl into somewhere on the border. The murder of the people at the Kanawa settlements had been discovered. The problem was that a thing such as the Gargoyle would not stop killing until, like a mad wolf, he would be killed.

Wetzel and Jonathan were absolutely dedicated to killing the Gargoyle and ridding the border of the absolute worst scourge to hit the border ever. On the last night before they were to leave, the bordermen and Colonel Zane were sitting on the porch of the Colonel's cabin. The Colonel's wife had made a fine supper of fried chicken and baked ham. The Colonel's sister Betty had brought out some apple pie, and Jonathan was churning homemade ice cream. All in all it was a nice quiet evening, which happened all too seldom on the border. Wetzel had been persuaded to play a few tunes on the fiddle, and Betty and the Colonel danced a reel to the music.

It was hard to picture that this clearing had been the site of bloodshed over the years. The Indians had burned three cabins on this site. The Colonel had vowed that no more cabins would be reduced to ashes because of Indian raids. As they sat there enjoying the evening, a whistle came from the direction of the fort, and a minute later Sam Brady stepped upon the porch.

"Hello, Colonel. Good to see you, Jack, Lew. Glad to see you got back with your hair."

"Nary a scratch, Sam. I see you still got your hair."

"Hope to keep it, too, Jack. Good to see you, Lew," Brady said, shaking hands with Wetzel.

"Sam, you heard any more about that big ugly son of a bitch we've been hunting?" Wetzel asked.

"Not a thing since he hit that settlement last week. He even mutilated a seven-year-old boy, for God's sake. I sure wish I could be there when you catch up with him."

"Well, if I had my way I'd save you a ringside seat, Sam. I've made up my mind that now that this raid on the Shawnee's village is over that monster is next on my list."

"What's up with Girty?"

"Not a damn thing. He got his hide out of the village somehow the minute the shooting started. He's precious shy of his skin."

"Well, I'll say one thing for Girty. He's never even been accused of anything close to what this beast has done," the Colonel said.

"Well, he needs killin' all the same," Wetzel said.

"Amen to that," the Colonel remarked. He remembered the reports of the siege at Boonesboro and stories of other atrocities, although a lot of them had been committed by Girty's brothers James and George. James Girty was known on the border as Buzzard Jim because of the death associated with him.

"When you leavin', Lew?" the Colonel asked.

"First thing in the morning, I reckon, Colonel."

"Well, I wish you good luck, Jack and Lew," Brady said. "Kill that animal as soon as you can."

"You can count on that, Sam!"

After his visitors left, the Colonel and his family sat on the porch enjoying the evening.

"I hope Lew and Jack can find that evil man," the Colonel's wife said. "I hate to see anyone killed, but this man deserves it."

"Yes, he does, Bessie. He's taken I don't know how many lives, and he enjoys torture."

"What makes a man like that, Eb?" Betty asked.

"I don't know, Betts. Maybe some day in the future there will be doctors who can look into a man's mind and figure that out. Right now the only sure cure we've got is to kill a man like him so he can do no more harm."

"Have you heard anything from General Washington, Eb?" Bessie asked.

"No, but I expect to hear by the end of the week. It's hard for a courier to get through with all the patrols the British have out. But I'm sure he'll be pleased."

FORTY-EIGHT

In Washington's camp was jubilation. The success of the settlers on the western border cut the Redcoats' ability to attack Washington from the rear and to extend British influence in the Americas. But with the jubilation came a worry. Washington was not naïve enough to think that the British wouldn't try again. Also the Gargoyle was still out there, and so was Simon Girty. Word of atrocities throughout the western border had turned up all over the border country. However, Washington had little time to dwell on the problems in the Ohio valley. General Gage and General Howe were doing their best to surround him and end the Revolution. Daniel Morgan's frontiersmen had been raising havoc on the British throughout New York and New Jersey. The frontiersmen under Morgan were the main reason why Howe waited to attack.

It had been a running battle since the first day of the war. The time had come for the Continental Congress to put up or shut up. Washington had told them that the money to outfit his army and pay them had to be there or the Revolution would fall apart.

:::

Along one of the creeks that fed off the Ohio a dozen or so miles south of Wheeling, a little boy was spending a quiet Sunday afternoon fishing. So far he hadn't caught anything, but the sun was warm and, like all country boys, he enjoyed lying on his back staring up at the sky and seeing shapes. So far he had imagined he could see a ship on an endless ocean of blue, then a parade of long-necked animals that he couldn't identify. It had been a long lazy day. The boy was just thinking that he'd better get back because the evening chores would need doing. He pulled in the line and was just turning toward home when a huge figure stepped out of the willows about twenty yards downstream and turned toward him. The boy screamed and took off running for home. He believed the devil from hell had just appeared on the riverbank.

The boy screamed all the way home. His father heard him coming and grabbed his shotgun. The boy ran past his father and into the cabin. The father, after looking all around and seeing nothing, stepped back into the cabin and closed. As an afterthought he barred the door. Something — he didn't know what — had scared his boy half to death.

It took hours before the boy was able to talk coherently about what he had seen. Basically he had seen a big man, bigger than any man he'd ever seen. But it was the man's face that had frightened the boy nearly out of wits. It was a face badly disfigured. A scar had covered all one side. An eye had been cut out. And the scar tissue had healed over. The boy's father wouldn't have been surprised to hear that the monster had horns. Now the father knew that the boy was, like any boy, prone to imagination but he had never lied to his father in his life. He had seen something. For three days the father carried his shotgun with him to do chores and even to escort his family to the privy. Nothing. He had almost begun to think the boy had imagined what he seen on the riverbank or had greatly exaggerated. Then one evening after chores, his wife was cleaning up the supper dishes and the pioneer was enjoying his after dinner pipe. He was brought out of his chair by a terrified scream from his wife. She dropped the plate she was drying and ran to him. He grabbed the shotgun and stepped out on the porch. Nothing was in sight. However, the dog was raising Cain so something had badly disturbed him. His barking and growling said that there was something in the woods surrounding the clearing that was not quite right.

Nothing was to be seen, however, so he returned to his wife's side to calm her.

"What was it that frightened you, dear?" he asked tenderly.

"There was a terrible face at the window. It was a huge, terribly dis-figured face, and cruel. It looked like a demon right out of hell."

"Well, whoever it was is gone now, so don't let him frighten you. We'll keep the door barred, and tomorrow we'll pack up and go see Colonel Zane. I'm sure that he'll know what this demon is. Between him and Jack and Wetzel they keep a pretty close eye on what's going on in the valley. I'm getting damn tired of hiding in the house while whatever this thing is goes prowling around out there peeking in windows and scaring you and Jeremy half to death. If I could get a shot at him I'd fill his britches with buckshot. I'll bet that would darn well discourage him!"

The rest of the evening went by uneventfully. The pioneer slept with one eye open with the dog on watch and the ten-gauge fowling piece loaded with buckshot at his side.

FORTY-NINE

Colonel Zane stared at the man in front of him almost in disbelief. On traveling cross-country from Virginia he had come across a clearing where some settler had build a cabin and barn and begun raising a family. The traveler knew the family well and had planned to stop for some company and maybe a piece of the wife's apple pie. What he found at the clearing chilled him to the bone. Not a living thing was left. The family had been murdered, the women stripped naked and violated, and the pioneer and his sons scalped. Even the family dog and the daughter's kitten were left dead.

The cabins had not been burned for some reason. Either the monsters that had done this had been disturbed and not had time to set fire to the homestead, or the fiends wanted to send a message to the settlements. It was anybody's guess. One thing the traveler had found left no doubt about who had committed the dastardly act: huge footprints larger than any the traveler had ever seen. The Gargoyle. Every day another sign of his depravity appeared. The Colonel knew that the bordermen were out there hunting the monster and his cohorts. In the meantime, the Colonel could do little. He had sentinels out to guard the fort against surprise. The families in the clearing lived in comparative safety, but it was the outlying villages that were at the mercy of this beast of the frontier.

The frontier was growing; there were farmers, rivermen, builders, carpenters. The border would expand westward, but only if people could bring their families west without fear of death from an Indian hiding in the coverts, or renegades attacking isolated farms and homesteads. Too many graves marked the hillside above Fort Henry. Within forty miles of Fort Henry the undergrowth covered the ashes of different settlements that had been burned by evil men or the Indians.

Indians had attacked isolated travelers many times. The only way to have a chance of getting through was to come with a large group of wagons with heavily armed men to fight off the Indians if they attacked. Word had come down from Fort Pitt that a small group of wagons had been attacked and burned, with no survivors. Some of the most vulnerable pioneers were the flatboats that plied their trade on the Ohio. Yet the boats were very important to the wellbeing of the settlements, bringing news from the outside world, supplies such as sugar, gunpowder, high-quality rifles, medicine, and once in awhile a letter from loved ones back home in civilization. Doctors were almost nonexistent on the western border so the settlers had to make do. Mrs. Zane was well known for her skills in sewing up knife wounds, arrow wounds or extracting bullets.

One afternoon, Tom Meyers and his brother were headed downriver with a load of supplies for Fort Henry. It had been a lazy trip so far as the river was low at that time of year and the rapids were down to slow eddies. However, there was always the threat of snags such as a tree limb broken off and floating in the water. Also, because the river was low, hidden sand bars and rocks were a danger. Tom was handling the tiller and his brother was riding the bow when the heavy bellow of an overcharged rifle sounded from the bank and a bullet whistled over the raft. Tom's brother took cover behind some nail kegs, grasping his rifle, looking for a shot. Again the rifle roared, and this time the bullet plowed into the side of the boat. Tom's brother fired, and a red body plunged down from the cliffs with a long, strangling death cry. By this time they were around the bend of the river and out of range of other Indian rifles. It had been a close one; the bullet from the Indians had plowed into the raft not a foot from Tom's head.

The rest of the voyage downriver came off without incident. Tom felt a tremendous relief when they pulled up at the dock at Fort Henry. He made arrangements for the raft to be unloaded, and then the rivermen went off to find Colonel Zane. They found him just coming in from a hard day in the fields.

"Hey, Tom, how's life on the river these days?"

"Not so good, Colonel. We dang near got our hair lifted this trip."

"You don't say. What happened?"

"A bunch of Injuns tried to stop the raft. I only seen one but I'm sure there were more there. Jim shot one, but one bullet came from another place on the bank."

"Well, at least you made it all right. We needed those supplies."

"I got a letter here for you, Colonel. It's from Fort Pitt. Somebody said it had come overland from the Colonies."

"It's from a good friend of Bessie and me in Boston."

"I imagine it's hard to get a letter out of the Colonies these days," Tom said.

"I'm sure it is. Well, you get the supplies unloaded and come on over and I'll settle up with you. You boys gonna stick around for few days or are you leaving to go back up to Pitt?"

"Oh, I reckon we'll stick around for a few days, Colonel. We don't have another trip downriver for about two weeks. If you've got anything you want to order from Pitt get it ready and we'll bring it down next trip."

"Well, I can't think of anything right offhand but I'll let you know. Bessie said something about cloth for some curtains."

"Well, see what she wants, then let us know."

After Meyers left, the Colonel opened his letter. As he had thought, it was a letter from Washington. The General congratulated Colonel Zane on the successful raid on the village but also had some disturbing news. Another spy had been captured and had divulged some very troubling information to save his life. Four more loyalist spies had been dispatched from General Gage to prepare another army to build up to attack the settlements in the fall. The Gargoyle had been ordered to attack and kill every frontier family he could find. Also they were ordered to burn the settlers' cornfields and granaries in the fall to disrupt the food supplies the pioneers depended on for the winter.

Such a plan on the part of the renegades could spell disaster for the pioneers.

When the snows of winter came, starvation could become a real possibility. The only thing then would be to kill the livestock, smoke the meat, and hope it would last till spring. Then when the following spring came, there would be no animals to pull the plows to replant the fields. Colonel Zane had faced trouble that threatened his settlement before, but this news worried him badly. Again it boiled down to the borderman killing the Gargoyle. If he was dead the Colonel believed that Simon Girty and his brothers would not be much of a threat. Either they'd pull out of the Ohio country altogether or they'd hole up in some Indian camp or other. Simon Girty had never been accused of cowardice. When he deserted his post it was not from cowardice; it was because he believed the cause was lost and he didn't believe in sacrificing himself or his brothers uselessly. But with the death of the Gargoyle, if that could be accomplished, Girty and his brothers would cease to be a factor at least for this year.

That evening Wetzel and Jonathan stopped by to report to the Colonel and to drop off a couple of gifts for Noah's birthday. The Colonel's oldest boy absolutely worshiped the ground the bordermen walked on. His greatest fear was that by the time he grew up, the outlaws and Indians would be gone and he'd never get the chance to be a borderman like his uncle. Never mind that he'd heard stories of scalping and burnings and such. He only wanted his chance for adventure. He was in absolute awe of Jonathan's friend Wetzel. As long as he could remember he had heard stories about the hunters' hunting and killing of Indians. Wetzel always had stories for him about Indian ghosts, bars, and bufflers. Deep into the night the boy would drift off to sleep with Wetzel's stories traveling through his dreams.

FIFTY

One evening, about twenty miles into Ohio from Wheeling, a group of five Delawares had halted for the night. They started a fire and cooked some venison steaks, washing them down with cold water. Then at twilight they sought their blankets, leaving one on guard. The darkest hours past and a slight grey shone in the east. The birds began to twitter. Then suddenly two huge shadows leaped from a thicket into the midst of the sleeping Indians. The sentinel died on his feet with a knife in his heart. One other Indian made it to his feet but died with a tomahawk in his forehead. A huge shadow sprang upon the last Indians with an inhuman roar. Both were cut down with the slash of a tomahawk. The camp lay quiet without a shot being fired. The bordermen scalped the Delawares and, dipping the warriors' eagle plumes in blood, stuck them in the bark of a tree. It was a way of telling the Indians that no quarter would be given. The quiet of the forest reigned again in the glade . . . just one more bloody chapter in a tragic time.

FIFTY-ONE

The bordermen's hunt for the Gargoyle was an exercise in futility and exasperation. They had been checking the trails and watching the various camps and villages without one sign of their quarry. There should have been a sighting or a track or something. It should have been impossible for a man of the Gargoyle's size with a hideously deformed face to hide, but he hadn't been seen. Yet the monster's depredations continued. Jonathan had made several hurried trips to consult with Colonel Zane and learned of various sightings including the family that had been scared out of their wits by what they thought was a forest demon. Colonel Zane had received a letter from Washington's headquarters with disturbing news about other depredations on the western border by agents of the British Crown. After Washington had attacked Trenton and embarrassed the Crown, taking prisoner the cream of the crop of the Hessians and capturing the huge amount of supplies, the British were determined to destroy Washington and the Continental Army at any cost. Clearing the western border was Howe's top priority.

Colonel Zane was most concerned now about protecting the food supplies, the granaries, hay and wheat fields, and the livestock. In the meantime the Gargoyle was continuing his depredations on the white settlers. A family murdered, travelers terrified, another border skirmish, a family frightened out of their wits by what they thought was a demon. Wetzel spent his time observing the Delaware and Huron bridal paths and water trails. He knew that sooner or later their quarry, if he were still on the border, would show up in one of those villages. After the attack by the frontiersmen on the Shawnee village, the Indians would be busy for months replenishing supplies and rebuilding homes against the coming winter. They would have little time to consider war plans. However, in the Delaware towns and the Huron village Pipe and Half King was railing against the white settlers. And Wingenund had all he could do to hold the warriors back. If the Gargoyle showed up in Wingenund's village he would not be welcome. Wingenund was a brave and implacable fighter in war but was not a killer of women and children. He was an implacable enemy of white settlements and an enemy of Wetzel but he would try to avoid the massacres that Pipe and Half King were famous for.

Wetzel and Jonathan decided to try the caves along the Ohio about twenty miles south of Fort Henry. If the Gargoyle was planning to continue his raids on the border he would need food and shelter. If he wasn't getting either from the Indians then he would have to find it somewhere else. Simon Girty and his brothers also knew about the caves and would probably have used them at various times during his time on the border.

The Ohio River was a highway to the flatboats but a hiding place for the renegades and evil men who were bent on the destruction of the settlements. The bordermen spent two days checking the caves. They found where someone had been living, but the huge footprints of the Gargoyle were not there. It was probably a trapper or a hunter of some kind. Wetzel and Jonathan knew both Girty's print and his brothers' and there were not any belonging to their quarry.

That night in camp Wetzel and Jonathan were trying to come up with a plan to ferret out the monster. "This man ain't like any other renegade on the border, Jack," Wetzel was saying. "He knows the woods and he's got a hole somewheres around here. It's got to be within traveling distance of Fort Henry. He killed those people on the river trail and they seen him at that settler's place on the Snake's Creek. Now what's in the middle of this area where a man might hole up?"

"I've been studying on that. I wonder if those folks that seen that son of a bitch on Snake's Creek knows how lucky they are?"

"Not likely, Jack. From what I hear the boy was the first one to see him. I bet that kid thought he'd met the devil himself." Wetzel couldn't help smiling. It wasn't that long ago that he was a boy fishing at his favorite place on the river. But that seemed like a hundred years ago in a different place and at a far different time.

FIFTY-TWO

The summer days dragged on. The hay was cut and stored in the barns, the grain was stored in granaries and wheat was ground into flour. The word came down from Pitt that the war news wasn't good. Washington was on the run, pursued by Howe and Gage. Cornwallis was chasing the Colonists through New Jersey. Washington had victories at Trenton and Princeton, showing that the British could be defeated. Howe now decided to destroy the Colonial Army. He would need another fifteen or twenty thousand more men.

The word had come down to Colonel Zane that there were already five more British agents on the border planning the fall of Fort Henry, Fort Pitt, and Boonesboro. The British were still smarting over the deadly defeat at the Shawnee village. It was not easy for King George to admit that the upstart colonists could rub the Britishers' noses in the dirt and continue on with their settlement of the western territories.

One afternoon as Wetzel and Jonathan were about a mile north of Colonel Zane's cabin, Wetzel happened to look down at the sandy bank of Wheeling Creek. There in the soft sand was the track the bordermen had been seeking for months — the huge track of the Gargoyle. No other man on the border had a foot that size. They trailed the monster to a thicket about two hundred yards above the fort where he was within easy range of the village. Any person in front of the fort, in the courtyard, or on the path leading to Colonel Zane's cabin would be an easy shot from there.

The trail headed down to the bank of the river. Wetzel and Jonathan, after reporting to Colonel Zane, got what supplies they needed and took the trail. After crossing the river they started a small fire to dry their buck-skin garments. The bordermen were now hopeful that the end of the Gargoyle's bloody trail was in sight. It was forty miles to the safety of an Indian town. Simon Girty and his brothers were nowhere close to aid the monster in his flight from the Wheeling area. Both Wetzel and Jonathan were determined to end the Gargoyle's bloody trail before the winter snows made pursuit impossible.

Wetzel had long ago dedicated his life to live to kill the Indians and renegades who made the people in the settlements and in the outlying farms live in fear. Jonathan for his part had dedicated his life to help his brother realize his dream of opening the Ohio country to settlement. The future generations would build cities, raise families, and cultivate the western country. Both Wetzel and Jonathan knew that there was not a lot they could do to aid Washington in waging the revolution. Their part would be to rid the border of the Girtys, the Gargoyle, and the Indian chiefs who did not want peace but a bloody war of cold-blooded murder. Killing the Gargoyle would go a long way to ending the war on the border.

Many evenings, when time permitted, were spent at the Colonel's cabin talking of the time when the Indian border war would be a thing of the past. Wetzel alone never planned for this. He was and always would be a killer of Indians. He once told a minister friend that if there were a god for him, he would be out in the forest under the trees.

FIFTY-THREE

The morning dawned bright and sunny. The bordermen had a quick breakfast of corndodgers, jerky, and fresh water. They put fresh powder in the pans of their rifles, checked the flints, and were ready for the day.

The Gargoyle's trail led straight west to the Delaware towns. The monster avoided the soft ground when he could. He would pick hard rocky ground that would hide his track. He tried every trick he knew. It would be hard to shake these wolves off his scent. He walked backward in his own prints, walked along fallen trees only to drop off on hard ground. He would walk in water when a creek could be found. All of his tricks had to be sorted out but steadily, steadily the bordermen tracked their enemy. On top of sorting out the trail they had to watch out for an ambush. There was no doubt that the man they hunted would kill at the first opportunity. All cover had to be scrutinized closely before continuing on the trail.

Slowly the day dragged on. At that time of year during the middle hours of the day it became very warm. The animals went about their business undisturbed, which surprised the hunters and told them their quarry was a very experienced woodsman. When they came to a large open area Jonathan went around one side, Wetzel the other. This made it difficult for the man they hunted to ambush them. In addition to the bordermen's caution, every bird, every squirrel, every deer, even a fat old groundhog had a story to tell. If squirrels played along the ground or scolded from tree limbs it told the hunters that no man concealed himself near or the squirrels would be hiding. No blue jay screamed from a tree, and if the old groundhog sensed man near him he would be hiding not hunting for delicacies in the grass.

At twilight the hunters had to stop for the night. They made camp along the log of a huge old cottonwood. The fallen forest giant provided them with dry wood for a small, hot fire. The bordermen dug a hole and built their fire at the bottom of it. That way not one flicker of light escaped to help an enemy locate the hunters. By dark the bordermen were wrapped in slumber. Both knew that the next day might bring a bloody battle that they hoped would be the end of the Gargoyle's depredations on the border.

The next day about noon they found where the Gargoyle had been joined by a group of six Indians herding about twenty horses. Their trail struck out for the Delaware town. The bordermen were tremendously disappointed because, unless they could come up with their quarry shortly, which seemed unlikely, the monster would again be safe in the Delaware village. Wetzel and Jonathan trailed the renegades with all possible speed but couldn't close the gap between them. Around dusk it was plain the fugitives were in the Delaware camp. Wetzel and Jonathan made their way to the top of a high bluff that offered concealment while providing a clear view of the open yard between the dwellings, which was well within the range of Wetzel's rifle. If the beast showed himself the hunter's unerring aim would end his career once and for all. For three days they watched. They saw Simon Girty consulting with a Redcoat officer and the lofty Wingenund but no sign of the man they were after.

FIFTY-FOUR

On the third afternoon the bordermen could see that for some reason the village was the scene of much activity. About four o'clock a group of nine Indians with another four men in the garb of frontiersmen rode into camp. The bordermen knew that these men had to be Tories or they would already have been bound to stakes. Pipe and Half King were prominent in the group coming out of the teepees to welcome the new arrivals. Simon Girty came out to shake hands with the visitors. The question was, who were they? They were not Girty's brothers. None of the men fit the huge stature of the Gargoyle. It was plain, though, that the visitors, whoever they were, were very important. That afternoon there was a great gathering of important people in the center of the village. Pipe was there, and so was Wingenund. The Delaware chief stood with folded arms surveying the gathering of warriors. He was too far away for the bordermen to hear but it was plain that he held great respect from the gathering of chiefs and elders.

One of the buckskin-clad figures stepped up to Wingenund, and the Delaware chief ordered him back. It was plain that something was up. The bordermen wished that they knew what.

That afternoon a British officer arrived with a guard of seven regulars. It was clear that this officer was an important man. His tent was set up for him and two guards posted outside. That night there was much feasting and celebrating. Something was being planned, but it was impossible for the hunters to find out what. They were there to find and get a shot at the Gargoyle. That was their primary mission. However, while they waited they would watch and see what went on in the Delaware town. In the morning when the sun was chasing the mists out of the Delaware town the gathering of chiefs was evident. Then the British officer came out of his tent and Wetzel and Jonathan could see the gold braids and medals on his uniform from where they were three hundred yards away.

"Jack, that struttin' turkey cock is up to no good. If we weren't here for another fella, I'd say we ought to wind up his ball of yarn right now."

"I know, Lew. I wish we knew if the Gargoyle was still in the village. I ain't seen him since we got here. But he's got to be down there. We been watchin' for five days and ain't seen him leave. He's got to be there."

"Well, it ain't likely that one British officer can do us much harm. At least not right now. I guess we'd better hang tight and see if we can get a shot at who we came for. But that Redcoat will bear watching, you mark my words."

After an afternoon of speech making and much ceremony the Redcoats left the village, heading back to the east. Still no sign of the Gargoyle. The bordermen spent the next day searching for the man's trail and finally found only a trace of it heading for the Ohio. But that was all. He had managed to ride out under cover of darkness and hide his trail. Now the border was under two threats. The British, on the one hand, were cooking up some deviltry to again threaten the border along with Simon Girty. The Gargoyle had given them the slip and was again on the prowl. The bordermen started back to Fort Henry with heavy hearts. Yet both Wetzel and Jonathan knew that the battle for the western land had only begun. Colonel Zane would not give up and neither would they. Somewhere in the forests of the frontier a human beast trod the moss and leaves and sooner or later the bordermen would find him.

FIFTY-FIVE

Colonel Zane was satisfied with the progress of the summer at Fort Henry. The granaries were full. The threat of the Shawnee and the Redcoats had been neutralized by the attack on the Shawnee village. The only thing left to do for the summer was to find the Gargoyle and destroy him. His bordermen were searching the forest for the monster, but so far he had managed to avoid the hunters on the trail.

On one particular evening the Colonel was in earnest conversation with Jonathan and Wetzel, who had just come in after another frustrating time trying to find the Gargoyle. They were having a second cup of coffee when a man came running from the fort, shouting "Colonel, Colonel."

"What's wrong, Henry?"

"The Porters' place is on fire! Somebody set fire to both the house and barn! Nobody has done any shootin' but Porter is about as mad as any man I've ever seen."

"Jack, Lew, I want you to see if you can pick up a trail to find out who in the hell pulled this off."

"Colonel, you'd better get some guards out and watch the rest of the fort's granaries. We can't do a lot to stop the raids on the outlying farms but the supplies inside the fort have got to be protected," Wetzel said.

The Colonel nodded. He grabbed his rifle and accoutrements and headed for the fort. Off to the south he could see the glow in the sky that marked the Porter place. He found the fort in a state of near-chaos. Everyone was sure that they were about to be attacked by the Indians or the British. Everyone wanted to know what Wetzel had to say and if he and

Jack were out after whoever had set the fire. The Colonel tried his best to reassure the pioneers with what little information he had. The gates swing shut and riflemen were posted on the catwalk. The Colonel's wife and his sister Betty had come to the fort to be sheltered behind the stockade walls.

The pioneers waited behind the walls for God knows what. Too many times the settlers had had to fight for their very survival. The cemetery on the hill had grown over the years from death by Indian attack. Too many families had been left without fathers, too many wives without husbands. But the pioneers were of sturdy stock, and they were nothing if not survivors.

When the sun came up it found the pioneers tired but safe and sound. Jonathan and Wetzel had come in to say that there was no large number of Indians in the woods. Whoever had set fire to Porter's granary was long gone. The pioneers, relieved, headed back to their farms, and the Colonel and his family headed back to the Colonel's cabin. Jack and Wetzel stopped by for breakfast, and the Colonel's wife and Betty were busying themselves pouring coffee and frying bacon and making pancakes. After breakfast Jack and Wetzel were drawing the charges in their rifles to put in fresh powder and making sure the flints were all right.

"So what's the plan, Lew?"

On matters dealing with the Indians and renegades the Colonel trusted Wetzel's judgment completely.

"Well, as I said before we've got to protect the fort's stores above all else. Might be a good thing to build a couple of extra storage bins for grain and bring it in from some of the farms that aren't to far from here. We also need to harvest as much hay for the livestock as we can. We depend on the supplies here at the fort more than anything else. It might have been an isolated instance or the British might be cooking something up to attack all the farms on the border. Jack and I found the trail of the varmints that hit the Porters'. We'll be pulling out around noon. We'll trail 'em for a ways and see what we can find out."

"Well, let me know. Washington said the British might be working with the renegades to destroy our food supplies. Word has it that Fort Pitt,

Fort Henry, and Boonesboro might be hit. In the meantime we've still got the Gargoyle to worry about."

"Well, at least he wasn't involved in burning the Porters'. There's no trace of his tracks, and anyway it ain't his style. The Porters got a twenty-year-old daughter — whoever did it had no interest in anything but burning the barn."

"Well, keep a look out for him anyway!"

"We'll do that, Colonel. Stay close, Betts. That old Gargoyle out there would just love to get his hands on you," Wetzel said.

"Oh, you don't think he'll try to carry me off, do you, Lewis?"

"Most likely he might," Lewis said with his soft smile.

"Well, I want you to find old Mr. Gargoyle and shoot him for me. Will you, Lewis?"

"I'll be more than happy to shoot him for you, Betts. Just as soon as I can find him."

"You're the only ones who can find him. You and Jack."

"Well, we're gonna do the best we can, Betts. Now promise me you'll stay in the house till this thing is over."

"I will, Lewis. I don't want to even see Mr. Gargoyle."

After Wetzel and his brother left, Colonel Zane spent the rest of the afternoon writing a letter to Washington. After it was finished he went down to the fort. He wanted to see if Sam Brady might be there. He found the scout at the gunsmith's shop.

"Hello, Sam. Got a minute?"

"Sure thing, Colonel. What can I do for you?"

"Sam, I've got a message I need to get through to the Washington headquarters. It's very important that it gets delivered, and I believe you're the only man except for Jack and Lew who can make it. Will you do it for me?"

"Colonel, you know I'll do anything I can to help. My rifle will be ready later this afternoon, and I'll pull out as soon as it is."

"I'm not trying to hurry you, Sam. It's important that this letter gets through. Are you sure your rifle will be ready? Otherwise I've got two or three rifles that you can choose from!"

"Should be ready in a minute, Sam," the gunsmith called from the back room.

"All right, Colonel. I'll get a knapsack and a few things to eat on the trail and pull out this evening."

"Good. If you want I'll have Bessie put up a few things and they'll be ready when you pick up the letter."

"That would be much appreciated, Colonel. I'll be there in about an hour."

"Good. We'll be at the cabin waiting for you."

The Colonel headed up the path to the cabin. He felt confident that Brady would get the letter to Washington.

Sam Brady was one of the most trusted men on the western border in frontier times, not only by Colonel Zane but also by Daniel Boone. Other than Wetzel or Jonathan Zane, no other scout commanded more respect.

FIFTY-SIX

Wetzel and Jonathan followed the trail of the people who had set the fire at the Porter farm westward. They were not trying very hard to hide their trail and the bordermen managed to close the gap. They knew right away that they were following four Indians and two white men. Wetzel knew that Simon Girty or the Gargoyle was not with the bunch they were trailing. The men they were following wore boots. Also neither Girty, an experience woodsman, nor the Gargoyle would step in soft soil or mud on the bank of a stream like these white men did. The Indians left little trail, but the white men left a trail like the track of buffalo. The bordermen knew that by evening they were within a few hundred yards of their quarry. Not far ahead, perhaps a mile or so, was a place with a hollow under a cliff. There was a spring there so it would be a likely place for the fugitives to stop for the night. Sure enough, that night after dark the hunters crept up on the camping place, and they could see the glow of a fire ahead. It was decided to wait until near dawn to attack the camp. Indians always get sleepy near dawn, Wetzel said. The night hours crept by. The moon rose to its zenith and then made its journey across the sky. The night wind blew softly across the glade and fanned the embers of the fire. It didn't warn the travelers that another wind, the wind of death, was in the forest and approaching the glade. The bordermen crept up to the fire. No sound, not twigs, cracking leaves rustling, no footfall was there to warn the weary men. Finally the bordermen were in position. Wetzel rose to his feet. Jonathan also was ready. Then with a roar Wetzel leaped into the glade. The travelers sprang up only to be cut down with the bordermen's tomahawks.

One of the white men tried to flee. Wetzel's tomahawk twinkled in the fire-light and then thudded into the runner's back. With a scream he flopped down on his face. The fight was over in seconds. Not one escaped.

The bordermen found a British dispatch pouch on the white men. Although empty it told Wetzel and Jonathan that this man was a British spy or commando working with the renegades on a mission of destruction, thus confirming Washington's belief that an attack on the settlements' winter supplies would force the border settlements to abandon the forts or face starvation.

"There are at least five of these sneaks who won't enter their happy hunting group with their hair on," Wetzel said as he scalped the Indians. The bordermen headed back to Fort Henry to notify Colonel Zane of what they had learned.

It has been said that Wetzel's habit of scalping his enemies made him no better than the Indians he hunted. There was a method in the hunter's madness. The Indians believed that if a man lost his scalp in this life he would enter the happy hunting ground without it. However, the Indians also believed that should a man's eyes be put out he would enter his heaven blind, thus unable to hunt. Although Wetzel never went beyond scalping, this was what made him so feared by the Indians.

FIFTY-SEVEN

The next afternoon at Little Creek, a small settlement thirty miles or so east of Fort Henry, the settlers had just come in for the evening meal. Suddenly a great cloud of smoke rose over the wheat fields. A cry of Fire! Fire! could be heard. The men and women ran out to try to extinguish the flames. As they reached the fields a sheet of rifle fire burst from the trees ringing the fields. Men, women, and some older children died in their tracks. Some were wounded and tried to crawl away from the flames but died in the fire. Among the attackers was a giant figure covered in war paint with a horribly scarred face, an awful caricature of a human being who reminded the one or two survivors of a demon right out of Satan's domain. He was laughing in glee and swinging his bloody tomahawk like a madman. One of the settlers hid in a root cellar along with his wife and daughter. After what seemed an eternity, the fire had burned out and the settler ventured out. A scene of utter carnage greeted him. The fields that had been gold with wheat were now blackened from burning. Broken, scalped, and bleeding bodies were everywhere. Only five or six people had survived. They stood around not really knowing what to do. Finally, it was decided that the best thing was to try to make it to Wheeling and the safety of Fort Henry. All had lost loved ones in the attack. All had seen their homes and summer's work go up in flames. All the men wanted revenge on the fiends that attacked women and children. But all knew they were farmers, not bordermen. Finding these murderers could not be accomplished by pioneers, only Wetzel or Jonathan Zane.

At Boonesboro Simon Kenton and Jacob Wetzel had surprised a

group of five Indians and three white men getting ready to set fire to Daniel's grain field. Three of the invaders had been killed, and Jacob Wetzel had scalped all three. One white man had also been killed. By his clothing he was identified as a British regular. But the man was not in uniform, marking him as a covert spy. This had made it open season on him. Kenton took the man's musket and bullet pouch and powder home to Daniel Boone. It was obvious that what Colonel Zane and Washington had feared was coming true. The British felt that they no longer had the strength for a full-scale attack on the settlements, so they had recruited renegades and Indians to destroy as much of the grain and corn as was possible. People had to eat; livestock had to be fed. If the lifeline could be cut off then the settlements would wither and die. Boone put out settlers to watch the wheat and cornfields and others to cut and put into barns as much hay as possible. Boone also sent men to the blue licks for a lot of additional salt to help in the drying and curing of meat. Deer, elk, and bear, and when they could be found, woods bison could be butchered and salted down to provide sustenance for the pioneers. As much corn as could be harvested would be there to help with keeping the livestock alive and healthy for the winter. It was hard for Boone to understand how an English gentleman could be a party to the starvation of women and children.

FIFTY-EIGHT

In war there are certain things that civilized men don't do. A man does not kill woman and children as a deliberate act. You do not poison water supplies or cause starvation deliberately. But King George had sent his army to the Colonies to quell the revolution against the English Crown by any means possible to accomplish their goals. He said, however, "I don't want to hear about it." Daniel Boone was by all standards a gentleman. He fought Indians and killed many of them during his lifetime but never for revenge, even after his brother Squire Boone or his son Israel had been killed by Indians. That is why Boone could never be classed as a border-man. To Wetzel and Jonathan Zane, Indian killing was the business of their life. But even Wetzel, as merciless as he was, would not make war on women and children. And he would not use starvation as a weapon. No, that was reserved for supposedly civilized King George, Howe, Gage, and Cornwallis.

Daniel Boone sent a message to Colonel Zane about the attack the Indians had made against Boonesboro crops. Daniel Boone knew about the plot the British had been cooking up for some time. But he didn't know exactly what could be done to stop them. Simon Girty was involved, and the renegade's woodcrafts made it hard to ferret out the British agents among the tribes. The Gargoyle had dropped from sight since his last atrocity at Little Creek. It seemed to Jack and Wetzel as if the earth had swallowed the renegade. No trail, no sign of him. No settler had seen hide nor hair of the monster anywhere in the Ohio country. None of the families in out-lying cabins were the kind that would hide a murdering renegade. They were all hard-working Christian family men. Most of them had come out here with Colonel Zane when he first opened the valley and erected Fort Henry. Most of the men had lost family members to the Indians and British. That's why Jack and Wetzel trusted every man in the valley. But there was sure one fact that was impossible to get away from: the Gargoyle had found a way to do his killing and devilments and then drop out of sight. It was a mystery that confounded the bordermen.

One afternoon Colonel Zane had an unexpected visitor from Fort Pitt. An officer in the Continental Army, Daniel Morgan had done a lot to keep the British busy back in New Jersey and New York. Morgan was a huge frontiersman. He and his Green Mountain Boys had spent his time making life miserable for the British all over the Colonies. Washington had asked Morgan to come out to Fort Henry to take custody of the soldiers who had been captured at the Shawnee village. Also he brought news about how the war was going. Howe had been trying to trap Washington for quite a while. For a man who a lot of people had thought would be beaten by the British and hanged by now, the General was proving he was more than a match for the best the Redcoats had. He had quite a string of small victories, but now he was facing a worse enemy than the British, a lack of funding to keep his men fed and outfitted. The Continental Congress so far had not provided the funding Washington needed. In addition, Franklin was in France trying to draw up support for the revolution from the French. France was still smarting from losing the French and Indian War to England. Franklin was approaching the French about providing ships and soldiers to help Washington and for some money to pay his troops. There was one sure thing — without help the Continental Army was in for a hard time of it.

The bordermen slept as much as they could during the day. At night they were out scouting the edge of the fields and watching for an enemy trying to creep up and take a shot at some unwary settler on the way home from an evening at the settler's store or somebody who had been out visiting a friend or some young couple out sparking.

The Colonel looked with great affection on his bordermen. Jonathan was his brother, of course, and Wetzel his good friend. After the hunter's family had been killed by a wandering band of Delawares, it seemed that Wetzel would die of the shock. It took many months of care by the Colonel and his wife to bring him back from the depths of depression. From that time on, the giant hunter had been the right arm of the fort's defenses. During the winters, Wetzel spent many hours at the Colonel's cabin. The Colonel and his family welcomed this silent man of the forest as they would the closest of family members.

Irv Lampman

FIFTY-NINE

One evening Jonathan and Wetzel had just got out to the corn field when a slight sound too low for ordinary men had struck Wetzel's ear like a gong. Out on the far edge of the cornfield something was moving. It could be an old buck deer sneaking down to the field to spend an evening munching at Colonel Zane's expense, or it might be something else. Right next to the corn was a field of ripe oats. Also there was a granary there that was full of winter wheat.

Wetzel went to the right of the field and Jonathan to the left. No sound was there to warn the invader that slowly, steadily, surely, the Wind of Death was moving across the end of the field. The waning moon might have seen the approaching tragedy and, as it was helpless to affect the outcome, continued on its lowly way across the sky. Where the long prairie grass met the edge of the forest a huge shadow showed, then sank back into the grass. Near the granary a light showed somebody was lighting a torch. Suddenly a giant figure moving like a bounding panther leaped from the shadows with a roar and pounced upon the one holding the torch. The torchbearer and another Indian went down under the weight of the attack. Meanwhile another figure sprang upon the other two Indians, a tomahawk swung in a whirl, and an Indian twisted and fell. The shadow raised his tomahawk to strike.

"Hold it, Jack! Let's save this fella till Eb has a talk with him. He's a white man."

The man fell face forward into the grass, plainly thanking his God for sparing his life, if only for now. He took one look at Wetzel's glittering eyes and his knees buckled.

"You got something you want to tell us, fella?"

The man couldn't talk he was so paralyzed with fear. He did shake his head vigorously.

"Well, I think the commander of this fort would like to have a talk with you," Wetzel told him. "If you don't want to be agreeable and tell us what we want to know then you and I'll have a little talk. I'd sure like that!"

The man nearly had to be carried to the fort. Colonel Zane was summoned. The Colonel was glad to see the first live British agent he'd had a chance to interview. He was surprised to see the British agent was a very young man, not much more than a boy.

"So, young man, what do you have to tell us?"

"I don't know. What you want from me? I'll tell you what you want to know or at least what I know but please keep that mad man away from me."

"Oh, you mean Lew. Well, you don't have to worry about him as long as you talk to me. But I'm warning you: you were not in uniform. Are you British soldier?"

"Yes, I'm on a mission for the King."

"Then as you were not in uniform you can be hanged as a spy!"

"Please, mister. I'm just a soldier. I didn't know I had to wear my uniform. This fellow Girty gave me this outfit."

"Simon Girty?"

"Yes, sir!"

"What were you supposed to be doing out there tonight?"

"We were supposed to help the Indians set fire to the grain fields and the granary."

"Now I want to ask you something, son, and be very careful how you answer; otherwise I'll turn you over to Wetzel."

"I'll not lie, sir! What is it you want to know?"

"Have you seen a big man ugly man with a disfigured face?"

"No sir, I haven't. I've only seen Mr. Girty."

"All right, son, where's your uniform?"

"In my knapsack over there."

"I suggest you get it on. You'll be turned over to General Washington soon as possible as a prisoner of war. If I find out you are lying, I'll send Wetzel after you!"

"Don't worry, sir, I am not lying."

"I believe you, son. You'll be held in the long room over the fort. You have nothing to fear from us. We treat our prisoners as humanely as possible."

"When will they come for me?"

"I don't know, son, but for you the war is over. Either you will be held somewhere as a prisoner of war or sent back to England. Consider yourself very lucky."

After the Redcoat was taken away to the long room, Colonel Zane turned to Wetzel and Jonathan.

"Well, we'll keep doing what we're doing, Colonel," Wetzel said. "But if we are busy here, we can't be out hunting that damn renegade."

"I know that, Lew. I've sent a letter direct to Washington and I'm gonna see if I can find a couple of scouts from Pitt to help down here. I need you men in the woods hunting for the Gargoyle."

"Well, let us know, Colonel. We're going back out till dawn. I don't think they'll try it again tonight but with Girty involved who knows."

Colonel Zane headed back up to his cabin to try to get another hour's sleep or so. He did feel relief in that at least they knew who they were up against. But it felt as if it was taking a long time to get a handle on things. The Gargoyle was still out there. Their food supplies could be attacked any time. Hard times, the Colonel said to himself. But someday peace would come. That was the hope the pioneers had to hold to. Somehow there must come an end to the border war.

The days seemed to stretch on forever. A week of cold wet weather set in. This would make it hard for the conspirators to set fire to any more fields.

SIXTY

A few miles south of Wheeling along the river was a well hidden cave known only to a few chiefs of the Delaware. In years past it had been used as a ceremonial cave and later as a burial cave for the old ones or "the ones who came before," as the Delaware called them. There a small group of buckskin-clad men had taken up residence, most prominent among them the man Wetzel and Jonathan Zane had been searching for all over West Virginia and Ohio. Simon Girty was also in attendance, and the rest of the men were all the scum of border society. A worse lot of border vermin could hardly be found anywhere on the frontier. Besides Simon Girty, Jake Hanlon was in attendance. Buzzard Jim Girty was there to lend support to his brother. Simon Girty was speaking.

"I have received word that a column of Redcoats will be ready to mount a siege against Wheeling in the near future. The tribes are only waiting for them to arrive. It probably will be ready sometime next spring. In the meantime our job is to mount a series of skirmishes and threats to deny any security to Eb Zane and his settlement. That is, if we can do it without getting killed by those damn bordermen of his. We are to continue burning the outlying farms, the granaries and grain fields, and slaughter livestock when we can get away with it. Put the carcasses in the streams to foul the water supplies. We must do our best to make life hell on earth for the border settlements."

"Am I to understand that I can have a free hand to attack the farms and forts anywhere I want to?" the Gargoyle asked.

"Not the large settlements. Not at this time. However, any outlying farm or small group of farms are fair game, as they've always been. This is total war! It's a matter of the survival of King George's interest in the Americas. And it is a matter of our safety. If the colonists win on the border, all of us will be decorating cottonwoods within six months, you can count on that."

"Well, I'm heading downriver to Haley's Landing. I'm gonna hit them next week. Haley's got a daughter I'd just love to get my hands on," the Gargoyle said with a hideous grin.

"Well, just be careful. The word's out that Wetzel and Jack Zane want you bad. You know them boys ain't gonna quit until they take your hair."

"Well, I been thinking of leaving this country for Canada. It ain't like I don't stand out in a crowd. Once they find out about this cave my life won't be worth a pinch of powder."

"Well, you can relax. Even damn few of the Injuns know about this place. The only white men know about it is right here. Can't see tracks out there on those rocks coming up here. You can't see smoke at night so if you don't light fires during the day time it's gonna be hard for anybody to find you in here, even those border tigers."

"Well, I'd just as soon shake the dust of this country off my feet as soon as I can. Personally I'd like to make enough gold to spend my declining years in the South Seas somewhere."

"Well, if we can pull this off we can all retire to wherever we want to."

"Well, I hope it's over soon. I'm getting damn tired of hiding in the ground like some damn groundhog or something."

"Well, go get some of those homesteads. There ought to be enough gold, whiskey, and willing young settlers' daughters to keep you busy."

"We'll be heading out first light for Haley's Landing. It'll take us about a week to get there. We'll wipe it out. Haley's got some gold stashed around there too, I'll bet. Anyway, there won't be anything left but ashes by this time next week."

"Well, I'm headed for Canada. General Howe is putting together a whole damn division of British regulars to bring down here to hit Wheeling and Boonesboro. I'd kinda like to get my hands on Ed Zane's sister.

She's about the prettiest little filly on the border," Simon Girty said.

"There's a lot of men on the border would like to get their hands on her. Ain't likely though, unless her brothers and Lew Wetzel are dead," Jack Hanlow commented.

"Never you mind. If we get those Britishers down here and the Delawares come in with us, we'll have it."

SIXTY-ONE

And downriver at Haley's Landing people went about their business unaware of the horror that would soon descend upon them. The Haleys were good people who had set up a trading post on the river to provide supplies to the pioneers heading down the Ohio to settle new homesteads farther south. They kept food stuffs, powder and lead, rifles, pots and pans, anything that settlers might need to till the land, to set up housekeeping, to raise their families in this beautiful, green, fertile valley. And it was beautiful. The trouble was savage men trod the forest paths with murder on their minds.

:::

The renegades pulled out the next morning for their assignments. The Gargoyle headed south for Haley's Landing. It would be a long trip, and the Gargoyle wasn't exactly comfortable being that far from the cave. He knew that the bordermen were in the woods, and it would not do to have them on his trail.

However, the trip downriver went fine and the afternoon of the fourth day found the Gargoyle and his three henchmen hidden in the trees just above Haley's Landing. It was decided to wait until dark, as the best time to find the family all together was at the evening meal. However, the best-laid plans sometimes go astray, and so did this one. A tow-headed country boy, the Haley's son, was on the river fishing. The renegades could not see him but from where he was on the riverbank in a clump of willows he could hear them talking. He heard their terrible plans for his family and, slipping away, he headed down the river to warn his family. His father and mother, after hearing the terrible words the boy had heard, barred the door. When the Haleys had first set up their store they had dug a tunnel under the house that led down to the river. The men figured to fight it out as long as they could, then take the tunnel down to escape. There was a raft waiting there to take them swiftly out of harm's way. The women spent the rest of the afternoon packing some meat and freshly baked bread to take with them on their flight from danger.

The men waited with loaded rifles behind the rifle ports in the shutters. They didn't have to wait long. About 5:00 p.m. men were seen taking up positions in the barn and in the doorway of one of the storage sheds.

"Ho, the house."

"We hear you. What do you want?"

"We're here to take your property in the name of King George."

"You'll never do it, you son of a bitch. And if you do you'll leave a good portion of your blood in this ground, and we'll burn it to the ground before we give it to you. So come ahead, you black-hearted villain; we're ready for you."

"Now don't be too hasty. I'm willing to promise you safe passage east to the Colonies or downriver to Fort Henry."

"We know who you are, murderer! You'll never take a living person out of this cabin."

"Well, die then. Fire!" came the hoarse orders from the Gargoyle.

Rifle fire erupted all around the cabin. Bullets thudded into the stout logs of the cabin but did little damage. The defenders were all good shots, and two of the renegades were dead and one wounded by dark. The Gargoyle was enraged. He had expected an easy victory, and it was turning out to be anything but. At dark he decided to fire the house. The outlaws started a fire and, with a make-shift bow, shot arrows of fire into the dry shingles of the roof, onto the porch, and into the door of the cabin. The cabin caught easily and was soon blazing brightly. The fire made the Gargoyle nervous because it could be seen like a beacon in the darkness. However, there was no help for it. The firing from the house continued for another hour and finally stopped. It was morning before the fire had burned down enough to go poking through the ashes. No bodies, no gold, nothing. The family had just disappeared. The Gargoyle was absolutely beside himself with anger. He actually howled and foamed at the mouth with frustration. Finally, the tunnel leading down to the river was discovered. The family, no doubt, was long gone on a raft or boat of some sort. Worse than that, no doubt they would carry word to Colonel Zane and the bordermen at Fort Henry. The Gargoyle knew that he had a very little time to get away before that damn Deathwind would be yapping at his heels. The renegades left on the run.

They hurried up river until they were about eight miles above the cave then took to the river. The Gargoyle knew that there would be no way to find where he left the water, for the rocks along the water at many places left no tracks. But the Gargoyle knew there were border tigers on his trail, and a chill ran up his back. Canada was looking better all the time. He wondered how in the hell he ended out here on the border anyway. He'd been a pirate and an outlaw in the Colonies. He'd barely got away in the middle of the night to avoid a noose. Now here he was with that borderman, the one they called the Wind of Death, on his trail. And if Wetzel caught him there would be no mercy.

SIXTY-TWO

Two days later the Gargoyle and his remaining henchmen were safe and sound in the cave. It was a week before he could relax without jumping out of his skin at every sound, every bird that sounded in the wood, every twig that cracked at the cave entrance. He spent every day looking over his shoulder and trying to stay out of sight.

The family from Haley's Landing had arrived at Fort Henry ragged, tired, and frightened but otherwise all right. Colonel Zane had sent Wetzel and Jonathan right out to Haley's Landing to see if they could pick up the renegade's trail, but he hadn't heard back. Colonel Zane had talked to the family and reached the conclusion that it had been the Gargoyle who attacked the family. But who had been with him? Not Simon Girty, as Girty was known all up and down the river. It was probably Jake Hanlon and the one everyone knew only as Bones. A vicious bunch. The Colonel hoped Jack and Wetzel would be able to flush out the border vermin that were forcing every man, woman, and child on the border to live in fear. Life could not return to normal until this threat to the settlements was wiped out.

The bordermen were searching every nook and cranny for the Gargoyle and his henchmen. No stone would be left unturned in their search.

Silas Zane came over one evening to report that all the grain that could be harvested was in the fort's storage bins. Two wagonloads of salt had arrived from Boonesboro. The women had been busy putting up preserves, and Silas said that a new well had been sunk inside the floor of the blockhouse to provide a supply of fresh water in the event of a siege. At the conclusion of the meeting between Silas and the Colonel it was decided that all that could be done to prepare for a siege had been done. Now all that was left to do was wait.

In the meantime life went on as normally as possible. Young couples came to Colonel Zane to announce their love and their intentions to marry and the Colonel, in lieu of a pastor and ever the matchmaker, performed the ceremonies. Of course, this meant cabins needed to be raised, farms plotted out. The women planned showers for the brides-to-be, and the young men with a twinkle in their eyes planned a chivaree to harass the young couples on their wedding nights. It was all in good fun, but the Colonel oversaw everything to make sure it didn't get out of hand.

Meanwhile, back in the Colonies things weren't going well for Washington and the Continental Army. Word had come down that the Continental Congress was deadlocked on how soon funds would be forthcoming. Benjamin Franklin had returned from France with a promise of aid but no gold. He was told that the French Navy would arrive as soon as possible to blockade the harbor to block Cornwallis's escape by sea. Gage and Howe were both pursing Washington with equal vigor, hoping to end the "insurrection," as they called it, before the winter snows brought the war to a halt and forced them to spend another winter in this "god-forsaken wilderness," as the English gentlemen called it. Cornwallis had voiced his opinion to his subordinates several times that the whole of the Americas wasn't worth spending one English sovereign or the life of one British soldier. He had lost too many of his soldiers to the long rifles of the colonials. His plans of a siege at Boonesboro had come to naught, and so far the food stuffs at Fort Henry were stored safely in the granaries. Simon Girty had notified him that one of his young operatives had disappeared along with important dispatches. All in all, for Cornwallis as with Washington, this blasted war was not going well.

SIXTY-THREE

Clothing was inadequate, to put it mildly, and you could track the soldiers through the snow with the blood from their frozen feet. Starvation was an ever-present threat. Guns were doubtful whether they would fire; fuel for the fires was not always plentiful. Washington petitioned Congress for the funds to keep his army available. Some of the men had not been paid for months; still they hung on.

Back on the frontier, Colonel Zane and the bordermen worked to make sure that Fort Henry was kept in a state of readiness. Wetzel and Jonathan continued to search every trail leading into Ohio and approaching Fort Henry. Daniel Boone came by to consult with Colonel Zane and to say that Simon Kenton and Jacob Wetzel were not having any more luck searching out the Gargoyle. He and his henchmen seemed to have fallen off the edge of the earth. Wetzel and Jonathan did not believe that the man had left the border country. The British were in too deeply to cut and run now, and they were depending on the renegades and their Indian allies to destroy the food supplies, the wood supplies, and other necessities of life that the pioneers depended on. But watching the river, searching the woods — nothing bore fruit.

It seemed sometimes as if the Indians believed the Gargoyle was an evil spirit come to haunt the people of the forest. They believed that, because the Gargoyle was working with the Redcoats, it would bring disaster upon any who associated with them. This made it extremely hard for Simon Girty to convince the Indians to go to war with the settlers as long as the Gargoyle was in the area. Wingenund had not forgotten that

Deathwind was in the woods searching for the Gargoyle's camp. Through Wingenund was not a coward and had proved himself in war time and time again, the great chief was tired of the killing. The British were not interested in the plight of the Indian. If the British were successful in driving the settlers back over the mountains, then the Delaware would have to deal with the encroachment of the British settlers into the Indian lands. There was no victory for the Delaware, only a change of enemies.

Wingenund, unlike Pipe and Half King the Huron, did not relish war. The French and Indian war was the Delaware's baptism of fire. The Indian had seen his lands divided up among the white man. Whether it was British, French, or white settlements, the Indians always lost.

A letter came from Washington on September 5. A new group of settlers was coming over the trail from the Colonies to Wheeling, arriving in October. Seven families were coming west to start new lives. What was of most concern to the Colonel was that there were several young women among the families.

The Colonel knew that to a monster like the Gargoyle this would be almost irresistible. The Colonel sent an urgent message by Sam Brady to summon Wetzel and Jonathan to the fort to discuss these latest developments. The good Colonel was always glad to welcome new people to the border but, brave man though he was and accustomed to border war, he never ceased to dread the danger of new, inexperienced families being exposed to men like the Girtys, Jack Hanlow, and the Gargoyle.

When Wetzel and Jonathan arrived at his cabin Colonel Zane informed them about the new arrivals headed to Fort Henry and his concerns about their vulnerability to attack.

"Lew, what's your advice about how to get them through?"

"Well, Colonel, I'm thinking this might just be what we been needing to bring this big ugly out of his hole and give us a chance to wind up his ball of yarn once and for all."

"What do you mean, Lew? You aren't thinking what I think you are?"

"Well, Colonel, we've been after this man for going on two years. We've tried every way we can to ferret him out, and the devil has winded us every time. Now if he knows there's a girl or two on those wagons he's gonna be after them. Maybe if we plan things just right we'll have a surprise for that villain. Now here's what I advise. First we need to meet those people right after they pull out so we'll know exactly what road they take. Then we can figure where those skunks will be most likely to hit 'em. Then all we got to do is wait. They'll camp somewheres close to the road the night before the wagons get there so they can set up their ambush. That's where we'll hit 'em!"

"Sounds good, Lew. Jack, you got anything you want to add?"

"Not a thing, Eb. If this works we'll have them in our sights. We've been after them long enough. He's killed enough people, and if we don't stop him he'll keep on killin'. Main thing is we've got to make sure those folks from the east are safe."

"Well, with that monster runnin' around out there ain't anybody safe that's headed out here," the Colonel said.

"Well, first thing is find out which trail they'll use. Can you send Sam?"

"I'll have him leave in the morning. Most likely they'll come overland to Fort Pitt. That means they'll probably come right through here. Probably, but we can't be sure. Sam will let us know. If they come that way they will probably come downriver on the Ohio to Fort Henry. We got to hope they come straight overland. If they do then our plan will work perfect."

"I wonder if those villains will know they're coming?" Wetzel asked.

"Oh, I'm sure they'll know. Girty has spies all over the Colonies, and the British will let him know the minute they pull out. More important is we need to be ready to meet them before they get too far out this way."

"Lew, have you noticed or heard any more activity along the trails or in the Indian villages? I know you've been checking them out pretty regular. Washington said to be on the lookout for some more spies moving in from the Colonies. He's figuring they'll be plotting a move against us before too long. He says in his letter that the Congress still hasn't approved any funds so he's got his hands full."

"How in the hell do they think he can keep fighting a war without being able to pay his men or supply them? Won't be long and winter will be on us," Jonathan said.

"I don't know, Jack. Personally I think we've got a bunch of politicians up there without the guts to make a stand."

"Well, there's been no sign of real heavy activity that I've seen in any of the Injun camps," Wetzel said. "I reckon they're waiting for Girty to make some plans."

"Do you think they'll be hitting us or Boonesboro before snow flies?" the Colonel asked.

"No way of knowing, Colonel. Right now, there ain't enough British to help the Injuns mount a full siege. Pipe and Half King are beating the drums for war, but Wingenund is holding back. If the Delawares come in, there'll be hell to pay, you can count on that."

"Old Wingenund is about the only Indian on the border that don't want war, 'cept maybe Logan," the Colonel said.

"There's something in the wind, Colonel; I just don't know what for sure yet. I ain't got no mercy for Wingenund, you know that, but he ain't no coward. I'll give him that. So there's got to be some reason why he ain't wanting war right now."

"Well, whatever the reason we should count our blessings — if the Shawnees, the Hurons, and the Delaware go on the warpath with whatever men the Redcoats can come up with we'd really have a mess on our hands."

"That's the reason why we need to settle this ugly villain's hash right now. I know he ain't the reason Wingenund's holding back, but he's got to be one piece in the puzzle. But either way if I get a chance at him I'll kill him, and you can bet on that. And if Jake Hanlon or Simon Girty is with him, so much the better."

The giant borderman's voice was cold and dry as a winter wind. His face was stony and gray and his eyes burned with an unearthly fire.

"Well, I'm counting on that, Lew. I'll be glad when a man can let his wife walk down to the settler's store without worrying about them."

"Eb, you keep a close eye on Bessie and Betts till this thing's over. And even if we do get that ugly son of a bitch we've still got the Girtys to worry about. But first things first. When's Sam pulling out?"

"I'll have him on the trail in the morning. I was just waiting till I had this meeting."

"Well, ask him to find out which trail they'll be on and where is the best place we can meet them no more than two days out on the trail. It's gonna take time to get this all set up."

"All right. Where you fellas gonna be?"

"I reckon we'll check out the Delaware town and the river trail. I don't expect we'll have any more luck finding that skunk than we have had, but it won't hurt to try. Besides that, we need to know if there's any sign of the Delawares painting for war."

"Damn it. We've been out her for ten years and not a day goes by we don't have to wonder what the Delawares got planned and when the Shawnees are gonna sneak across the river. I don't know about you but I'm getting damn sick of it," Colonel Zane grumbled.

"Well, I reckon everybody on the frontier feels about the same way, Eb," Jonathan said. "Maybe if we can get this monster it'll put the fear of God in the rest."

"Well, I'm sure that some day, maybe not in our day, but the day will come when they won't be a Shawnee in the bushes with a bloody scalping knife or a renegade waiting to run off with some helpless girl. There is too much promise in this valley to let a border war go on forever."

"When the Revolution's over, it'll go a long way toward putting an end to a place for Girty and his kind to hide. I'm sure the British have been backing him in his work stirring up Indians and recruiting renegades."

Simon Girty and his brothers had a terrible, almost debilitating fear of Wetzel. They had seen too many of their gang members cut down by the hunter, and they knew that he had no mercy for the renegades and their kind.

The borderland was a bloody country where no quarter was asked or given. The land was lush and green with mountains seeming to rise to the sky, rocky cliffs, and rushing streams. Herds of deer, bison, and elk were plentiful, along with streams brimming with fish. No wonder the pioneers wanted to establish homes here; no wonder the Indians wanted it kept the way it was, as it had always been.

George Washington was faced with the real prospect of losing the borderland along the Ohio to the British. This would not be tolerated. That was why no mercy would be shown to the Girtys or the Gargoyle, the border monster.

SIXTY-FOUR

Wetzel and Jonathan pulled out to check out the Delaware town before daylight the next morning. Two days later found them on a hill overlooking the village of Wingenund. The village looked normal. Warriors lounged about the tipis or slept in hammocks. Children ran laughing from tipi to tipi. Women hung clothing out to dry. Some of them stood around, like women have for time without end, and gossiped about the weather and warriors and each other. Several white traders lounged in front of tipis, trading with the Indians for furs and whatever the warriors might have. These men were not renegades but simply businessmen.

No sign of the Gargoyle, Simon Girty, or any other renegade could be seen from the bordermen's place of concealment.

There were four or five Redcoats in the village, but that was no surprise. The Colonel and the bordermen had known that the British and the Delaware had been in cahoots for some time. All in all, after a week of keeping the Delawares under surveillance, there was no sign of either Girty or the Gargoyle; at least it appeared that no plans were being made for the Delawares to go to war. Wingenund was seen standing around talking to some of the lesser chiefs, and once or twice with the British officer that appeared to be in charge. But no war dances, major councils, or war preparations were apparent. The front sight on Wetzel's rifle covered Wingenund's noble face a couple of times but the hunter reluctantly could only let the chief go. Many years before, when Wetzel was a captive in the Delaware camp, the chief had whipped and tortured him. From that day on Wetzel and the chief had been sworn enemies. Several times Wetzel had had the opportunity to snuff out Wingenund's life but could not kill him for one reason or the other. But the hunter swore the Delaware's life was his, and that some day he would claim it. Of course, Wetzel was a sworn foe of all Indians but Wingenund especially. Wingenund had a reputation of being an implacable foe of the white man. There were times that Wingenund had tried to intervene to save a white captive, such as the case of Colonel William Crawford who had been burned at the stake by Pipe and Half King. Wingenund along with Simon Girty had tried his best to save Crawford's life but to no avail. Perhaps it was the timing. Not many months before Colonel Cresap had massacred Logan's whole family. This so infuriated the Indians that any white man who fell into their hands was doomed to a cruel, terrible, painful death. Colonel Crawford was doomed the minute he was captured.

Wetzel and Jonathan finally decided to head back to Fort Henry to see if Colonel Zane had heard anything from Sam Brady. It had been more than two weeks and actually almost three since the bordermen had left Fort Henry, and if Brady had left on schedule then he should have made contact and returned with information about where Wetzel and Jonathan could meet the settlers on their trip west.

The Colonel was glad to see Wetzel and Jonathan and to hear that there was no sign of the Delawares preparing for war. Sam Brady had brought news that the travelers would be coming overland and would be leaving August 26. They would travel on the only trail that allowed the wagons to get through. They would be at Cottonwood Creek on the eighth of September and wished to meet the bordermen there. Brady had made sure that no one knew that Wetzel and Jonathan were being sent to escort the travelers; only his second in command would know that the most famous Indian fighters on the frontier would be their traveling companions. The leader had been told of the danger posed by the renegades. He was told that his people would most likely be attacked by the monster of the frontier coming for the sole purpose of capturing the two oldest daughters and to take whatever gold they might be carrying to help them get set up in their new home. The leader of the travelers knew the danger the wagon trail faced but he also knew that all of the families had invested everything in this endeavor and could not afford to wait until a safer time.

On the night before the bordermen were scheduled to leave they met with Colonel Zane to look at the map and go over the plan.

"Colonel, we've got about all we'll need to get those folks through. I figure those frontier vultures will hit the train at Delaware Lookout. That's about here. We'll be scouting ahead and the day before the train gets there we'll hit the villain's camp. We hope that those renegades will be lying quiet before the settlers ever get there. I figure they'll be about six or seven strong."

"Who do you figure they'll have with them?" the Colonel asked.

"Probably the Gargoyle, Jake Hanlon and Bones, maybe two or three Injuns," Jonathan said.

"No doubt about it, a bad bunch," Colonel Zane remarked. "The main thing is to kill the Gargoyle and Jake Hanlon. If those two are laid quiet maybe we can rest easy this winter."

"If they show up you can write those two off, Colonel. Maybe we'll be lucky and Simon Girty will join the party. I don't expect him, though. He's too busy over to Wingenund's camp. 'Sides, he's knows we've been hunting that big ugly fella, and Girty's too shy of his skin to take a chance in getting in a fight with us."

"We'll pull out tomorrow morning. Have you got everything ready for those folks when they get here?" Jonathan asked.

"I'm in the process of putting up five or six new cabins. We'll lay out farms next spring. It's too late for them to plant crops this fall anyway."

"Good. I hope we can get everything — people, wagons, livestock, all of it — here but if we don't they need a place to stay anyway when they get here. Getting the people here safe has got to be the most important. The fort needs its new people moving in. I'm not sure how many people are coming exactly," Jonathan said.

"Probably six families. Four or five people per family. From what I understand they'll be six not long after they get here," the Colonel said with a twinkle in his eye. "I understand that we'll have a wedding not long after they arrive."

"Well, that's fine, Eb. The fort needs young couples if it's goin to grow and prosper," Wetzel said.

"Now we've just got to make sure they all get here."

"Well, I'm depending on you and Jack. Kill those damn renegades. I'm getting damn sick of our people living in fear."

"Amen, Colonel, amen. I'll guarantee one thing. If we get a chance we'll kill every one of those villains."

"Well, have a good trip. Let me know if you need anything."

"Will do, Colonel. I expect we'll have some good news for you when we get back."

"I sure hope so, Lew. I sure hope so."

Colonel Zane and his bordermen shook hands. Each knew that the coming fight would be a hard, bitter battle with no quarter given. Each man was acutely aware that this could be the last handshake they'd have and the last time they might see each other. The Colonel had no doubt in the ability of his bordermen. The determination of Jonathan and the ferocity of Wetzel were without question. Yet he knew that this was a bad bunch. The Gargoyle was a huge man who had killed men with his bare hands, and Jake Hanlon was an expert with either knife, rifle, or tomahawk.

The Colonel never ceased to hope that peace would come to the border and Jonathan would settle down and perhaps even Wetzel would give up his quest after the Indians and live a life as a pioneer. Ah, well, that would have to be far in the future. The Indians and renegades weren't ready for peace yet, not to mention the Revolution was still raging. But maybe some day.

SIXTY-FIVE

And in a cave along the river an ugly giant of a man had just got word from a British spy about the new settlers coming from the east. He heard that the travelers carried gold that was needed to buy land and build homes. They also had a couple of pretty young women with them, all that was needed to bring the Indian renegades down on them. They would be at Delaware Lookout by the eighth of September.

"I reckon the Delaware Lookout is the best place to hit them. There's plenty of cover there and those tenderfeet won't be expecting any trouble. They'll be thinking of the new homes they're gonna build and the new lives they're gonna have. They'll figure that Eb Zane will have everything set up for them, and he probably will. Only they ain't never gonna live long enough to see Fort Henry. We'll kill every mother's son except those two girls I heard about. They'll do to warm our beds when the winter snows move in."

"Well, just save one for me," Jake Hanlon said with a lecherous grin.

"You can have the leavings," the Gargoyle said coldly. "Be ready to leave by this weekend."

The renegades began making preparations to trek to Delaware Lookout. All were looking forward to having the gold from the wagons, new rifles, and whatever else they might find. Every lecherous fiend had visions of a beautiful girl to be his slave and cater to his every wish.

But what didn't get through to the whiskey-besotted brains of the renegades was that Deathwind was on their trail. He was an enemy who couldn't be seen or shaken off a track. He could kill a man at two hundred fifty yards with the long rifle. He could split a man's skull with a tomahawk or gut him with the slash of a knife. In ten years of bloody border war with every Indian warrior swearing to take his scalp, he was still on the trail. Like a wolf he took the scent. And like a buzzard he would circle till the time came to strike. Then he and Jonathan would descend like eagles with talons outstretched to maim and kill.

SIXTY-SIX

As Jonathan and Wetzel headed east from Fort Henry it was a typical late August morning. Early in the morning it was rather chilly, but as the sun came up it spread its warmth, chasing the fog off the river and from the surrounding countryside. Squirrels scolded from the trees, crows cawed from a distant hilltop, a blue jay added his raspy cry to berate these intruders to what he considered his domain. A huge old whitetail buck suddenly leaped up and bounded away. The bordermen spent long minutes checking out the trail ahead. The bounding buck could well alert a hidden Indian that something had disturbed him, be it a panther or a man. But as nothing was amiss Wetzel and Jonathan moved forward, still with that cautious step that hardly disturbed the leaves, never cracked a twig, or moved or crushed grass.

The long rifles were carried ready for instant use, fresh powder in the pans, flints clamped tightly in the jaws of the hammers. The long rifles were not like the Brown Bess muskets carried by the British. These weapons were long, fully six feet in Wetzel's case. Long barrels provided deadly accuracy up to two hundred fifty yards. They could be loaded even while running.

The hunters headed eastward. As the sun reached its zenith, their faces shown with sweat. At noon they stopped for a quick lunch of corn-dodgers, a sandwich Mrs. Zane had made for them, and fresh cold water from a spring that bubbled forth from the rock. The borderman's life was a hard one, bereft of pleasures like wives and children. But the wilderness had its own simple pleasures. The animals, the birds, the solitude, and the fresh cold water all made the bordermen content. On this day neither Jonathan's nor Wetzel's mind was on the beauty of their forest home. Wetzel's face was cold and hard. His eyes burned with an almost unearthly fire. A dark terrible gloom shaded Jonathan's face. Both men moved forward with a cold, deadly purpose. Both men had lost many friends and relatives to the renegades and Indians. Wetzel's whole family had been destroyed by them; Jonathan's brother Andrew Zane was killed, and another brother Isaac was still missing and presumed dead. No mercy was there in the bordermen for these border wolves they hunted. If they managed to catch these human hyenas they would kill them like one would a rabid wolf or mad bear.

This had not been an easy trail, and the hunt for the border monster had stretched for two years. Many good people now lay under the moss and leaves; some had not even had the luxury of a decent burial. Men, women, and children had died under the tomahawk of the beast of the frontier. Both Wetzel and Jonathan were determined that the killings would cease.

That evening at twilight the bordermen tired. They cut some heavy willow branches and leaned them against a log, covering them with pine branches as the flickering in the west promised rain. About 11:00 p.m. the storm broke with fury over the forest land. Thunder and lightning danced among the clouds, and wind made the trees whip back and forth in a frenzied manner. But as it always does, the storm finally blew itself out and the bordermen were able to sleep as only tired men can sleep.

Morning found them again on the trail. The woods were fresh from last night's rain. Birds twittered among the trees. Water still dripped from the leaves. An old panther shook himself to get the water off his fur. He started to wash his face but, seeing the bordermen, hissed at them and glided silently away.

"Quite a storm last night," Wetzel said. "It probably washed away any trail we might have found. No sense looking for it. There's only one place for that bunch of skunks to hit the homesteaders. That's at Delaware's Lookout. We'll detour around in case there are any of them already there and meet the wagons a few miles east of there."

Jonathan nodded his agreement. "We can save a few miles if we cut off up here a ways and head over that ridge."

Wetzel nodded. "We'll have to go careful though. There's no way of knowing for sure which way those villains are coming. We don't want to scare 'em off before we're ready."

The hunters moved cautiously ahead. Squirrels darted off with their bushy tails in the air. Once a covey of quail flushed and flew off into the woods. The bordermen had to wait many minutes to make sure the quail hadn't alerted some quick-eyed Indian scout. After assuring themselves that no Indian guarded the trail ahead they proceeded on their way. Once an old black bear challenged them. He had probably been trying to get at the honey in a bee tree he'd found. The bordermen waved their hats and rushed toward him. After a few huffs and growls the old bruin decided that discretion was the best policy and took off for other parts.

Jonathan grinned. "Sure acted like a tough old cuss. Glad we didn't have to shoot him."

"We didn't need rifle shots to warn every Indian in the woods that we're around," Wetzel said. "Most times a black bear will run at a waved hat. Not always, though. I've seen more than one bear that was meaner than sin. Then you'd have to shoot him. This fella just decided that the honey wasn't worth the fight."

It was hard going over the ridge, but by the middle of the afternoon the bordermen were over it and back down to the valley floor. They'd saved about twenty miles by going over the ridge instead of following the trail around. Also they managed to avoid country where an ambush would have been easy. Now they were on the other side. A few hours later they were well satisfied with the distance they'd covered, and after a small supper crawled into a thicket and fell asleep. Jonathan awakened once during the night and listened to the forest sounds. The hoot of an owl, the buzzing of insects, the croaking of frogs all made a symphony for the borderman. Long ago he'd learned to enjoy the forest sounds like few other things in his life. His brothers, the Colonel, Silas all had their families. Only Andrew had been a borderman like himself and enjoyed the wild places.

The Colonel had always hoped his brother would give up the borderman's life and go into some other endeavor, but the wilderness and the wild life as Wetzel's companion with its danger and excitement was his lot in life.

SIXTY-SEVEN

Morning found the bordermen again on the trail. They moved slowly and carefully now, as there was no way to know how close they were to the Gargoyle and his renegades. Another two days should bring them to the wagon train and the homesteaders. So far the plan was working as well as they could have hoped. Around noon they ran across the tracks of four Indians headed south. Wetzel would have liked to track the Indians down, but there was no time for that. Anyway, the Indians were traveling south away from the homesteaders. They should pose no threat to the travelers. Wetzel and Jonathan forgot about them for the time being and pushed on to their meeting with the homesteaders. Along about 4:00 p.m. they noticed a column of smoke off to the west but didn't attach any importance to it as it was far away from the trail they were on. Anyway it seemed to be too small to be more than a small brush fire, maybe set by the lightning they had seen off to the west the night before. They both knew that the most important thing now was to meet up with the homesteaders to keep them from heading blind into Delaware Lookout. Wetzel and Jonathan both had no doubt that if the homesteaders got to Delaware Lookout they would lose their wagons and die right there. The hunters made up their minds to travel most of the night to get to the wagon train about the middle of the morning. A couple of times the bordermen slipped into the bushes at an unfamiliar sound in the night. However, nothing came of it and they proceeded on their way. Dawn found them about twenty miles east of Delaware Lookout. They could detect the smell of smoke in the air and a few minutes later they broke into a small valley with a camping place off the trail. Several wagons were pulled up, and the homesteaders were in the process of having breakfast. A rotund, ruddy face man noticed them first and came to greet them.

"Hello, neighbor. My name's David Patterson. We're on the way to Fort Henry. I have a letter from a Colonel Zane; perhaps you know him?"

"My name is Jonathan Zane, Eb's brother. This is Lew Wetzel with me. We're here to escort you to the fort. However, I've got some news for you. We need to talk."

"Certainly. You fellas take a seat over there by my wagon, and I'll have the cook bring you some breakfast. We can talk then."

Wetzel and Jonathan gratefully accepted the offer of breakfast. They had not even stopped to eat the night before, as they had wanted to reach the wagons as soon as possible. After issuing orders that they were not to be disturbed, Patterson got himself another cup of coffee and came over and sat down by the bordermen.

"Now, gentlemen, what can I do for you?"

"Mr. Patterson, I hate to tell you this but no more than twenty miles from here some of the worst renegades on the border are gonna be waiting for you. Someone from the Colonies, probably someone you trusted, has let the renegades know that you are coming. They want gold, and they want your young women."

"My God, man, what can we do?"

"Absolutely nothing except pull these wagons off the trail into that willow grove over there and wait. Wetzel and I will hit the renegades tomorrow morning about daylight."

"But there's only two of you. How can you hope to fight that vicious bunch? Why don't I get some of the men together, and we'll all go and wipe out these outlaws?"

"No offense, Mr. Patterson, but you folks are pioneers. These men are experienced woodsmen and killers. You folks wouldn't have a chance. We know what we're doing and you men would only get in the way. Now take my advice, hide your wagons and protect them. We'll be back after we've dealt with these vermin."

"Well, I have to take your word as to what to do. Colonel Zane said I was to trust you and Wetzel completely, so I place myself and my people in your hands."

"Good, I'm glad you've seen what has to be done here. We'll be back tomorrow night. In the meantime just keep quiet and wait. Make sure your men are armed and ready for a fight in case one or two of the varmints sneak through."

"Sir, your name is Wetzel. It seems to me I've heard something about you in the newspapers back east!"

"Don't believe everything you read, Mr. Patterson. Just fort up now and be ready to move when we get back!"

Patterson shook hands with the bordermen and returned to get the settlers ready to meet an attack as best they could. There was no doubt, inexperienced as they were, the men would not shirk from a fight. The bordermen, after grabbing a couple hours of needed rest, started back down the trail to Delaware Lookout. Each was ready for the struggle to come and felt hope that at last they would finally come to grips with the monster and his henchmen.

The eastern newspapers all tried to romanticize the western border of the time. Men like Daniel Boone were already legends. *Poor Richard's Almanac* was one of the papers that tried to paint a rosy picture of the adventures waiting for the brave and daring among the young men. Unfortunately, it didn't say how many pioneers had found death from a bullet, arrow, or tomahawk. But daring men have always been needed to protect the weak and vulnerable. And they most likely always will.

SIXTY-EIGHT

Meanwhile at Delaware Lookout preparations were in full swing to attack the wagon train when it arrived. A better place for an ambush could hardly have been found to suit the renegades' purposes. Huge boulders ringed the glade on both sides of the trail and were crowned with ferns, wild rose bushes, and scrub brush. There was a cleft in the cliff where a renegade or Indian might conceal himself. Huge ash and hickory trees ringed the glade. The Indian and outlaws concealed themselves and waited in anticipation for the unsuspecting settlers to roll into their trap.

Jack Hanlon was there to back up his partner, the Gargoyle, and Bones, the vicious little murderer from New Orleans. It was said you knew he was coming by the stink of death that lingered upon him from the blood of his victims. There was no sign of Simon Girty or his Indian brothers. Girty only felt secure in locations like an Indian camp where he could not be got to by his enemies. Girty knew that the bordermen were on the trail of the Gargoyle and sooner or later they would corner the monster. He didn't want to be anywhere near when that time came. Girty was well aware that a price was on his head and that Wetzel and Jonathan Zane had both sworn to kill him at the first opportunity that presented itself.

The Indians had picked places where they could conceal themselves and not be detected until the last possible minute. Jake Hanlon had chosen a spot next to the Gargoyle at the base of one of the boulders where both could pour a directed fire into the settlers while not exposing themselves. Bones, the little rat, had picked himself a place in the upper branches of a pine tree. From there he could fire down into the middle of the settlers with deadly accuracy. It was a very deadly, efficient ambush that the renegades had planned; they had every right to expect it would be successful. But they didn't know that just a little ways away were two men who had every intention of putting an end to them and their vicious plans.

Wetzel and Jonathan had approached Delaware Lookout very slowly. By evening they knew exactly how many adversaries were there. They had known that the men they hunted were all desperate renegades with murder on their minds. There would be no quarter given in the fight. The men waiting at the glade all had taken the lives of innocent men, women, and children. The Gargoyle, Hanlon, and Bones had all kidnapped helpless girls and, after using them for a time, had murdered them and left them in unmarked graves. All had killed and scalped men who only wanted to put down roots and raise their families in peace.

That night as the moon came up and shed its pale light over the forest the renegades lay wrapped in slumber, except for one Indian they had left on guard. This Indian, about three hours before dawn, had trouble keeping awake. He awakened his companion, then sought his blankets. The darkest hour came and went. A slight gray appeared in the east. The birds had just begun their sleepy twittering. The Indian guard stood and stretched. Then from far back in the depths of the forest a soft low moan like the whisper of the night wind breathed through the woods. The Indian sentinel straightened and listened. Again the same low moan came floating on the night air, rose to a wail, then died away. The Indian guard awakened his companions with a whispered word, "Deathwind." The Indians sprang to their feet. Click. Crack! Click. Boom! Two rifle shots thundered through the glade. Two of the Indians fell without a sound. Bones leaped from his blankets only to fall like a rag doll. The remaining Indian was locked in a struggle with a tall, tigerish figure wielding a knife and a tomahawk.

Meanwhile a huge form leaped upon the Gargoyle and Jake Hanlon with a roar that was scarcely human. Then began a terrific whirling struggle that gave no quarter. Jake Hanlon was an experienced knife and tomahawk fighter who had killed many men in fights in saloons from New Orleans to the Ohio Valley, but he soon realized he was way over-matched.

The giant form he was facing began a whirling, sweeping attack on both Hanlon and the Gargoyle that seemed to come from everywhere at once. Twice both Hanlon and the Gargoyle tried to run only to be pulled back. A tomahawk slipped under Hanlon's guard and broke his collarbone. Another lightning blow smashed his forearm.

Over all the noise of the conflict, the screams of Hanlon, and the hoarse yells of the Gargoyle rose a deep booming roar not unlike that of a mad bull.

At last a tomahawk got by Hanlon's guard and buried itself in the renegade's forehead. The outlaw fell like a log, blood spurting from a great number of slashing wounds. His body convulsed and then lay still.

Wetzel now closed in on the Gargoyle. Jonathan Zane had killed the last Indians and now turned to see if his companion if needed help. The Gargoyle was a huge man who had killed many men with his bare hands. And he fought with fear and desperation like any animal does when cornered and wishes only to survive. Wetzel closed with him in a wrestling whirl, then began a macabre dance. Across the glade they went, each struggling to break free to land a killing blow. "Your race is run now, you murdering son of a bitch," Wetzel roared.

The white face, the eyes glowing like wakening furnaces, all served to terrify the renegade. He was now feeling some of the terror experienced by his countless victims. Suddenly, Wetzel caught the monster's arm in a vise-like grip and broke it like a brittle stick of wood. The beast screamed again. A slash of a knife across his face caused the blood to spurt. The Gargoyle put up his arm to ward off a blow, and that arm was broken. Wetzel now stepped in and caught the frontier fiend by the collar and one ankle and lifted him high in the air. He was smashed down over one of the boulders, and his back splintered like a dry tree limb. Again he screamed. He felt himself dragged across the glade to the cave where the fire pit from last night's fire was still smoldered with glowing coals. Wetzel tossed in several pieces of wood and a bright flame licked up. The monster was tossed bodily into the pit. With his broken back he could not help himself. The fire caught his buckskin garments and flared up hungrily. The monster's body began to burn, and his screams echoed from the surrounding hills. Jonathan stood riveted to the spot. Never had he witnessed anything like what he had just seen. Wetzel stood watching the writhing of the renegade, his buckskin garments soaked in the blood of the outlaws. Finally he turned away. Without speaking he scalped the dead Indians and stuck the eagle feathers in the bark of a tree after soaking them in blood. "Come on, Jack, we'd best be on our way." Jonathan followed his companion out of the glade. The Gargoyle's body still sizzled and popped in the fire. As the bordermen left the glade, several great dark birds sat on the limb of a dead oak. A feast was coming. The largest bird, as if at a signal, swooped down and fastened his beak in the breast of Jake Hanlon!

::::

The American Revolution was showing signs of branching out into a world war. Ben Franklin was asked to leave by England for it was well known where his inclinations were. France had been persuaded to come in with its navy on the side of Colonists and keep the English navy occupied all over the empire. Cornwallis was busy pursuing the Colonials all over South Carolina aided by the soldier called "Bloody Butcher" Tarleton. Daniel Morgan would soon meet him at a place called the Cowpens.

And so the stage was set. The defeat of Cornwallis and Tarleton would ultimately lead to a town called Yorktown.

SIXTY-NINE

By 1:00 p.m. the bordermen had the wagons in sight. They hailed Patterson and received a call back. Patterson expressed thankfulness that the bordermen were safe and that the renegades had been destroyed but he shuddered and shrank from the giant borderman and the dark horrible stains that covered his buckskin shirt and the tufts of hair that hung from his belt. Though Patterson was new to the frontier he knew what they were. Scalps. The beast of the border who had terrified the settlers for over two years and who had claimed many helpless victims was dead. Nowhere on the border was there someone to mourn for him. A few weeks later when the word reached Washington that the Gargoyle and Jake Hanlon were dead, the General sent his thanks and congratulations to Colonel Zane, Wetzel, and Jonathan. Daniel Boone sent his thanks from the people of Boonesboro and his congratulations. Everywhere on the border there was celebration.

In the valley of the Delawares and in the camp of the Shawnee was a terrible gloom. Simon Girty and his brothers knew that safety eluded them as long as Lew Wetzel and Jonathan Zane trod the forest glens and the grass-covered plains.

Everyone on the border knew a long and bloody struggle lay ahead.

There would be a siege at Fort Henry before the winter snows. After a terrible battle Simon Girty and his Indians would be driven off. In the Colonies the Revolution still raged and Valley Forge lay ahead. But in the hearts of the people of the frontier beat an indomitable will. Yes, there would be bloodshed. The long rifles would again speak their piece. But in the end Colonel Zane believed that this beautiful valley — with its promise of wheat fields shining golden in the sun, corn fields growing and ripening and cabins springing up along the river — would become his vision born when he and his dog came out of the bluff and gazed upon it.

Late one afternoon, a week after the death of the Gargoyle, Wetzel and Jonathan stopped by to notify the Colonel that they were leaving to check out a rumor that the Shawnees were massing to march on Fort Henry. The good Colonel shook hands with his bordermen and tried to find the words to thank them. His brother and Wetzel both knew that the Colonel knew that the people of Fort Henry owed them more than they could repay. Some day when the Indians and the renegades were forced to the peace table there would be no need for a borderman, but not now. Now they were the greatest importance. The Colonel watched the tall figures of Wetzel and Jonathan walk down to the fort and disappear around the bend of the path. He remembered the last words Wetzel had said to him. "We'll be back in a few days and we'll have all the information you need. Keep your eyes open, watch the river, and try not to worry any more than you can help. We'll be ready for whatever comes."

The Colonel knocked the ashes from his pipe and, whistling, went in to supper. As night descended over the valley, the call of a whippoorwill echoed down from the hill. A great horned owl flew over the bluff, echoing his booming cry down from the treetops on his search for dinner, some unsuspecting mouse or rabbit. Peace and tranquility reigned, at least for now, over Fort Henry.

SEVENTY

The next day a courier arrived from Washington. Word had reached the General that the group of spies that Cornwallis and the British high command had sent in would in the near future be making a concerted effort against Fort Henry. No one knew exactly when or where the attack would come from, but it was certain Simon Girty and his henchmen would be involved. The big question was how many Indians, what tribes would he be able to enlist to join the attack. Sam Brady had talked to a friendly Cherokee and had learned that there was talk of a huge move against Fort Henry. Redcoats had been seen in the Shawnee towns, the Delaware camp of Wingenund, and in the camp of Tarhe the Huron. The Colonel decided to wait to get a report from Jack and Wetzel before making any decisions on the fort's defenses.

They still had extra soldiers who had been stationed at Fort Henry waiting for an attack. There was a guaranteed supply of fresh water from a well that Silas Zane wisely had dug inside the wall of the stockade. A cannon was mounted on the roof of the blockhouse on a swivel so it could cover the total yard in front of the fort.

Food would not be a problem as the storehouses were full. Colonel Zane had ordered all scrub bushes around the fort to be removed so they couldn't be used for cover by their Indian adversaries. There were about twelve heavy gauge shotguns in the fort's arsenal. When loaded with buckshot, these were devastation waiting to happen. They would tear through a group of Indians or Redcoats with terrible effect. These weapons would be placed in strategic places around the stockade.

With all the preparations completed there was nothing for the pioneers to do but wait. The days dragged on. Nothing had been heard from Jonathan and Wetzel, but Colonel Zane knew that his bordermen would arrive to let him know when an attack was imminent. Word had reached Colonel Zane that the British were bringing in reinforcements from Canada along the river overland and that a troop ship would be arriving from England. This was good news in that it showed that all was not well with King George's plan to crush the Colonists this year. The British commander in the field had not yet learned that the tactics employed for centuries in feudal warfare in England would not work in the wilderness warfare of Colonial America. While the Americans lost many of their men, men that Washington could little afford to lose, the British casualties were horrendous.

The British still relied on the Brown Bess musket. While it was a huge caliber weapon that would inflict a terrible wound, it was a comparatively short-range weapon. The Kentucky long rifle, on the other hand, fired by a man skilled in its use, would kill easily out to two hundred fifty yards or more put the British at a terrible disadvantage.

Almost all the Colonial army was made up of farmers, storekeepers, hunters, trappers, and blacksmiths. Every man on the frontier hunted for squirrels, deer, bear, turkey, and all the animals that would provide meat for the table. Washington knew this and was using this to his advantage.

Also while the British regulars relied on bayonets to frighten and demoralize the opponent, the Colonials were expert in the use of tomahawk and knife. This added up to a bloody, bloody war called the American Revolution.

The British had spent a large amount of time and money recruiting the renegades to build a force of Indians to attack the settlements and Fort Henry in particular. Colonel Zane knew that his fort occupied a strategic place on the river and the Redcoats would spare no expense in driving the settlers out and burning the settlement to the ground. In the year 1777 George Washington had sent all the aid he could to help the settlers. The British knew if the settlers surrendered the Redcoats would not be able to control them. Every man, woman, and child would be murdered. For that reason Colonel Zane and his brothers had vowed that the Indians would not be allowed to take anyone alive out of the fort.

SEVENTY-ONE

One morning the Colonel had just sat down for lunch when he heard a familiar step on the porch. He opened the door to see Wetzel and Jonathan standing in front of his door. Both bordermen looked tired, and their buckskin hunting clothes were ragged and torn. A dark, terrible gloom covered Jonathan's face, and Wetzel's eyes burned like coal fires. By the bordermen's demeanor Colonel Zane knew that the news was not good.

"Glad to see you, Jack, Lew. What news do you have for me?"

"Eb, I hate to tell you this but Girty's got a force of three hundred Indians and one hundred British getting ready to march on Fort Henry," Wetzel said. "I expect them within two weeks. We've got that long, maybe a little less, to get ready!"

"Well, we knew it was probably coming," Colonel Zane said. "But it's never easy when you've got women and children to think of."

"Well, we could take them overland and back to the Colonies. Trouble is, there's no way of knowing how safe they'd be back there, and I ain't sure Bessie would go, Eb," Wetzel said.

"She's pretty set in her ways," Jonathan commented.

"If we did decide to pull out, take the women out of here, what are the chances of getting through?" Colonel Zane asked.

"Not good, Colonel," Wetzel said. "Girty's got spies out everywhere by now. The Redcoats have done their devil's work, and they want to wipe all traces of the settlements off the map. The Injuns will do their dirty work for 'em!"

"Well, that's that, then. We stay. Lew, I'm depending on you to keep me informed of Girty's movements. I need to know when he's a day, maybe two, away."

"Count on it, Colonel," the hunter said.

"Jack, I'll need you to watch the river. They may try to mount a surprise attack from across the Ohio at night by coming down from the north."

"Will do, Eb," Jonathan agreed.

"If Sam's at the fort send him over here. I've got a message I want to send to Boonesboro. I need to let Dan'l know what's going on in case Girty decided to hit him again. I don't think the Injuns have sufficient strength to mount two attacks, but we can't leave anything to chance," Colonel Zane ordered. The Colonel knew that the die was cast and he took charge as he always did. His bordermen would carry out his orders to the letter.

The Colonel set about getting his family ready for the siege. Bessie would get all her medical supplies ready to take to the fort. Over the years she had developed an admirable skill at treating bullet and knife wounds. The Colonel had some of the young men move their prized pieces of furniture down to the fort, including Bessie's prized dining room set and her piano that had been brought overland all the way from Virginia. Colonel Zane was sure that all the outlying cabins would be burnt by the Indians, and he was determined that after the siege Bessie would still have her prized ties to civilization to restart her home with.

The Colonel had made a vow that at least some of the comforts of civilization would be taken west to the frontier. There was a set of fine china that Bessie took great pride in, bringing it out when distinguished visitors stopped by — both George Washington and Thomas Jefferson had sat at Bessie's table in the Colonel's cabin. Daniel Boone was a frequent visitor when he could get away. Once or twice Daniel had brought his wife Rebecca with him for both Bessie and Rebecca enjoyed visits, which on the frontier were all too scarce. Difficulties in travel, dangers on the trail, from Indians to renegades who would like nothing better than to catch women travelers between settlements.

For this reason Colonel Zane had long ago made up his mind to provide creature comforts to his loved ones. The cabin could be rebuilt. In fact, it had been rebuilt more than once. But china, piano, and silverware were not as easily replaced. Betty packed her best gowns and girlhood treasures to go with the family's belongings into the fort.

One afternoon a rider was seen approaching. Every foot he rode toward the fort he was under the keen eyes of the frontiersmen inside the stockade. Every eye was looking over the sights of a long rifle. The men who held the rifles were sturdy pioneers who knew they were standing at their posts to defend wives, children, fathers, mothers, and sweethearts. These were not bordermen but farmers, blacksmiths, trappers, and shopkeepers. They were not professional killers, but each man was ready to send a bullet into the heart of any man who threatened his loved ones.

SEVENTY-TWO

"Ho, the fort" came an authoritative voice.

"Ho, yourself. Come on in but keep your hands where we can see em," Silas Zane called.

The gate swung wide, and the man rode on into the courtyard.

"What can I do for you, sir?" Silas asked.

"I come from General Washington. I need to speak to your commandant."

"What name are you looking for?" Silas asked.

"I believe the name mentioned was Zane!"

"You wait here. There's coffee on the stove in the blockhouse and some food if you need it. I'll be back with the man you wish to see in an hour or so," Silas told him.

Silas found the Colonel working in his workshop putting the finishing touches on a cabinet he was preparing for Mrs. Zane.

"Hello, Silas. What's up?" the Colonel asked.

"We've got a visitor. Says he's from Washington, but I ain't so sure."

"Why's that?" the Colonel asked.

"Nothing I can put my finger on 'cept he didn't ask for Colonel Zane or Eb Zane. Just Zane. Now if he is from Washington, why didn't the General tell him to ask for you specifically? It just didn't ring true."

"Well, let's go talk to him. If he is from George we should be able to figure it out pretty quick. I should hear from Jack or Lew today or tomorrow. The fort's ready as it will ever be. We need to be on the lookout for any trick Girty might try to pull."

As they arrived at the blockhouse they found the visitor sipping coffee and having some beef stew that the fort cook had prepared.

"Hello, sir. I'm Eb Zane. What can I do for you?"

"I bring greetings from General Washington, Colonel. He asked me to warn you of a coming attack and has asked me to escort you and your people back east to safety. There is no way your settlement can survive against such a determined force of Indians and British regulars combined."

"George was here not long ago, and I told him we would not abandon our home and land here and he said he understood. Why would he change his mind now?"

"Perhaps he was unaware of the size of the force preparing to come against you!"

"Perhaps. Well, you make yourself comfortable here at the fort. I want to consult with my scouts. Jack and Wetzel should be in tonight or tomorrow, and we'll see what they have to report."

The Colonel and Silas noticed that when Wetzel's name was mentioned their visitor paled visibly. Both thought this was highly suspect as only two types of people had reason to fear Wetzel. One was Indians, and the other was white renegades.

"We aren't making a move until we hear from Jack and Lew. There's no way George would order us to abandon the fort. I think we got a skunk in the hen house," the Colonel said. "I reckon he'll be a dead skunk pretty quick," Silas said.

"If Lew comes in you can count on that," Colonel Zane agreed. "Lew and Jack neither one have much tolerance for renegades."

"Eb, I don't think there's a family in the Ohio valley that would want to just give up all we've worked for and pull out with our tails between our legs and sneak out and head back east."

"Silas, I don't think so either. Well, I expect Jack and Lew tonight or tomorrow. They'll know what we can expect. To tell you the truth I don't believe one word from that fella that says he's from Washington.

Just then a pioneer came running up the path from the fort. "Colonel, that fella from Washington's camp just jumped on his horse and left out of the fort like his tail was on fire. He didn't even wait to let anybody know where he was headed."

"There you've got you answer, Eb. He was a damn renegade. Otherwise he'd have waited for Wetzel and Jack," Silas said.

"Girty must be getting pretty damn desperate to pull a trick like that," Colonel Zane mused.

"Well, desperate or not he's damn cunning. He'll be watching. I hope Lew comes in tonight. We're liable to be up to our neck in Indians any time now," the Colonel said.

"Did Jack tell you about Wetzel's battle with the Gargoyle?" the Colonel asked.

"No, he just said that the bastard was dead."

"Well, Jack told me in all his life on the border he never seen anything like it. It must have really been something. He said Lew broke his arms and damn near chopped him to pieces. Then he picked up all three hundred pounds of that monster and broke his back over a rock. Finally, he threw the renegade alive into the fire pit. A fitting end it was for that beast!"

"Yes, it was. It's a terrible thing for a man to die like that but if any man ever deserved it, he did!"

"Maybe it'll make the Girtys think about what's coming to them when Lew catches up with them!"

SEVENTY-THREE

That evening Lydia Boggs and her father Captain Boggs came by for a visit. Betty and Lydia went into the cabin to talk over whatever teenage girls talk about while the Colonel, Captain Boggs, and Bessie sat on the porch enjoying the evening. It was a warm late August evening. The mists had just begun to rise over the river. A whippoorwill called from down the valley, and owl hooted and the drone of insects all seemed to lull them into a sense of tranquility. The Colonel and the captain smoked their pipes. Conversation was really not needed. Suddenly a soft footfall sounded on the path. Two tall figures were approaching.

"Evening! Jack, Lew, I've been expecting you. Bessie, bring some coffee."

"Evening Colonel. We have to report that Girty, a hundred Britisher and two hundred fifty Injuns will get here day after tomorrow, the first of September. We've got that long to get everybody inside the fort."

"Well, we knew it was coming. We'll be ready! We had a visit while you were gone, Lew. A man came in said he was from Washington."

"What did he have to say?" Jonathan asked.

"He said that the General wanted us to abandon the fort and head back east."

"What did you tell him?" Jonathan asked.

"I told him I wanted to wait for you fellas to come in. Next thing you know he got on his horse and flew the coop."

"Eb, it's a good thing you waited. There's signs of a force of Indians heading east of here, probably planning an ambush," Jonathan said.

"Well, we'll have our coffee and then get the womenfolks down to the fort.

Captain, you best get your wife and Lydia down there too. I'll ring the warning bell so people get started in from the outlying farms and cabins. Lew, you got any suggestions?"

"Nope. Just get ready for one hell of a fight. Girty's under pressure from his Redcoat bosses. He's got to wipe us out to justify keeping the British out here on the border."

"Anybody seen Major McCulloch?" Wetzel asked.

"No, but I suspect he'll be here in the morning."

"Well, when he gets here I'd like to see him. We need to lay out a plan for after this fight is over. Winter's coming and we need to try to get Girty's bunch before the snows move in."

"All right, Lew. I'll send him to you soon as he comes in. Jack, you got any ideas?"

"No, Eb. Like Lew says, we need to get ready for one hell of a fight."

Captain Boggs got Lydia on the way to the fort then hurried to his cabin to get his wife. Colonel Zane got Bessie and Betty ready and headed down the path to the fort.

Upon arrival at the stockade the Colonel rang the bell to summon the pioneers to the fort. The notes pealed out over the valley. The settlers knew that the Indians were on the way and that to some of their number it would be a death knell.

Morning found most of the pioneers inside the stockade. That particular morning the sunrise was spectacular, bathing the valley in that vermilion color that because of what was coming looked like the horrible color of blood. Two or three of the settler's cabins were at some distance from the fort. Jonathan and Wetzel hurried out to alert them to the danger and urge them to hurry to the stockade.

By late afternoon almost all of the settlers were inside the stockade. Only Major McCulloch and Sam Brady had not yet arrived. Colonel Zane was hoping that McCulloch or Brady would come in before the expected attack would begin. He needed either Brady or McCulloch to man the cannon. Jack was to command the colonial militia in the blockhouse. Wetzel would be free ranging wherever he was needed the most. Water barrels were filled to capacity. The livestock inside the fort were secured. The women were busy tearing bandages, and Mrs. Zane had set up a makeshift hospital in the corner of the blockhouse.

All was in readiness for the battle to come.

SEVENTY-FOUR

That night was overcast, almost as black as a tomb. The mist came off the river, making it damp and cold. Just as the sun broke through a war whoop sounded. The lookouts saw hundreds of Indians urging their horses into the water. They were covered with war paint, and their war bonnets were full of eagle plumes. They were whooping and screaming as they came.

Just as the Indians reached the riverbank a tremendous shouting and screaming of the war cries came from the top of the bluff high above the fort. A second later the settlers, Indians, and Redcoats were transfixed by the sight of a horse and rider stark against the sky. Then the horse and rider plunged off the bluff, sliding down the hill into the cottonwoods and pine trees at the base of the cliff. No one believed that a horse and rider could survive such a leap, and the settlers were amazed a second later to see both horse and rider dashing out of the trees and racing for the fort. A mighty cheer sounded. It was Major McCulloch. From that day onward, to the Indians he would be forever known as the Flying Chief.

The gate to the stockade swung wide to let the major and his mighty steed in and then was closed behind him. A mighty cheer and liberal slapping on the back greeted him, but there was precious little time for celebration. Simon Girty and Half King approached the fort, staying just out of rifle range.

"You in the fort. I'd like to speak with Eb Zane."

"I'm here, Girty. What can I do for you?"

"We've got a large enough force here to take the fort. I'm willing to offer you safe passage back over the mountains if you'll surrender yourself and your weapons."

"Not a chance, Girty. We know what you've got in store for anybody that you get your hands on. You know what happened to that animal you were running with. Wetzel's after you now, and you're going right where the Gargoyle is gone. Come on, you son of a bitch. Do your damnedest."

"Suit yourself." Girty raised his hand and then dropped it. War whoops sounded from hundreds of throats, and the Indians started on the run for the fort. Instantly white puffs of smoke blossomed like huge flowers from rifle ports all around the fort. "Bang!" the little bulldog cannon roared from the top of the blockhouse. Colonel Zane had ordered that the gun be loaded with musket balls, a dozen or so. The lead shot spread terrible devastation in the Indian ranks. "Bang!" went the cannon again, and the Indians retreated back out of range.

The Redcoats were content to stay under cover and fire on the stockade. Their Brown Bess muskets were not as accurate as the pioneers' long rifles, so they had to be content to fire on the stockade.

Wetzel could be seen stalking from one rifle port to the next. Every shot from his deadly small-bore speed to the heart or forehead of an Indian. He was there to encourage, here to replace a wounded man. Just his being there gave encouragement to the pioneers. Two warriors tried to put a ladder against the stockade. "Boom! Boom!" Both barrels of a shotgun sounded, throwing both invaders back in a bloody squirming heap.

The yelling of the Indians, the hoarse yells of the pioneers, the roar of the cannons, and the crack of the rifles all blended into one incredible roar of sound. The smell of black powder smoke almost was strong enough to choke off the breath of Indian and pioneer alike.

By noon the early September heat hung over the battle, so hot it made it hard to breathe. The Indians withdrew to the riverbank to hatch some other devilment. Colonel Zane went from rifle port to rifle port trying to encourage his people. So far the defenders had fared pretty well: only two dead and five wounded. The Colonel saw Jonathan standing by the water barrel. His brother's face was powder-blackened, and his dark eyes sparkled.

"How's it going, Jack?"

"Pretty well, Eb. The folks are holding up as well as can be expected."

"Have you seen Lew?" the Colonel asked.

"He was over there by Will Metzar's station the last I saw him. Why?"

"I just want to ask him something. I thought I saw a small mortar when the British pulled up this morning. I'm afraid they may try to move it up after dark. If they get it within range we've got a big problem."

"Why don't you come with me? We need to come up with an idea."

Jonathan turned his rifle port over to one of the other men and followed the Colonel. They found Wetzel talking with Will Metzar.

"How's it going, Will?"

"Fine, Colonel. Killed me a dozen Injuns this morning, and so far nary a scratch. Had one close shave, though. Bullet came in that port hole thar and knocked the hammer off my spare rifle."

"Well, I'll send over an extra from the fort stock. Keep your head down."

"Lew, can I see you a minute?"

"Sure thing, Colonel. Watch yourself, Will."

"Sure will, Lew."

"What's up, Colonel?" Wetzel asked.

"I want you and Jack to get up on the wall and see if you can spot a mortar or small cannon. I saw the British pulling something by a team of horses. If it is a cannon of some sort, we're gonna have big trouble if they get it set up."

"We'll have to find a way to stop it or we'll get blown right out of our socks," Jonathan said. "We can keep them from getting it set up today, but after dark it's another story. Lew, you got any ideas?" Jonathan asked.

"Here they come again!" somebody shouted from up on the catwalk.

Immediately began a terrible roar of war whoops, hoarse yells, the combined roar of rifles, the bang of the cannon, the boom of the shotguns, the screams of the wounded, and overall the acrid smell of powder smoke all combined to make a hellish scene of human conflict. Jonathan and Wetzel both were firing as fast as they could load their rifles. Some of the Indians had built ladders to try to scale the stockade and gain the run of the fort. "Bang!" came the roar of the cannon. Indian warriors were thrown hither and yon, then either lay quiet or writhed in agony on the ground in front on the fort.

Jonathan was loading and firing from a porthole. Wetzel was stalking from rifle port to rifle port, his fearful yell sounding above all the rest. The terrible fire in his eyes was awful to behold.

The rush against the fort lasted about twenty minutes, and then the Indians withdrew again to the riverbank. The Redcoat officers and Indian chiefs gathered under a huge willow tree to plot strategy. Simon Girty joined them a couple of minutes later. Threatening looks were turned toward the fort. Wetzel and Jonathan were talking it over, deciding the placement of the Redcoats' small cannon.

"They have to put it where it can be hidden until it's ready to be fired. I'd guess they'll put it right behind that little knoll with the oak trees," Jonathan commented.

"That's where I'd pick too!" Wetzel said. "Moon won't be up tonight till around nine if this overcast breaks. I hope it won't. That'll give us a chance to slip out and kinda throw a kink in their plans."

"I like your thinking," Jonathan said. "What's your idea?"

"Well, two things. First we'll have Will Metzar, Hugh Bennet, and a couple of others get a diversion going like they're planning to bust out of here. We'll slip out and plant a couple of small kegs of powder under that cannon. Then we'll spike the barrel of that gun. At a hundred fifty yards I can put a bullet right into those kegs. When they fire that cannon with a plugged barrel it's gonna take the fun out of their morning. Then I'll put a bullet into those kegs. My guess is they'll fire it right about sun up. First the cannon blows up. Then I'll shoot one of those kegs of powder. That ought to upset their apple cart."

Twice more during the afternoon the Indians made an effort to reach the stockade and enter the fort. Both times they were beaten back. The

Redcoats were content to stay undercover and fire continually at the fort. From that far they really couldn't do much damage. Girty knew that if the small cannon couldn't break a hole in the stockade in the morning he would have trouble holding the Indians together to continue the siege. So far the Indians had lost many warriors both killed and wounded. The ground in front of the fort was littered with dead Indians. Several minor chiefs had been killed and several wounded. It was plain that barring something spectacular the siege would fail. Girty hoped the little field piece would provide that something.

So far Girty's campaign against the settlements had been a disaster. Boonesboro still was like a thorn in Girty's side. The plan to bring the cannons into the Ohio valley was a total debacle. The Gargoyle was dead and Wetzel and Zane were on his trail. Girty had thought more and more of heading for Canada lately. He had no allusion as to what would be his fate if he remained in Ohio and somehow fell into Wetzel's hands. A cold chill ran up the renegade's spine.

SEVENTY-FIVE

Twilight came quietly. The cook fires glowed cheerily from both the Redcoat camp and the Indian camp. Indians cleaned and repaired weapons. Wounds were bandaged, and death songs were sung. It was a dark night. Suddenly firing broke out from one of the port holes of the stockade. Indian guns returned fire. It was way too dark for accurate shooting, but the Indians were successful in driving the settlers back into the fort.

The rest of the night went by uneventfully. The cannon was set up in a little clump of trees about one hundred fifty yards from the fort. Girty and the red-coated captain set firing the cannon for daylight. The weapon had been cleaned and loaded at sundown so it wouldn't have to be done in the dark. The Redcoat captain stopped by Girty's tent in the wee hours of the morning.

"All set, Girty?"

"Ready as I'll ever be, Captain. That gun should open up that stockade like a huge battering ram. I'll have Half King and Red Fox ready to charge through into the fort as soon as the hole opens up. If everything goes right the fort should be ours a couple of hours after sun up."

"What do you propose to do about prisoners, Girty?"

"I'm afraid there's very little I can do, Captain. Pipe and Half Kind are wild for blood. If the people in the fort had surrendered there might have been a chance for them. But not now. Half King and Pipe have both lost some of their best warriors to those damn bordermen firing from the fort. They won't rest till every one of those people are dead and their scalps are drying on the chief's lodge poles."

"Well, you leave me out of it, Girty. I'm a soldier not a damn butcher. Some of these people have children. I won't have it on my conscience. If I thought there was a way to stop this massacre and still take the fort I'd stop it right now, but as far as I can see there isn't."

"Well, Captain, you Redcoats started this border war against the settlements. King George wants to wipe out these settlements out here. Don't start complaining now if it gets bloody. You people expect the Indian to fight a civilized war. Well, let me tell you, Captain, Pipe and Half King don't fight a civilized war."

"Well, just the same it makes me sick."

"Well, just stay out of the way, Captain. I'll fight your damn war for you. After it's over you can go back to England, collect your medals and try to live with it."

The captain went back to his tent, and Girty tried to grab a few hours' sleep before dawn. His sleep was filled with nightmares of a huge border-man with burning eyes chasing him with a bloody tomahawk.

He awakened sometime just before dawn. He got himself out of his blankets and headed over to the cannon. The Captain and some of his men, presumably the gun crew, were already there.

"All set, Girty?"

"All set, Captain. I'll go on over and get the Indians read to head for the fort."

"We'll fire in five minutes!"

Girty headed for Half King's tent. He had just reached the Hurons when an ear-shattering explosion shook the ground. Cannon carriage and several Redcoats were sent skyward. A second later a clear, ringing rifle shot sounded from the fort and another explosion shook the earth. Redcoats, Indians, and pieces of cannons were thrown around like chaff.

A tremendous shout and cheering came from the fort. Girty ran over to where the gun had been emplaced. He counted seven dead Redcoats. Only pieces of the cannon remained. The Captain was picking himself up about twenty feet from the gun. That distance is what saved his life. Anyone closer to the gun was killed.

"What, what the hell happened?" the Captain gasped.

"Those damn bordermen again! They spiked the gun! Then they put a couple of kegs of powder under the cannon. Wetzel put a bullet into the powder! Damn him! Damn him!"

"Damn the whole bloody border country. Well, what's to be done?"

"Well, we can keep trying, but I'm afraid all we'll do is lose more men!" Girty grumbled. "There's no way we're gonna breach those logs in the stockade without getting our men shot all to hell. I'm afraid it's a lost cause for now, Captain."

"What about the Indians? Will they try another charge?"

"I'll ask them, but I doubt it."

"Well, I've got a hell of a problem, Girty. I've got to go back and tell my superiors that these damn settlers out here have defeated King George's regulars."

Back in the fort was elation. Everyone knew that they had avoided disaster. They knew that had the cannon been brought to bear against the stockade not a man, woman, or child would have survived. As usual, they owed Wetzel and Jonathan more than they could ever repay.

SEVENTY-SIX

About noon long lines of Indian warriors were winding their way across the river. Next went the Redcoats. The siege of Fort Henry was over. The settlement had survived. The pioneers were powder smoke-blackened. Saddened by the loss of twelve of their number, they were never the less grateful to be alive.

Colonel Zane walked over to shake hands with his bordermen. Words could not express the thankfulness he felt toward these men. Wetzel stood leaning on his long rifle. Jonathan sat on the steps of the fort. His powder-blackened face showed the weariness of the past two days.

"Jack, Lew. I hardly know what to say."

"Don't say anything, Colonel," Wetzel said.

"We're glad to do anything we can."

"Well, just the same I'll never forget what you've done. Are you going to take Girty's trail?"

"Just as soon as we're sure there's no other problems here. I think we'd best hang around for a couple of days just to be sure."

The settlers began to take stock of what was left after the siege and what would be needed to put their lives back to normal. There were always funerals to be conducted. The cemetery on the hill above the settlement had grown over the years and doubtlessly would continue to welcome members of the settlement. The grain stores as well as most of the livestock had been protected because the Colonel had wisely stored them behind the stockade walls.

The blood-stained, smoke-blackened walls of the old fort would stand in mute testimony to the struggle it had seen for many years.

Wetzel and Jonathan scouted the woods around the fort until they could report that the siege had really been broken. A couple of days later a column from the Colonies arrived. They were relieved to find the settlers alive and well.

Wetzel and Jonathan stopped by a week later to say goodbye before leaving on Girty's trail. Colonel Zane again shook hands with his bordermen and thanked them again for all they had done. All three men knew that years of bloody strife lay ahead. The Revolution back east would continue. Washington would continue the Revolution for years, winning some battles and losing some. At that time no one knew that the Revolution would ultimately be successful and out of the ashes of the old would come a new nation. There would be more battles, more mountains to climb, but the pioneers would carry the nation westward to the Pacific.

A couple of weeks after the siege the Colonel could be found at his customary place sitting on the veranda of the fort, smoking his pipe. Part of his cabin had been burned and the Colonel, his wife, and children had taken up residence at the fort until repairs could be made. Betty was staying with Lydia Boggs in her father's quarters at the fort. Major McCulloch had stopped by that afternoon to let the Colonel know that he planned to join up with Captain Williamson to lead an expedition on the Shawnee towns in the spring.

Captain Boggs stopped by for coffee. And Hugh Bennett had come over to see if the Colonel would like to come for supper on the next evening.

The Colonel was joined by Bessie on the veranda, and the two of them sat enjoying the evening. A whippoorwill called from the bluff. The mists came up from the river, covering the valley with a ghostly veil. The old fort, blackened and bloody, glowered over the valley. That evening, just for a time, peace reigned over Wheeling and Fort Henry.

Afterword

The Indian wars in the Ohio Valley went on for another thirty-eight years.

The old fort at Wheeling withstood numerous smaller attacks and another siege in 1782. Betty Zane became the heroine of Fort Henry by running the gauntlet of Indians and British to save the fort.

Colonel Zane lived to see his settlement grow into a thriving village. He was awarded a contract to cut a road through from Fort Henry to Maysville, Kentucky, known as Zane's Trace. He died in 1811 and is buried at Martins Ferry, Ohio.

Betty Zane, Jonathan, Ebenezer and Ebenezer's wife, Bessie, are also buried at Martins Ferry, as is Silas Zane.

Wetzel alone never married. He remained a roamer of the forest, Deathwind to the Indians, and an implacable enemy to the renegades. He lived until 1808 and now rests in the McCreary Cemetery at Moundsville, West Virginia. Jonathan finally married and lived out his life at Wheeling and at Zanesville, Ohio.

People say sometimes on a summer night you can hear a sad mournful wind blowing over the hills and vales of West Virginia.

Historical Notes

While researching historical sources, I came across a reference to the Draper Papers that are housed at the University of Wisconsin. Upon contacting the Historical Society, I asked them for whatever information they had on Lewis Wetzel, the Wetzel family, and the Zane family from Wheeling, West Virginia, preferably Colonel Ebenezer Zane. I was told there was volume after volume on the Wetzels and the Zanes. The archives of Ohio and West Virginia are filled with references to the Zanes, the McCullochs, and most of all, the Wetzels. I also learned that Theodore Roosevelt once referred to Lewis Wetzel as the greatest one-man army known to man. Zane Grey, himself a relative of the Zanes, researching material for his early frontier novels, wrote three books about Wetzel and Betty Zane, *The Spirit of the Border* and *The Last Trail*.

In one of the most famous frontier novels, *The Last of the Mohicans* by James Fenimore Cooper, a reference was made to Hawkeye's reloading his long rifle while on the run. This was one of the traits that Wetzel was known for and a trait used by Cooper to build the character of Hawkeye, the pathfinder.

The year of Wetzel's birth is disputed as anywhere from 1750 to 1763. As he was a scout for Washington's army and a well-known scout and Indian hunter by 1777, it was most likely 1750.

Daniel Boone, as an old man, once commented to a family member, "I spent a lot of time in the woods, fought Indians when I had to although I had many Indian friends, but next to Lew Wetzel, I was but a babe in the woods."

Lewis Wetzel died in Mississippi in 1808. His grave was located in the 1930s and remains were interred in West Virginia next to his brother Jacob. A new monument was erected along with the inscription "Lewis Wetzel – Indian Fighter."

Wetzel was a product of the time in which he lived. Both the Indians and the renegades waged unrelenting war on the white settlers of the Ohio country and were enlisted by the British during the War of Independence. Wetzel was Colonel Zane's right-hand defense against these vicious killers. One of the stories told in this book is an absolute fact. Not far from Wheeling was a large grove of trees that was a favorite place of the frontiersman for shooting turkeys. However, several of the pioneers had been killed while stalking their feathered quarry. Wetzel went out alone to find the Indian who was doing the killing. About halfway up the bluff was a large cave. Wetzel circled around, coming up on the cave from above. Finding a good place, he waited. Before too long the sound of a gobble came from the cave, and the head and shoulders of an Indian warrior rose up. Taking quick aim, Wetzel fired and the Indian fell like a stone. No further settlers were shot while turkey hunting. The Wind of Death had exacted payment for the dead settlers.

Daniel Boone told another story. A small herd of horses had been stolen from Wheeling. A group of frontiersmen persuaded Wetzel to go with them to recover the horses. They managed to come upon the Indians just as they joined up with a larger party. The other pioneers beat a hasty retreat. They asked Wetzel to go back, to which he retorted, "Not likely! I came out here to find Injuns. Now that I've found them, I ain't goin' back with my tail between my legs. You fellers go back to the fort. I'll be along." A few days later, Wetzel showed up with the horses and several fresh scalps.

There has been over the years a great controversy among historians about how Wetzel made the sound of the "Wind of Death." Wetzel said he made it by blowing down the long barrel of his rifle. He said it was done with a whittled mouthpiece. He said he did this to scare the hell out of the Indians and as even Simon Girty said, "He succeeded."

Both Wetzel and Jonathan Zane scouted for the colonial army during the years 1775 until the end of hostilities in 1782. Both were present at Fort Henry during the siege of 1777, the year of the Bloody Sevens, and again in September 1782.

There is a place in Ohio called Wetzel Spring where a group of Indians pursued Wetzel, and the hunter killed four out of the five. One of the Indians called to his companions, "No catch that man. Him gun always loaded!"

I talked to a woman whose family dated back to the settlement of Wheeling. She said that in those days if there was someone, a widow or elderly people many times, Wetzel or Jonathan would hunt for them, protect them against Indians or wolves or any other marauding renegades or Indian animals. Although all the Indians and renegades feared Wetzel, both he and Jonathan were loved and revered by all the settlers.

George Washington, while entertaining guests at Mt. Vernon after his retirement, remarked to his guests that during the Revolution, the western border of the Ohio country was of extreme concern to him because the danger of being surrounded and attacked from the west would have been devastating to the Colonial forces. He said his force owed a tremendous debt of gratitude to the scouts of that area and particularly to one Lewis Wetzel, who killed a renegade who had been assigned the task of killing Washington himself.

During the Revolutionary War, one of the loyalists or Tories as they were called was assigned the task of killing Washington. If this had been accomplished, there might well have been no United States of America. Washington was to take part in a conference at Fort Pitt. As the General approached a grove of birch trees, the renegade prepared to fire. Suddenly the short, spiteful crack of a rifle shot was heard, and the body of the Tory dropped like a stone out of the oak tree where he had concealed himself. Two men in buckskin stepped from behind a boulder on the edge of the track. They were Lewis Wetzel and Jonathan Zane.

There was at one time a question of what caused Wetzel's hatred and war of vengeance against the Indians. In some references, it was the death of his father and in others supposedly the Indians murdered his whole family. It is documented that his father was ambushed and killed while crossing the Ohio country in the early 1770s.

One of the first stories about Lewis Wetzel comes from one of the older residents of Wheeling who is reporting on a story that has come down through the years from the earliest settlers.

When Lewis was about fifteen and his brother Jacob a little younger the boys were captured by Delaware Indians. Lewis was seriously wounded. After about two days in the evening the boys escaped. Hearing the Indians pursuing them the boys hid under a hollow tree. Knowing they needed weapons, Lewis returned to the camp and stole two rifles and ammunition. After a couple of days traveling, the settlers were overjoyed to see the boys show up. Reported but not confirmed was the story that Lewis had two Indian scalps on his belt.

At the time of the American Revolution and the border war, the Indian fighters, because their weapons were single-shot, fought most battles with a knife and tomahawk in close battle. Usually they would fire their first shot and then close with their foe with both knife and hatchet. Both Wetzel and Jonathan Zane were deadly fighters, never giving quarter or asking any.

One of the biggest problems of the frontier villages was the preservation of meat. For this reason, most of the hunting for bison, deer, and elk was done in the fall when the temperatures were cooling down from the oppressive heat of summer. Wetzel many times was asked to accompany the hunters to scout any Indians that were in the area of the bison herd or hiding in ambush for the settlers when they were hunting.

Daniel Boone lost one of his sons at a place called Blue Licks when the settlers had gone out for salt. Boone never recovered from the loss and in later years in Missouri when he tried to tell the story he could never do so without weeping. Lewis Wetzel's brother, Jacob, was a good friend of Boone and had advised against going to get salt at Blue Licks until a larger group was available to go.

There is an absolute wealth of information available through the Brady and Wetzel families. Although Lewis Wetzel never married, some of his brothers did and their descendants are living in West Virginia and Ohio till this day. There is a county in West Virginia named for Lewis.

Wetzel, of course, was a prized catch for any Indian chief. Twice Indians captured him, both times at Wingenund's camp. Both times he escaped but only after being tortured. This made him swear a particular enmity toward Wingenund. In the year 1782, it was Wetzel who killed Wingenund's son. This put an even higher priority for the chief's village to hang the hunter's scalp on his lodge pole.

One of the greatest problems faced by the frontiersman and their families was winter time isolation of the outlying farms. In the diary "Early Days at Fort Henry" by Harriet Bonnett Smith, she tells of an older couple that lived about four miles from Wheeling on a small creek. The snow had piled up that winter until it was impossible for them to make the trip to town. Colonel Zane sent Wetzel and Jonathan to check on them. The old man was down with the fever and both were in pretty bad shape. The bordermen rigged up a travois of sorts and pulling them through the snow managed to get them to the fort. Despite Bessie's best efforts, the old gentleman passed away not long after they arrived at the fort but his wife lived several years.

On the Western border or the Ohio country during Revolutionary times, there were several Indian chiefs that rose to prominence. First, of course, were Wingenund and Half King the Huron, also Big Beaver and Tarhe. Tarhe eventually was able to bury the hatchet with Wetzel mostly because of the influence of Isaac Zane, who married Tarhe's daughter Myeerah or White Crane. Zane lived with the Huron most of his life and helped to avoid bloodshed between the Huron and the white settlers on several occasions.

Anyone who has spent time in the woods knows a love for God's creation like nowhere else. The smell of the woods after a rain, the first twittering of the birds in the approaching dawn, the smell of wood smoke all let us share the sights, the sounds, the smells that our forefather's experienced so long ago. Although the borderman's life was a lonely one, bereft of wife and children and bloody though it was, the Lord must have planned the forest as some compensation for the loneliness.

At Wheeling on the Ohio River, one of the greatest dangers the pioneers faced was a sudden attack from across the river. Because of that a lot of time had to be spent making sure no surprise attack could succeed. Wetzel and Jonathan scouted both the river crossings where it was shallow and far back into the forest at least two to three miles. It is to their credit in all of Wheeling history, including both sieges 1777 and 1782, no surprise attacks ever succeeded.

Many references can be found saying Wetzel was unbalanced, mad for blood of the Indian. Nothing could be farther from the truth. His moaning sounds in the woods and terrible yells were all a way to exploit the superstitions of the Indians. The shaman of the Indian villages believed that the Great Spirit had sent the Wind of Death to punish the Indian people for some great wrong they had done to displease him and so the warriors of the forest held him in almost reverent respect.

During the frontier days of the 1760s through the late 1790s the primary occupation of the bordermen was the scouting and killing of Indians. However, there were times when the bordermen were called on for other purposes such as the search for two lost children, a boy and a girl who had wandered away and were feared dead. Jonathan, Wetzel, and Sam Brady searched for two days in the forest around the fort. Most of the pioneers feared the children had been killed by Indians, taken captive or attacked by wolves or panthers that frequented the forest surrounding the settlement. However, the children were found alive and in pretty good shape by Sam Brady and Jonathan in a cave along the Ohio, a couple of miles below Fort Henry. They were cold and wet and mosquito bit, but otherwise all right and was returned to their parents. This account can be found in a diary journal, "Early Days at Fort Henry" by Harriet Bonnet Smith.

One of the happiest times in the life of the pioneers was a cabin or barn raising. The men worked and the women would bring food by the ton including venison, wild turkey and hams. The children would play and in the evening likely as not, someone would play a fiddle and lovers would spark by moonlight. This was done under the watchful eye of Colonel

Zane, Wetzel or Jonathan. Small amount of spirits were allowed but no drunkenness would be tolerated. The Colonel was always opposed to gambling or alcohol to access.

Although justice on the border during the frontier days was harsh, there was at times mercy for lawbreakers when no loss of life was involved. Once two young men stole a group of horses from Colonel Zane and tried to sell them to a group of Tories that were camped in the area. The normal punishment on the frontier for stealing a horse was a trip to the nearest tree and they would be hanged and that was that. However, the boys' mother went to the Colonel and pleaded for mercy for her boys. Bessie interceded on her behalf and the Colonel relented. After sending Wetzel and Jonathan to reclaim the horses the boys were sentenced to three months lockup in the long room over the fort and with a warning what would happen if they should repeat the offense when let go. This account can also be found in Smith's journal.

Over the course of the twentieth century and into the early part of the twenty-first, we have been told of the Wild West. We have grown up with the tales of cowboys, cattle drives and gun fighters. We've been taken through books and movies to the streets of Tombstone and the OK Corral. We've heard of Custer's last stand with the 7th Calvary and Custer, Sitting Bull and Crazy Horse. But somehow the history of another time, the struggle on the western border in the 1760s through to 1800 has been forgotten in these days of radio, television and the web by a whole generation. The sacrifices made by these brave people in their attempt to establish homes in the wilderness should always be part of the western story. Without them, the Wild West may never have happened. And in the hills and valleys of Western Virginia and Ohio, men still talk in hushed tones of Wetzel, the dark and terrible borderman — the true Deathwind of the Border.

Irv Lampman

CPSIA information can be obtained at www.ICGtesting.com
Printed in the USA
BVOW04s1332090315

390897BV00002B/3/P